DEADLY TARGET

SCVC TASKFORCE, BOOK 9

MISTY EVANS

Beach
Path
Publishing

Deadly Target, SCVC Taskforce Series
Copyright © 2018 Misty Evans
ISBN: 978-0-9994740-9-9
Cover Art by Sam Fanderclai
Formatting by Beach Path Publishing, LLC
Editing by Elizabeth Neal, Patricia Essex

ACKNOWLEDGMENTS

This is my 50th published novel.

5-0.

Ten years ago, my first book was published and I had no idea I would still be writing (as a career) and turn out so many stories! The great thing is, I still have plenty more in my head. Who knows what the next ten years will bring?

There are so many people to thank it would take another book to name them all.

To Mark, Ben, & Sam, who saw it all, stayed by my side, and continued to encourage me to stick to my dreams and tell my stories my way – I love you forever. I would not be here without you (and the dogs).

Every book is your book.

To my friends who picked me up a hundred times and stood me back on my feet after crushing rejections, who shared ideas and brainstorming, who would not allow me to give up – you are worth far more than gold.

To my editors – you've taught me much and helped make my stories shine, thank you. I rely on you to polish and glean the best from every book.

To my cover artists and formatters – your gifts and skills are invaluable.

To my readers – I am humbled by your love of my characters and storylines. Thank you for letting me share what the crazy voices in my head say.

A special acknowledgement to my street team ladies, Nikki, Brenda, Danille, and Ruth for lending me their names for Victor's sisters.

To my characters, who are real to me – shine on, you weirdos, and I'll keep writing your stories.

Shine on, everyone.

Love & light,

Misty

"We are all broken,

that's how the light gets in."

~ Ernest Hemingway

1

For Victor Dupé, perfection was a moving target.

Forget fifty shades of gray, there had to be at least one hundred shades of blue. Winter Blue? Sea Sprite? Southern Evening? What he really wanted to know was who sat around thinking up names for all these paint colors? Maybe he was in the wrong business.

Or maybe he should stick to solving crimes rather than renovating a house.

With at least a dozen different swatches of blue on the wall, he tried to decide. He'd already purchased several gallons of Southern Evening, but which shade was best for his vintage craftsman bungalow?

Did it really matter? *Who's going to see it besides me?*

Buying the house and remodeling it had seemed like a good idea. He was tired of living in a condo and was ready for something more permanent. He'd always thought by the time he reached thirty-nine, he would have a wife and kids. A nice house. A dog.

The FBI had had other plans.

In reality, he didn't blame his job for the lack of family and a home of his own. It was his own fault for loving his job more than the idea of marriage and kids. He'd assumed he would have time to settle down and start a family. Now, with his 40th approaching, an irritating itch had set up under his breastbone since meeting Olivia Fiorelli at a Christmas party the previous December.

The deputy US marshal, nicknamed the Rock Star Agent of Organized Crime, had stirred a passion inside him he hadn't realized was dormant. Just as committed to her job as he was his, they had talked for hours over drinks. He'd laughed more that night than he had in the previous year, maybe longer. Her dark beauty had drawn him in, her take-no-prisoners attitude a total turn-on. He liked strong-willed women who knew their worth and had no qualms expressing themselves. There was a mystery about Olivia. A mystery he still hadn't solved.

It wasn't the only mystery he hadn't solved. He glanced at the wooden dining room table he'd purchased at a local antique shop, dozens of papers spread over the stained and scarred top. Something about stripping wallpaper and fixing the bricks in the fireplace had made him long to pull out the one case in his life he had not solved. Yet, anyway.

It's just a distraction. Whenever he got into something over his head, he circled back to the past, looking for answers. He knew subconsciously it was his way of processing the trauma he'd survived, the young boy in him believing if he only had answers to that one mystery, the answers for everything else would fall into place.

With Olivia, and definitely with this house project, he was in over his head. While he was no stranger to one-night stands, that night with Liv had set a chain of events into play. Hence, the reason he now had a mortgage and rundown house to fix up and was standing in his living room staring at too many fucking samples of blue paint.

Only a woman could do this to him.

Only Olivia Fiorelli.

Taz, Victor's Lab mix, lifted his nose and whined at the front door.

Yeah, he had the dog from his "Things to Have by Forty" list, but Taz was only a loaner.

"What is it, buddy?" Victor glanced out the bay window and saw a familiar car pulling into the drive. His pulse accelerated and he grinned. Huh. What was she doing here?

After their one night of heated passion, he and Olivia had texted every day, talked for hours on the phone, and even met briefly for coffee. Every time they'd set up an official date, she'd cancelled. The reason—excuse?—was always work. Each time she had invited him to her place, work had come up for him, so he couldn't fault her. Even their coffee date had been cut short when she'd gotten a call from her boss. It seemed like the universe was conspiring against them.

She exited the car with a white bag and a six-pack. The bright pink logo of his favorite bakery in Laguna Beach was visible on the side. Late afternoon sun glinted off subtle copper streaks in her hair, the long, brunette strands pulled back in a ponytail. Kicking the driver side door shut with her foot, she gave his house a once over, her gaze stopping on the six swatches of beige next to the front door.

Normally, he had no problems making decisions. That's what made him the efficient director for the West Coast FBI. It was how he kept all of his hand-selected California Taskforces running smoothly. But when it came to paint...

Taz rose to his feet, a low growl issuing from his throat. Olivia had never been here, had never met the dog. Victor hoped Taz would like her as much as he did. "Down boy." He ruffled the dog's ears. "Best behavior, now, you hear?"

Victor threw open the door just as Olivia started up the wooden steps. He couldn't keep a smile off his face. "Are you any good at picking paint colors?"

She smiled back and held up the contents of both hands.

"That's what sugar and beer are for. They dull the brain and give you a good excuse when anyone asks why you picked clashing colors. You can blame it on too many carbs causing poor decisions."

Taz sniffed at her, now wagging his tail. "I thought you were working today."

"I thought you were too," she said. "I ran into Cooper and Celina buying diapers at the grocery store with their little girl. Cooper said you're on a two-week vacation, and planned to work on your house, so I decided you might want some help."

She lived in Carlsbad, not far from Cooper Harris, head of the SCVC Taskforce, and his wife, Celina, who'd once been on the taskforce and still worked for the FBI as a forensic photographer. Another reason Victor rarely saw Liv. His office was in LA, his new house Laguna Beach. From his place to hers was only forty-five miles, but with traffic on the freeway, what should take an hour or less often was double that.

He held the door open and motioned for her to come in. "I'd hoped to have a few things fixed up before I invited you over, but I'm really glad to see you."

"From the looks of things," she said, eyeing the living room swatches, "I got here in the nick of time."

"You don't like blue?"

"Blue is great for bedrooms. With your west facing window in this room, I think you could get away with something bolder. Something a little more fiery."

She liked things hot. With her Italian heritage and olive colored skin, she gravitated to dark reds, deep oranges, and gold. Today, she had on a brilliant yellow tank top under a flannel shirt that reminded him of the sun. Her worn jeans molded to her hips and disappeared into black leather boots with three-inch heels.

Maybe she's the right color palette for what I need.

"What's in the bag?" he asked, even though he didn't care as long as she'd brought it.

4

"Cannolis. What else?" She laughed.

Cannolis and beer, what a combination. But that was Olivia—big smile, sexy laugh, and weird taste in food.

He took the six-pack and led her to the kitchen. Although he'd moved in weeks ago, boxes were stacked on the counters and floor. He'd managed to unpack a couple of plates, some glasses, and a plastic bag with disposable silverware. Rooting around for his bottle opener, he hoped the mess didn't offend her.

"Aha." He found the hammer-shaped opener and popped the lids off two beers.

Olivia accepted one, eyeing the novelty opener. "Why am I not surprised you have a tool that does double duty?"

"It was a housewarming gift from Cooper's team. Apparently, they thought I'd be doing a lot of drinking while rehabbing the house."

Olivia clinked her bottle against his and they drank. She cleared a spot on the table, set down her beer, and opened the bakery bag. As she drew out the cannolis, Victor tore off two paper towels, making plates out of them.

They ate in silence, Victor studying her under half-lidded eyes. She was sultry and beautiful. In direct contrast to the sunny tank top, she wore a flannel shirt with the sleeves rolled up to the elbows. She looked like the sexiest home-improvement contractor he'd ever seen.

She caught him staring at her ample cleavage and smirked as she licked cream from one end of the cannoli. Teasing.

That was all it took. He remembered the feel of her tongue on him, those lips scorching every bit of skin they'd touched. In that instant, his mind went back to that night and all they'd shared. He had no doubt that was her intention as she slowly bit into the pastry and grinned wider as she chewed.

Taz sat patiently at her feet, his big tongue hanging out the corner of his mouth. He'd been part of a dog fighting ring and had lost teeth before being rescued when Victor and his team had slipped in to arrest several of the participants. If there was one thing Victor hated, it was bullies and those who hurt others, human or animal. He'd made sure the dozen dogs received proper medical care and were taken to a no-kill shelter. Once Taz was on his feet again, the shelter's manager asked him to foster the dog, who needed to work on his people skills and manners in order to be a better candidate for adoption.

Taz was obviously becoming quite adept at his people skills since he gave Olivia pleading puppy dog eyes, hoping for his own cannoli. A tiny bit of drool ran out the side of his mouth onto the floor.

Watching Olivia, Victor figured he wasn't much different, although he hoped for something more than a bite of cannoli. Finishing his pastry, he checked the corners of his mouth to see if he'd been drooling himself. *Maybe a little.*

"So what color do you suggest for the kitchen?" he asked, trying to get his big brain back online.

"Hmm." She glanced around, slipping the dog a piece of her cannoli. "Pumpkin, maybe, or squash."

"Are we talking paint or food?"

"The woodwork is really beautiful. In here, with the lighter fir trim around the windows and on the cabinets, I think the best colors would be in the warm, fall category."

She licked the ends of her fingers and toyed with her beer bottle.

Once again, the brain in his head had trouble focusing as the blood ran south. "Well, I don't have either of those, nor anything fiery for the living room."

"Guess that just leaves us one option, doesn't it?" she asked, her dark eyes teasing.

Please, God, let her be thinking what I hope she is.

One of the things he'd loved about Liv from the start was the fact she didn't beat around the bush. While she didn't always come right out and say what was on her mind, he seemed to be able to read it anyway.

She had a few crumbs on her tank top. He leaned forward and teased them off the fabric, letting his fingertips brush against the bare skin above the soft cotton. "You seem to be the expert," he said, tipping his face closer to hers. "So, unless we're making a trip to the hardware store, it looks like we're painting my bedroom this afternoon."

Her breath hitched, those piercing eyes searching his face. He caught the scent of beer and chocolate on her breath. "Do you have all the tools you need?"

I have you. "Maybe you should check my toolbox and see."

"That's a terrible pickup line." She laughed, low and sexy. "Totally cheesy."

"I never was good at them."

She kissed him then, letting her tongue outline his lips. "I don't work for free, you know. I expect dinner in exchange."

Holy hell, he'd give her anything she wanted. "Is that all?"

"Where's the bedroom?" She grabbed his hand and dragged him out of the kitchen and toward the stairs. "Dinner is only the beginning, *polpetto*."

"I love it when you speak Italian," he said, following her up the steps to the bedroom loft. "What does that mean?"

"Meatball."

Meatball? What the...? "Seriously?"

She laughed and yanked him inside where they collapsed onto the mattress lying on the floor. He hadn't set up the head-board and rails yet. "Trust me," she said, as she took off her flannel shirt and went to work on his belt. "It's a term of endearment. There's not much we Italians love more than a good meatball."

God, this woman. He'd barely known her a few months, but there was no doubt in his mind, he was totally head over heels for her. Just gone.

Helping her remove her tank top before he pulled her down beside him, he once again realized perfection was a moving target.

And right now that target was a beautiful US deputy marshal who had her hand down his pants.

OLIVIA FIORELLI WAS NOT this kind of girl.

She'd only known Victor a couple of months. The first time she'd slept with him she chalked it up to a wedding, which always made her sentimental, and too much booze, which never failed to lower her inhibitions.

But today? Right now? One beer wasn't enough to use that excuse, so maybe she should use Cooper, Celina, and their baby. They had all survived a hostage situation before Christmas the previous year, reminding Olivia how precious life was and how quickly it could be taken away. Afterwards, she'd attended Cooper and Celina's impromptu wedding at their house, and found herself totally infatuated with the man whose bed she was currently in. Seeing the happy family earlier had triggered her ovaries to do the hula. She longed for a man. A strong one who supported her and wanted kids as much as she did. A man who wouldn't hold her crazy, criminal family against her.

Unfortunately, those men were few and far between.

With those pesky, demanding hormones coursing through her system, and the realization she was about to turn thirty with no marriage or family in sight, she'd done what any respecting kickass woman would do—picked up a bag of comfort food and some alcohol and drove straight for hell.

Because that's where she was headed.

Good Catholic Italian girls did not sleep with a man before marriage. An old-fashioned idea but one that had been ingrained in her head by her mother and father. That past conditioning didn't die easy.

As Victor unsnapped her bra and cupped her heavy breasts, she considered letting herself off the hook. It wasn't like she slept around. She wished she could be casual about sex like some of her friends, but that had never been her style. Along with the fact that the first guy she ever fell in love with, Johnny Valducie, had gotten the crap beat out of him when her father caught them making out in the basement. Totally traumatized—poor Johnny —and she had been too. Johnny never spoke to her again and for good reason.

It was after that when she realized her father wasn't the man she thought he was. That for all his talk about being an important person at his job, and all the nice, expensive things their family enjoyed, her father was nothing more than a mid-level gangster. Not just a gangster, a *hitman*.

Yes, he loved her, but that love—and subsequently hers— came at a price.

All these years later, she still sensed his shadow hanging over her every time she felt the pull toward a serious relationship. Two thousand miles away and her job in law enforcement standing between them, and her father's presence was just as intimidating as it had been growing up.

Victor's kisses stole her breath and took her mind off the weight of family guilt and past consequences. Maybe that was why she kept throwing herself at him. He offered absolution, wiped away the pain and embarrassment of who her father was, what he had done. What she was, and could never be again.

Daddy's little girl.

As Liv sank into the heady oblivion of Victor's touch, the heat he was building inside her took over. Mindless. She could submerge herself totally in her body, rather than her head where thoughts never stopped and over-analyzing was her constant companion. She could forget for a few minutes about all the crap and pretend she wasn't keeping a secret that would ruin everything she had with Victor.

"So good," she whispered in his ear. His fingers undid her zipper, slipping in to touch her panties. "I'm so glad I came."

He chuckled deep in his chest. "Oh, you're going to come all right."

He slipped a finger inside her and she gasped as a vibration tickled her skin. Another vibration pulsed a second later, but she was too far gone to immediately recognize what it was. Her body insisted it was only Victor's skilled fingers at her hot center and —*Mother Mary full of grace!*—he was hitting all the right places.

But the third time, she realized she heard music. A very specific series of notes, as in the ringtone of her latest informant, and future WITSEC client.

The burner phone was in her back pocket, the one she was laying on.

As if he could read her mind, Victor mumbled, "Do not answer that."

She didn't want to, not one bit. What woman would trade the sexy director of the West Coast FBI for mobster–turned–informant, Alfonso Barone?

This was her job, though. No exceptions, no excuses. When her informants and protected witnesses needed her, she had to be there for them.

Victor wasn't about to let her off the hook that easy. As she reached for the burner, he grabbed her wrist and pinned it to the bed. His other continued to minister to her sweet spot and as the ringtone faded in the high-ceilinged room, Liv's eyes rolled up in her head, her back arching and her hips rising to meet Victor's skillful hands.

"Sweet...Jesus!" she screamed as the orgasm ripped through her. She rode the crest, Victor's fingers milking the release, stringing out the incredible sensation—one she'd denied herself far too much—and providing a safe place for her to fly apart.

In the aftermath, she floated down, softly, sweetly. His arms wrapped around her as he drew her onto his chest where she rested her head for long moments, pretending she was someone else. That she wasn't betraying the man who'd just brought her a few minutes of golden peace.

A man who trusted her, who admired her. A man she could fall in love with.

Once he knew the truth, he would be just like Johnny. He would never have anything to do with her again.

For good reason.

She kissed the side of his neck before rolling over and sitting up. The Barone phone was out of her pocket now and she snatched it up to see Alfonso had left a message.

"Critical information," was all it said.

Better than *imminent danger*, which was the 911 of her world. Critical information meant he'd learned something important, probably in conjunction with the mob bosses he was informing on. But with Alfie, it could also mean a new gravy recipe to try.

Italians and their sauces.

Liv stood, adjusting her pants, and walked toward the opposite wall. She dialed Alfie, even as she held up a finger to Victor. "Sorry, I have to take this."

Half undressed, he sighed, putting one hand behind his head as he watched her from his pillow. He didn't say anything, didn't complain, but in the depths of his gaze she saw his disappointment.

The phone on the other end didn't complete a full ring before Alfonso answered. "Hey, doll. Where you at? How come you didn't answer?"

"I do have a life, Alfie," she said. "What's this critical information?"

"Something big is going down. Not sure what."

She fought the urge to roll her eyes. Really? He'd interrupted her chance at sex for *that*? "I need something more specific."

"Yeah, yeah. I know. All I can tell you is law enforcement is being targeted."

Liv's stomach went south and she glanced at Victor. "Specifics, Alfie. Who is being targeted and why? How did you hear this? Who's behind it?"

"I got my feelers out," he said, slightly petulant, "but I need you to watch your backside, you hear me? This is big-time shit. Frankie B is involved. There's more than one target, if my nose is accurate, and the boss is pulling out all the stops. He's got someone on the inside helping him."

Frankie B—the Butcher—Molina. One of Alfie's bosses. Gino DeStefano's right hand man.

Alfie was holding back, she was sure of it, but what mob guy ever told the truth? There were many days when Olivia believed Alfonso was like her dad. He'd once been a CI too. For all she knew, Alfie was leading her on, dropping trivial pieces here and there to make her believe he was helping, when in reality, he was pumping her for more information than she was getting out of him. That's what her dad had done.

A cold prickle of dread scratched at the base of her spine. She couldn't deny that Alfonzo's critical information might actually jive with her undercover mission. She hadn't floated into Victor Dupé's world by accident—her contact at the Justice Department had sent her to keep an eye on him and see what ties he might have to the California mafia. Could Victor be Frankie's inside guy?

She turned away from the director's penetrating gaze and tried to interject a lightheartedness she didn't feel into her reply. "You worried about me, Alfie?"

"What can I say?" His Jersey accent was heavier today. "You know I like you, even if you are a cop."

"More like you're worried about me being a target because I'm the one keeping you and your daughter protected, ain't that right?"

He chuckled. "I'm still looking for those tickets to Hawaii, you know."

If he came through for the prosecution when the time came, Alfie and his daughter would disappear, officially part of the witness protection program. Everyone in WP wanted to go to Hawaii, Florida, or some other warm location. Exactly the places they'd told friends and family they'd like to visit, which immediately crossed them off the potential list of places to hide.

"You keep looking," she told him, "and I'll see what I can do."

Alfie wasn't the only one who could tell a partial truth.

"I'm serious," he said. "Whatever this is, it's going down soon, and it's going to be widespread. If nothing else, I don't want you caught in the crossfire."

His concern seemed genuine and it took her off guard.

In the next breath, he was back to normal. "We still on for tomorrow night?"

God save her, they had a standing dinner date. Alfonso liked to make his mother's gravy and the smell always brought back fond memories of her own mother and food. It was an absurd thing, but occasionally she got him to talk about the DeStefano mob and Frankie B's ongoing plans to eliminate certain cartels in an effort to control the drug trade in California. These were times Liv thought she was actually getting significant intelligence. Her boss encouraged her to keep attending the dinners in hopes Alfonso would eventually trust her enough to help her crack open the entire West Coast DeStefano operation.

"I'll be there," she said.

Just as she was hanging up, Victor's phone went off downstairs. He ignored it, crooking a finger to entice her back to bed.

She wanted to tell him the truth. About everything. But until she had concrete evidence that he was indeed the elite director he appeared, there was no point blowing her cover or admitting she purposely crossed paths with him in order to keep a close eye on him, just like she kept on Alfonso.

Victor would blow a gasket if and when he discovered the Justice Department was surveilling him, but that wasn't her biggest concern. She'd deceived him, and although the seduction had been voluntary, he wouldn't see it that way.

Once again, she was ready to forget, to lose herself in the game she was playing, but Victor's cell didn't stop ringing. A second ringing started up as well. His landline.

She pulled away, the ache inside her growing as she accepted the fact that the two of them were not meant to be together no matter how much she wanted him. "You better get that. It could be an emergency."

She didn't need to tell him that, but she couldn't help herself. Maybe this was God or the universe trying to save her from complete self-destruction.

A moment later, she heard him answer the phone downstairs, the change in his tone making the hairs on the back of her neck stand up. She threw on her shirt and hustled to join him, only to find the look on his face scaring her even more.

As he hung up, he was already racing for the front door. The dog ran in from the living room on high alert. "There's been an emergency. I'll call you as soon as I can."

She chased after him. "What happened?"

"It's not good." He stopped at the door, snagging car keys from the foyer table, his body language tight, controlled.

"Victor?"

His jaw worked and finally glanced at her. "Cooper's been shot."

"What?" She couldn't believe it. "Oh God, is he okay?"

Dumb question. Of course he wasn't.

Victor kissed her forehead. "He's in surgery. I've got to go."

"I'm coming with you."

Victor turned back. "You don't have to do that."

She grabbed the leash from its hanger and clipped it on Taz's collar. "We'll be right behind you."

2

Cooper was in critical condition.

Even with his siren going, it took Victor nearly two hours to drive south to the hospital. Due to the severity of the gunshot wound, Cooper had been transported to San Diego where a team of specialists continued working on him.

Victor, Olivia, and Taz hustled through the emergency room doors, Liv flashing her badge at the security guard and then at the nurse at the admitting desk when she called, "You can't bring a dog..."

Her sentence died before she finished it at Liv's stony glare.

Thomas Mann was waiting for Victor and waved them all into a small alcove that held a Virgin Mary statue.

"How's he doing?" Victor asked. Thomas had sent several updates to his phone while Victor was driving. "Anything new?"

Thomas, second in command of the SCVC Taskforce, wiped a hand over his face and then raked his fingers through his short hair. "Not much. He and Celina were taking Via to an Easter egg hunt at the park not far from their house. They'd walked there and just entered when he was shot. The bullet missed his heart by centimeters, punctured a lung, and he nearly bled out. It went all the way through but did a lot of damage on the way. No one else was hurt, and there was only the one shot."

It was deliberate and calculated. Not some random drive-by shooting, and done very publicly, with lots of witnesses. Kids and their families. The potential collateral damage made Victor shudder, but the shooter had known exactly who his target was, and thank the heavens for the fact he hadn't hit any of the children.

"How's Celina?" Olivia asked.

"She's a mess." Thomas shook his head. "He was shot right in front of her and Via."

Jesus. Who did that? But Victor already had a good idea. Gang members, mobsters, drug dealers. Someone making a point, sending a message. Through the years, Cooper had racked up dozens of enemies, but which one had decided to take revenge for him ruining their criminal enterprises and sending them to jail?

"The shooter?" Victor wanted whoever it was hanged, drawn, and quartered. "Do we have any leads?"

"Working on it."

Victor started for the waiting room. "Work faster. Someone saw something. I want to know who and what they witnessed."

Celina sat in a chair, bowed forward, head in her hands. Ronni Punto, FBI agent and full-time SCVC Taskforce member, sat next to her talking softly. Nelson Cruz, another taskforce agent, and his wife, Sophia, had taken Via home with them.

Celina looked up when they entered and rushed into Victor's arms. How strange that only a few years ago she was on the taskforce and would have never dreamed of throwing her arms around his neck. He didn't tend to show emotions with coworkers —or anyone else for that matter—and kept a respectable distance, but in this case, he was glad he could be here for her. The men and women on his Southern California Taskforce were not only the best agents from the FBI, DEA, NSA, and ICE, they were also family.

My family.

Celina sobbed against his chest and he hugged her close. "He's going to be okay. You and I both know what a tough SOB he is."

She nodded, stepping back. Her eyes were bloodshot, her face puffy from crying. "He was just standing there, perfectly fine, laughing at Via, and then the next second..."

Her voice hitched, her eyes darted around, as if witnessing the scene all over again. "All that blood, Victor. I know they say the bullet missed his heart but... he lost *so much* blood. Via was screaming and I couldn't stop the blood and I didn't know where the shot had come from or if they were going to shoot us too. Everyone was screaming and running, and I just...panicked."

Liv moved in and hugged Celina as Victor squeezed her hand. "I'm so sorry this happened," Olivia said. "We're going to figure out who did this and make sure they pay."

"Thanks for coming." Celina tried to smile. "I can't believe we only saw you a few hours ago. He was just buying diapers."

Celina was a tough FBI agent. She'd been through some pretty extreme circumstances in her career. But this? Seeing her husband gunned down in front of her and her daughter? This might take the cake. The shock of it was still too fresh, her mind a horrified, chaotic mess.

"Ronni is going to stay with you and I'm taking Thomas," Victor told her. "We'll follow up with the police, and start working on our own leads on who shot him."

She dashed a hand at the tears on her cheeks. "I want to help."

A spark of that kick ass agent he knew so well shone in her eyes. He squeezed her hand again. "I know you do, and the best way is to be here when Cooper wakes up after surgery. Your face is the first one he'll want to see. And he'll be hell bent for leather to get out of that bed and hunt down the perpetrator, and you're probably the only person, besides me, who can keep him here, no matter how badly he's hurt. You know how he is. I need you to keep him in that bed and listening to the doctor's orders. You feel me?"

She nodded, knowing he was right. "Let me know if there's anything I can do from here to help catch the bastard who did this."

"Any ideas who the shooter is? Did Cooper mention anyone he pissed off lately?"

The hint of another smile. "He pisses off a lot of people, so there could be more than one candidate." She tried to chuckle, but it came out more like a hiccup. "But no, there's no one I can think of. I've been racking my brain, but I'm drawing a blank."

He hated to do it, but he had to ask. "Any chance the person was after you? Or trying to terrorize you like before?"

She didn't miss a beat, her past always a shadow over her. A Mexican drug cartel leader had sought revenge on her at one time, hurting, and even killing several people close to her. "I thought of that, but since I've been a forensic photographer, I work behind the scenes, now. I don't go undercover, nor arrest people anymore, so the likelihood is very low."

Victor figured as much. "I put in a call to Mitch to come help." Mitch Holden was a national security expert who handled top secret, and very hush-hush, intelligence gathering. In the past several years, he'd worked with the taskforce on several assignments, but mostly was a stay-at-home dad these days with his wife and new baby. "We'll put out a net to trap this scumbag before he gets too far."

Mitch was married to a forensic psychiatrist who'd had great success using animal therapy to help juvenile delinquents. "I'll see if Emma can come too, and I want you to sit down with her and talk. Tell her what happened. This can bring up a lot of old stuff for you. Emma can help you deal with it."

He'd witnessed plenty of shootings in the line of duty, unfortunately, and seen the scars they left on those involved, whether they'd taken the bullet or watched a loved one or friend take it. Celina was going to need therapy, regardless of how resilient she was.

"I'll be fine. I have to be strong for both Cooper and our little girl."

"This is a direct order, Agent Davenport." He put a hand on her shoulder to soften his pulling rank. "You're tough as nails, Celina, but I also know how valuable you are to your family and my taskforce. Emma is your friend, as well as a top-notch psychiatrist, and you need both in order to help Cooper and Via process this."

His newest sidekick backed him up. "You are their rock," Liv said to her. "In order to be that rock, you need to accept support from your friends. Besides, Emma's going to want to know all the details anyway, and with your help, she'll be able to build a profile of the shooter for us."

"I don't know how." Celina sighed, the puff of air blowing up her bangs. "I didn't see anybody. All I know is what direction the shot came from."

Liv smiled. "From what I know about Dr. Collins, she's worked with less and still managed to help law enforcement catch their man."

Celina smiled back ruefully. "You're right. She has an amazing ability. It's almost like she digs into your mind and sees the scene herself, picking up on all the little things you didn't register in your consciousness."

Victor hugged her again. "Do you need anything before Thomas and I leave?"

Ronni stepped forward and took Celina's hand. Celina looked at her, relaxing slightly, and then back to Victor. "Just catch this bastard, Director. You can't let him get away with this."

"You think of anything, no matter who, what, or how insignificant it seems, you get in touch with me."

"I will."

He patted her shoulder again. "Take care of our boy. Thomas and I will keep you updated on anything we find. When Cooper comes to, tell him I'll be back, and if he doesn't stay in that hospital bed and listen to you and the doctors, I will kick him into it."

"Thank you," she said, giving him a hug. "I'm so glad you came."

That was what he did. Made people feel safe by protecting them, and when he couldn't protect them, he made sure justice was found. Emma Collins would tell him it stemmed from taking care of his four younger sisters after their mother was injured in a car accident and could no longer work. His father had been killed when Victor was only ten years old. Too young to have so much responsibility riding on his shoulders, but that was life. All of that for his family had groomed him to be the man he was. He stood up for the weak, protected the vulnerable, squashed evil.

"Call us if you need anything," Thomas said to Celina and Ronni.

Ronni nodded, her dark afro longer than Victor had seen in a while. "We will."

Steering Liv and Taz to the door, Victor stuffed down the burning desire to punch the wall as he left a very vulnerable part of his Taskforce behind.

OUTSIDE THE HOSPITAL, Olivia followed Victor to their cars. His jaw was tight, a muscle jumping in his cheek, and she knew he was holding back his emotions with great restraint. Thomas was parked in a different lot and they'd agreed to meet up at the secret office the taskforce kept downtown. Taz jogged beside her, both of them having to move quickly to keep up with Victor's long strides.

The sun was setting and a soft orange glow came from the west, the parking lot in shadow from the multiple story hospital. When they got to the cars, Victor said nothing, reaching for her and pulling her into his arms.

"What can I do to help?" she asked.

He released her and patted the top of Taz's head. "It means a lot to me that you came, but there's really not much you can do. Maybe put out some feelers with any of the lowlifes you know. Thomas and I will be working with the locals and checking through our recent cases that might involve someone wanting to strike at Cooper. Roman has his team checking the web for chatter concerning this to see if anyone is taking credit or knows anything."

Dr. Roman Walsh, Homeland Security. She'd heard of him, but never had the opportunity to work with him and his Domestic Terrorism Taskforce.

Her earlier conversation with Alfonso niggled at the back of her brain. "Did Cooper's team ever have any cases involving the Fifty-seven Gang?"

He gave her a curious look. "That rings a bell, but they're not an active case. Why?"

"One of my informants is feeding me information about a couple mafia bosses here in California tied to the Chicago Fifty-seven Gang syndicate. DeStefano is the leader's name. My CI told me something big is in the wind and it involves targeting law enforcement. That's what my call at your house was about. My source doesn't have details yet, but I'll stay on him, just in case."

He squeezed her arm. "I appreciate that. I don't think the SCVC Taskforce has tangled with DeStefano, but many of the criminals they go after have ties to both American and foreign mafias. Seems like everyone's an equal opportunity employer anymore when it comes to running drugs and guns, and other crimes."

She nodded, seeing Thomas driving past the lot. A For Sale sign was taped in the back window of the older sports car. "Taz can come home with me. When you're ready for a break, come over."

"It's going to be a long night. I appreciate you taking care of him. I usually have my neighbor let him out when I'm pulling an all-nighter, but he'll be happy with you."

She reached up and brushed a kiss across his lips. "Keep me updated and I'll expect you for breakfast, if not before. That's an order. You have to eat, even if you don't sleep."

He gave her a tired smile. "Text me your address."

She led Taz to the passenger side of her car. "You don't have it?"

"Should I?"

"A blue-chip agent like you? I expect you ran a background check on me the night we met. You probably know more about me than my mother does, although she doesn't speak to me much anymore."

He chuckled. "Hate to disappoint you, but I didn't even look at your Facebook page."

Her shock was genuine. "I don't have one, but I do have a pretty extensive file with the Justice Department. You might want to check it out. I've been told it's better than reality TV."

He raised one brow. "I see reality TV every day on the streets. I'd rather get to know you in person, rather than by some dry, textbook file."

Considering he knew her intimately, she took that as a compliment that he also wanted to become familiar on other levels. Yes, they'd been texting and talking since that holiday party, but they hadn't yet gone diving into either of their pasts.

Emotional dumpster diving, her college friend, Mandy, had called it. While few people's pasts were bright and shiny, some had a lot of gross, smelly issues they would rather keep hidden in a garbage can. Liv fell into that category.

She opened the car door and let Taz hop onto the seat. "See you for breakfast. I'll text you the address. I'm not far from Cooper and Celina's."

He waved and she drove off.

She sang along with her playlist as she finagled her car out of the city and onto the freeway heading north. Streetlights came on as darkness stole its way over the land. She opened the passenger window, allowing Taz to stick his head out.

A warmth infiltrated her chest as she thought about the fact Victor hadn't investigated her. With most men, she would've doubted his sincerity, but the director was different. She trusted him on many levels, and that was no small feat in her world. When you learned your father was a gangster as a kid, it was like finding out Santa Claus wasn't real.

She didn't trust anyone, especially those who claimed to care for her. Knowing she could trust Victor was better than gold.

But could she? The JD didn't have her investigating him for no reason. They hadn't shared any specifics on why they suspected foul play, and she had asked to no avail. The Justice Department was like God, moving in mysterious ways.

Still, it was in Victor's nature to be inquisitive and protective of his own boundaries, so it really wouldn't have surprised her if he had a complete file on her somewhere in his desk. Knowing him, he kept all the intel inside his head. But if he said he hadn't done a background on her, she believed it.

She hadn't needed to check into his past. She knew all about him, thanks to his prominence in the FBI and the way Celina had gushed about him when inviting Liv to the Christmas party. He hadn't become the West Coast director by playing small. Everyone in law enforcement knew Victor Dupé and his impressive record against the dark underbelly of the world of violent crime.

But she'd had an agenda at that party, another reason for knowing everything about Victor. She'd had the perfect opportunity to stay close to him, like her Justice Department superior wanted, but she knew better than to push too hard. She was simply to observe, interact, and report back if she discovered anything suspicious. So far, all she had come up with only verified the fact that the director had a clean nose and deserved every one of the commendations hanging on his office wall.

She prayed it would stay that way. That Victor would go on trusting her and they could develop their relationship. Maybe he hadn't needed to investigate her because she too, had a bit of notoriety. Tinker Bell, they called her, because she was the daughter of Felix "The Hook" Fiorelli. She hated it, as much as she did the reason for the moniker, but it had stuck, even in the US Marshal Service. No one dared say it to her face, but she heard it whispered behind her back.

Her father, and the Chicago crime syndicate he'd ran with when she was a child, had given her the fuel to become who she was. She had built her reputation with one goal in mind—wiping out the mob. From the eastern shores of America to the west, she was on a mission.

Tinker Bell that, you pieces of shit.

Alfie was going to help her with that. She'd been grooming him for the past five months. She was closer than ever to uncovering the final nails to put in Gino DeStefano's coffin. The men he had working to expand his empire in California would also go down, if she had any say in the matter. If she cut off the head of the snake, it would die.

Her house was dark when she pulled up. She hadn't left lights on, hoping she would be spending the night with Victor. Using an app on her phone, she disengaged the security system and lit the place up. Taz sniffed at all the new smells and she finally took him into the tiny backyard so he could pee.

Back inside, she cooked hamburger for him and gave him water. While he investigated the house, she put in a call to Alfie.

It rang three times on his end and she hung up. She waited a minute and called again, doing the same. That was their signal. Then she waited for him to call her back.

After five minutes, she grew frustrated, but this wasn't abnormal. He might be in a meeting, or, for all she knew, on the job. She'd like to believe he was home with his daughter, reading her a book. When she was very young, her father had often read to her at night before bed. Her favorite stories had been fairy tales. He'd liked those too.

That was always part of the problem. These guys were monsters on one hand, but they were also family men who fiercely loved and protected those around them. Her father loved her and her mother with deep conviction. She had never doubted that. But what he did to others...

Liv shuddered. The Hook had been a brutal killer.

She found an extra blanket in the hall closet and made a bed for Taz on her bedroom floor. Alfie would call when he could. She had plenty of work she could do to keep her mind off his warning about law enforcement being targeted by Frankie. Instead, she grabbed her laptop and logged in to several national databases. She started with Cooper Harris and began cross-checking him against the Fifty-seven Gang syndicate.

An hour later, the only hit she had was with Roman Walsh and the Domestic Terrorism Taskforce. They had brought down Uri Zion, a Russian mob leader, with the help of one Dr. Brooke Heaton, last fall. Part of the file was marked classified, but Olivia had no problem accessing the high clearance information with her code. She had to read one paragraph two times. It stated that Dr. Heaton was actually a relative of the Zion family. Who knew?

Apparently, Heaton hadn't known the connection before working on the case. Liv could guess her reaction when she found out, and felt a natural bond to the woman, even though she didn't know her. It wasn't every day you discovered you were a mob princess.

These days, the Russian mafia was virtually incestuous with its American counterpart, the former enemies finding an uneasy truce as they worked together to increase their power and control in all parts of the world. Everyone vying for the same resources, right along with the terrorists, and the street and biker gangs.

While Dr. Heaton had assisted the SCVC Taskforce on occasion, she was not considered part of the team. Nothing else in the file suggested an overlap between Cooper and anyone associated with the Chicago Fifty-seven gang and their empire that had stretched into Vegas and California.

Next, she ran a check between Gino DeStefano and the Zions. Maybe there was some small connection that could be teased out and lead her to a potential suspect in the shooting. It was farfetched, but she had nothing else.

Eventually, she gave up. She couldn't find any connection, not even a thin one. She washed up, found Taz curled on her bedroom floor, and read a text from Victor saying Cooper was out of surgery and in recovery. The operation had taken nearly four hours. Exhausted, she lay down on top of the covers and didn't bother turning off the light.

Hearing the click of nails on the hardwood floor, she opened her eyes to find the dog sitting in the shadows beside her. "What's up, Taz?"

Maybe he had to pee again. She'd never had a pet, although she'd toyed with the idea many times. She didn't mind being independent, but she hated being alone at night.

She took him out once more, standing under a partial moon while the dog sniffed around and marked the yard in several places. Back inside, he went right to the spot next to the bed again and gave her the same look.

Too polite to jump onto the bed, he was well-trained. Probably by Victor.

Laying down once more, she patted the space next to her. "You're not my first choice for a bed partner, but what the hell."

Some time later, her burner rang, waking her from a dead sleep. She snatched it up and fumbled to answer it. "About time," she yawned into the speaker.

"Hey," Alfonso said, totally indignant. "I took my daughter to the movies. I've been through enough hell tonight with pink ponies and talking unicorns. Don't give me grief."

There it was...that humanness about him that made him less gangster and more normal. "You were right," she played on his ego. "A law enforcement officer was targeted this afternoon."

"No kidding? Somebody you knew?"

Knew. As in dead. She swung her feet off the bed and scratched Taz's belly when he rolled over. "He's still alive, and yes, I know him in passing."

Alfie sounded surprised. "They didn't kill him?"

"Missed his heart by a few centimeters from what I understand."

"Huh."

"Any idea who did it?"

"You sure it was a hit? Nobody I know would miss. Maybe it wasn't one of us."

And she was the Holy Virgin. "It was a hit, all right, occurred right in front of his wife and daughter. Seems like a pretty clear message."

Alfie grunted. "We ain't the only ones to send those, doll, but if the shooter belongs to our group, he wouldn't miss."

It might not be related to the Fifty-seven Gang and DeStefano's syndicate. All the evidence pointed to someone else. Sometimes, however, evidence could be cloudy. "You think it's just a coincidence that you heard about a hit being put out on law enforcement shortly before one was shot by an unknown assailant?"

"Cops get shot every day."

She paced to her bedroom window, containing her annoyance at his flippant attitude. "Have you heard anything more about Frankie's plan?"

"All I know is that he's got a boner for taking over the Suarez cartel and Gino's given him the green light to do whatever he wants to either wipe them out or overthrow them. Fastest growing enterprise inside California at the moment, you know."

"So why spend time taking out an agent? That'll only put more heat on him."

A cynical chuckle. "He ain't worried about heat from you guys. He's got scarier people breathing down his neck. I asked my guy over some raviolis and he said Frankie and Gino need to clear a path for this cartel."

"Clear a path?"

"They have all the infrastructure the Fifty-seven Gang needs for buying and distributing a wide variety of products to certain clientele, if you get my drift. But it sounds like there's some high-ranking guy, Fed probably, putting the screws to them."

Everything in Olivia's body froze. "Which Fed?"

"I didn't get a name."

Of course you didn't. "I need to know who the target is, Alfie."

"Look, my guy was getting nervous from all the questions. I didn't want to blow it and act too interested. Besides, I should be in the know with Gino and Frankie and I ain't. Didn't want this guy to figure that out. The hit wasn't mine, and if I go badgering people to find out the who, what, when, and why, I could end up taking a swim in the Pacific."

Pushing him farther would be a waste of time and yet her skin crawled and she wanted to hit something over his lack of intel. She'd learned along the way when to press an issue and when to back off. Handling made men like Alfie required finesse and patience. Too bad she had neither at the moment.

"We're still on for dinner tomorrow night, right?" she asked, even though she already knew they were.

"Of course, doll."

"I'll be there. And Alfie?"

"Yeah?"

"You better have a name for me, or I'll make *sure* you take that swim."

3

Olivia woke to the sound of her phone dinging. She scrambled over Taz to reach her nightstand, the caller ID reading Victor's name and telling her it was four a.m.

When she answered, he said, "I'll be there in ten."

She and Taz hustled out of bed and she slid her robe on, yawning as she headed for the kitchen. Victor's voice had been rough and ragged, the toll of the night and his emotions apparent, even with a layer of steel under it. The members of his task-force were family, and nobody messed with his family and got away with it.

In the kitchen, she pulled out her bottle of Frangelico and two shot glasses, pouring an inch into each. Grabbing them with one hand, she headed into the foyer, turning on lights as she went.

She deactivated the security system and opened the door. Taz stood next to her, as if he knew they were waiting for Victor. The man in question pulled in moments later, parking behind her car. He was on the phone when he stepped out of his Cadillac SUV and stood for a moment by the open door.

"Yes, sir," he said. "Agent Harris is stable. Agent Mann and I have a list of suspects we'll be investigating today. I will keep you informed of any further updates."

There was a pause as he listened to the man on the other end. His gaze raked over Olivia, his expression one of controlled patience. "Yes, he is. Agent Harris and I have worked together for many years now, and he's always been one of my best agents. A good friend too."

Another pause and he glanced at her bare feet, his gaze lingering on her ankles before rising to her calves. "I'm about to do that right now. A couple hours of sleep and I'll be back on the case."

He said goodbye, disconnected, and tossed the phone on the driver seat. Leaving the door open, he walked straight to her. "Sorry. Had to update the director."

The director, as in the main guy in Washington. It was three hours later on the East Coast and Director Allen was probably already at his desk.

Victor opened his arms and Olivia went into them without hesitation, rubbing the back of his neck and letting him hold her. He nuzzled her ear, breathing deeply and hugging her tight. Next to them, the dog whined.

"Glad you made it," she said. "You have suspects?"

He released her and rubbed his eyes. "Sort of." He grabbed his phone, popped the trunk, and then went to withdraw an overnight bag. A beep of his key fob and the car was locked. He set down the bag and greeted Taz with a ruffle of his ears. "Have you been a good boy?" he asked.

"He's extremely well mannered," Olivia told him. She handed him one of the glasses. "You went all the way back to LA to get clothes?"

He downed the Frangelico in one gulp and picked up the overnight bag, following her into the house. "I keep spare clothes in my car at all times. I never know when I'm going to make it home for a shower and a fresh shirt."

Smart man. Because of her job, she often carried extra clothes, protein bars, and extra ammunition in her trunk. Came with the life of an agent.

"Nice place," he said, peering around once they were inside. "Do you like it here?"

She sipped at her drink and eyed him under her lashes. Leave it to Victor to make small talk at four in the morning when he was totally exhausted. *Such a kind, polite, amazing man.*

She took the empty glass from his hand and drew him down the hall with her. Her place was small, barely more than a surfing shack, but she'd made it hers through the years with small touches here and there. "I do. Carlsbad fits me, and it's nice to know Celina is down the road. How is she? Did Dr. Collins talk to her?"

"She's doing okay. Emma and Ronni stayed with her all night."

In the kitchen, she finished her Frangelico and set the glasses in the sink. "Can I get you something to eat? You must be starving. Eggs and toast maybe?"

"Throw in bacon and you have a deal."

She made a face. "I have sausage. Will that do?"

He pulled out a chair and sat at the breakfast bar. "I'll take it."

Good thing she'd gone to the market two days ago. Her ancient refrigerator was well-stocked with the basics. A rare occurrence. "So do you actually have any suspects, or were you inventing them for Director Allen?"

"The shooting happened in broad daylight at a kids' function. Parents all over the park were filming their children. It's already on YouTube, going viral, thanks to a couple enterprising souls who are more interested in likes on their channel than the horror of a DEA agent being gunned down in front of innocent children. The upside is that we confiscated multiple videos shot from different angles, and do actually have several potential suspects. We're running them through facial rec and following up on any hits we get. Two of the taskforce members are starting interviews with witnesses today to see if we can glean better details. Our three suspects are nameless at this point, and I can't guarantee any of them is our shooter, nor can I assume they are linked to criminal organizations, but they're all we have."

Factual, no emotion. Even in his current state, he was all business, his analytical mind going over the facts, or lack thereof, repeatedly.

Olivia heated a skillet and got out the toaster. "Coffee?"

Victor shook his head. "I've been running on caffeine. Got any orange juice? Whatever was in that glass was pretty good. Maybe I should just have another shot of that."

"Frangelico. Haven't you had it before?"

"Not that I'm aware of. You know me, I'm more of a beer guy."

After she broke a few eggs into the skillet, she poured him some juice. Then she put ice, a squirt of lime, and a couple shots of the liquor into a separate glass and set both in front of him.

"Frangelico for breakfast?" He chuckled. "Guess it's five o'clock somewhere."

She popped two slices of bread into the toaster. Taz sat patiently, watching the food prep. She passed him a piece and he gobbled it down. "I assume you're familiar with the Suarez Kings?"

His expression turned curious. "Of course."

"I heard from a source that Gino DeStefano and Frankie Molina are trying to take over the cartel for the Fifty-seven Gang. Various law enforcement officials are making this difficult for him, and Gino has no qualms about removing those obstacles. I didn't get a specific name, but I wondered if you, or one of your taskforces, was leading the charge and might be a target."

"The DEA and FBI have been trying to infiltrate the Suarez cartel for the past eighteen months to no avail. We know someone has been putting heat on the cartel, and there's been several bloodbaths between them and the Kings, but we've been focused on the cartel itself. Didn't realize it was a mob versus cartel war."

"I didn't either. Molina is pretty sneaky and crafty, and I'm guessing DeStefano is trying to accomplish the takeover on the down low."

Victor nodded. "We shut it down, Gino's got nothing. Again. He and some of his cronies have been trying to establish themselves in California for the past several years, as you know, but haven't gotten a true foothold in the drug biz. They haven't had much success in general, from what I understand, probably because of you."

He smiled at her, his tone teasing.

"Just doing my job," she said, ignoring the pride she felt at his acknowledgment. Maybe that wasn't the right word. Self-respect was more like it. She knew the mob from the inside out, and how to use that to her advantage when it came to stopping them. It was her duty, her responsibility, and she took it seriously.

The eggs were done, so she put them on a plate on the back of the stovetop to keep warm and started frying the sausage. Four pieces of perfectly browned toast popped up, and she buttered them while her thoughts ran in circles. Should she tell him what Alfie said? It was a lead, but a very slim one, and at this point she had nothing to link the information to the shooting. "And you're sure Cooper has never crossed paths with DeStefano or his gang in conjunction with the cartel?"

"I assume if you thought there was a connection, you already checked."

She shrugged, flipping sausage. "Not every FBI operation is open access to marshals, and I get it if you can't share details. I just have a feeling…"

He took a drink of the orange juice. "I didn't have a chance to double-check the records regarding Harris and DeStefano, yet, but I will."

"Also the Kings, okay?"

"Of course." He watched her carefully. "Is there something you're not telling me?"

Wow. He was good. She kept her eyes on the skillet. "My source claims Frankie is going after whoever stands in Gino's way. Like I mentioned before, it might include the law enforcement officer he credits for blocking his takeover attempts."

He tried the other drink, seemed to like it better, and took a second sip. "But you don't have a name or know the branch this law enforcement officer works for?"

Anytime you used informants, they could—and often did—lead you on a wild goose chase. Anytime one of them did not give up specific details, it made you question the validity of the intel.

She drained the sausage. Taking down a clean plate, she placed two eggs, two pieces of toast, and two sausages on it, handing the fixings across the bar to Victor. "I'm working on it."

"I appreciate the heads up, and I get where you're going with it—that Cooper may be the target," he said. The fact it was basically worthless information without specifics didn't seem to bother him. Or maybe he was just being kind, as usual. "I appreciate the breakfast too."

She made a second plate for herself and sat next to him. Taz joined them, taking residence under her chair. A small sausage might have slipped off her plate and landed in front of him and he gobbled it up, her partner in crime.

As she and Victor dug into their food, she realized she'd never had a man over for a meal before. Hell, she couldn't remember having any man, outside of a couple contractors, inside. She snuck a sip of Victor's orange juice, cutting a glance his way. He didn't complain, but moved the iced Frangelico out of her reach, giving her a grin.

It felt so right having him here, talking work, sharing a meal. So...normal.

The thought scared the sin right out of her.

"I will alert my teams about your info," he said. "And I'll

check with the DEA, just to be sure Cooper never worked a case involving the Fifty-seven Gang, DeStefano, or Molina before he joined my taskforce."

A brief feeling of relief spread through her. Victor hadn't blown off her concern or simply placated her. He was taking this seriously. "Thank you."

They finished in companionable silence. When he began to clean the dishes, she stopped him and led him to her bathroom, grabbing his overnight bag on the way. She started the tub filling and got out a clean toothbrush for him. "You wash up, and I'll be back shortly."

He glanced at the big tub and then at her. "You want me to take a bath?"

The only shower she had was outside, meant for washing off after a day at the beach. "Don't tell me you're one of *those* guys."

"Not sure I follow." But the look in his eyes said he was teasing her again.

"You think bathing is only for women." She narrowed her eyes at him. "A manly man only takes a shower, right?"

"Actually, I was hoping you had some bath salts or bubble bath to go in it."

"Nice save. When was the last time you took a bath?"

"Yesterday. I take one all the time."

"Liar."

He chuckled and raised both hands in the air. "Busted."

"You might like some lavender Epsom salts. They're detoxing and help you relax."

"I'd rather have you. Why don't you join me?"

"Because you're tired and need sleep. You told Director Allen you'd be up and going in two hours, and you've already burned thirty minutes of that."

He gave a mock salute. "You're right, but I'm so damn crazy about you, I'd rather spend the remaining hour and a half in this tub enjoying every inch of your skin. I'll take you over sleep anytime."

His chocolate eyes grew darker, a sexy intensity she recognized. "Although I'd love to, I'll give you a rain check. You need to take care of yourself, Victor, and if I have to force you to do it, I will."

He started to argue, and she was already feeling pretty weak about her stance thanks to those sexy eyes, so she whirled away and shut the door behind her. All the way to the kitchen, she had to draw in slow, deep breaths to keep from running back to him.

Scrubbing the pans, she decided she had to come clean. Tell Victor the truth. Everything about him made her feel safe and ready to take the next step with their relationship. The nagging doubts were still there, but when he was around, they seemed completely ridiculous and insignificant. That's what he did for her, giving her perspective and making her realize she needed a man in her life. Not just any man, but the right man.

There weren't many things she felt one hundred percent confident about, especially outside of her job. But she couldn't base a real relationship with Victor on a lie, and while the timing was poor, she couldn't go on without telling him the truth.

Wiping down the counters, she hummed softly, and when she was finished, she shut off the kitchen light. *I'm going to tell him everything.*

Her insides felt tight with doubt and fear because there was no way he would take what she was about to tell him casually. In fact, he might walk out the door, but it was a chance she had to take. Undercover work was one thing—you had to lie and deceive people for the higher good. Lying to Victor was wrong, even though she hadn't been investigating him seriously since that first night. Her instincts were usually spot on, and she'd known after talking to him for several hours at the Christmas party, that he was clean as a whistle.

Of course, her report to her boss with those words had only

garnered a 'stick with it' reply. Normally, she wouldn't have been annoyed because some of the best criminals were exceptional at creating a persona that made you trust them implicitly while they were doing illegal activities behind your back. She'd been duped once before, but never after that. Her bullshit radar was as superior as her shooting capabilities. She hit the bull's-eye every time.

I have to do it. For better or worse, she had to come clean.

The bathroom door was open, steam filtering into the bedroom. Crossing the floor, she glanced to her bed and her heart melted.

Victor was fast asleep, the dog lying next to him.

Taz peeked open an eye and his tail did a lazy wag.

So much for good intentions.

Liv crawled in beside them both and let herself drift off.

4

Victor came awake slowly, spooned around Olivia. Another warm body pressed against his back snoring softly. Taz.

It felt right. Comfortable. He couldn't remember the last time he'd woken up in a strange bed, outside of the occasional hotel room when he was traveling for work. In the past year or so, there'd been no women in his life, except his mother and four sisters, and he'd been okay with that.

Until Olivia.

His morning erection pushed into her bottom, and he breathed deeply into her hair on the pillow they shared, drawing in the scent of her shampoo. If only he could stay in this place, forget about the worries pressing into his brain already.

Olivia shifted slightly, sighing as her hand found his arm. She gently trailed her fingers over his wrist to his hand, pulling it tighter around her abdomen. Her bottom pressed back into him, an invitation.

He didn't need further encouragement. Snaking his hand down the edge of her nightgown, he eased the satin over her hip.

She wasn't wearing panties.

His hard-on grew even more painful.

Her moan was low and soft, her legs opening to allow his fingers access. He tickled her soft folds, enjoying her heat and the wetness he found. Part of his brain urged him to get up and check on Cooper, but his other brain, now situated at Liv's warm entrance, suffocated the demand.

He buried his face in her hair, nuzzling her neck and tracing his tongue down the knobs of her cervical spine. His fingers slid through her wetness and found the spot that made her catch her breath.

Along with her increased breathing, he heard panting in his ear. Taz was awake and leaning over Victor's shoulder to see what was going on.

"Down," he demanded.

The dog licked his face and he had to give the command again, but then Taz got the point and bailed. In his arms, Liv laughed. "For a second, I thought you were talking to me."

He chuckled, stroking her until she cried out his name, her orgasm tightening around his fingers. Once she came down, he maneuvered her onto her stomach, propping her hips on a pillow and plunged inside.

Their coupling was hard and fast, as if they couldn't get enough of each other. Outside of the interrupted hook-up the previous day, it was only the second time he'd had the pleasure of exploring her body. He meant to take it slow, but she did things to him that made that plan fly out the window. Every touch, every kiss, every moan made him lose control.

Victor never lost control.

What is happening to me?

His overactive brain finally shut down as Olivia bucked under him, crying out his name again on her second orgasm. He helped her ride it until she was nothing but a beautiful, quivering mass of boneless female under him.

And then she shifted onto her back, running a hand through

his hair and spreading her legs wide once more to take him inside. Gripping his hair, she found his bottom lip with her teeth and nibbled. The sudden assault sent him over his own edge and he thrust into her, burying himself into her heat one final time.

As his cock spent itself, pulsing inside her, he bent his head and kissed her deeply. Bliss infused him from head to toe, mindless and welcome.

In the aftermath, they spooned once more for a few quiet moments. Victor had nearly dozed off when his phone rang from the nightstand, the sound of Thomas's ringtone telling him who the caller was.

His temporary reprieve over, he leaned across Liv and retrieved it. "Thomas," he answered, dread in his chest. "How's Cooper?"

"Stable, sir, but that's not why I'm calling."

Olivia scooted off the bed and headed for the bathroom. The male in him enjoyed the sway of her hips under the body-hugging satin as she walked.

He swung his legs off the bed and sat up. "Did you get a hit on one of our suspects?"

Thomas's voice was strained. "Nothing solid."

"Then what is it?"

"There's been another incident."

Everything in him went south. He came to his feet. "What happened?"

"After you texted me about Olivia's intel on the Kings, I called some of my contacts. FBI Agent Vasco Marin met me at headquarters first thing this morning. He's working undercover with the Suarez Kings and agreed to update me on what they have in the works."

Taz appeared in the doorway, ears up. Olivia must've also heard the concern in Victor's voice. She appeared in the bathroom doorway with a frown on her face.

In the background, Victor heard sirens. "And?"

"And I should correct myself and say he *was* working under-cover. He's dead, sir."

"What?" Victor's guts turned to mud. "How?"

"You know I've been trying to sell my car? Well, Marin was interested. After we discussed the Kings, he asked if he could check it out. I had parked a block away, like I normally do, and it had started pouring. I lent him my FBI jacket and hat, and he went to take a look." Thomas blew out a heavy sigh. "The car exploded a few seconds after he climbed inside. I felt the blast all the way in here."

Now Victor's stomach turned over as he wrapped his mind around the obvious. "Someone put a bomb on your car?"

"They must have thought he was me when he got inside."

Victor lowered the phone for a second, trying to catch a mental breath. "Shit."

"Victor?" Olivia asked earnestly, coming to lay on a hand on his arm. "What is it? Is Cooper okay?"

He held up a finger and brought the phone back to his mouth. "Are you all right?"

"Physically? Yeah, I'm fine. Mentally? Not so great. A good agent just died because someone thought he was me."

Victor understood Thomas's reaction, but his main concern at the moment had to be about the safety of his taskforce member. "Are you safe?"

"Relatively speaking, I guess. The bomber almost certainly believes I'm dead at this point, but the first responders are here, and I have to give a statement."

"I'll handle the police. You stay out of sight. I want Mitch there, ASAP, to keep you under wraps. I'm putting the whole team on high alert." Victor believed in being prepared, and his team was trained for this possibility, but he'd never had to issue the directive until now. "Code Condor. I repeat, Code Condor."

There was a slight pause. "Yes, sir."

Victor checked the clock on the nightstand. "I'll be there in twenty minutes. Go to ground and don't come up until you hear from me."

They disconnected.

Olivia was now gripping his arm. "How bad is it? Do I want to know?"

"I need coffee and..." he started to say *you*, but caught himself. She had a job to do, a career, just like he did. She couldn't stay at his side 24/7. "Can you take care of Taz for a while longer?"

"Of course. Don't worry about him. I'll get you some coffee while you clean up."

He could see the questions in her eyes she didn't voice. He appreciated the fact she didn't badger him, and then felt slightly guilty he wasn't more forthcoming. "Someone tried to blow up Thomas in his car, except they killed a different agent. Not one of mine, but... Shit, it's still a horrible thing."

Her face clouded with consternation. "My God, that's terrible. Is Thomas okay? Who was the other agent?"

"Vasco Marin. FBI." Victor grabbed his overnight bag and headed for the bathroom. "Marin had information on the Kings and was meeting Thomas. Outside of tremendous guilt, Thomas is fine." He stopped in the bathroom doorway. "I have a feeling this is going to get worse. I need you to watch your back."

She patted the dog's head. "I need you to do the same. Seems to me like someone is targeting your taskforce, not me."

It was starting to seem that way. "I know you have work today, but..."

As if she could read his mind, she smiled. "I'll catch up with you as soon as I can, okay? You need me sooner, I'll cut work and run."

He would feel better if he could keep an eye on her. "Whoever targeted Thomas waited for him to show up at the office where the taskforce meets. The place has always been a secret, since the agents are often undercover. We used it like a safe house."

Understanding dawned. "Who knew about it outside of your group?"

"That's what's bothering me as much as anything. No one, especially a criminal, should've known the address."

"Do you think one of your agents was followed?"

Each of them was careful, having been trained like spies to use surveillance detection routes to ensure they were never followed to the meeting place, or home from it. "Unlikely, but anything is possible. I intend to find out."

"Thomas is your second-in-command with the SCVC, correct?"

"Yeah." He knew what she was getting at. "First Cooper is shot, now someone tries to kill Thomas."

"Systematic assassination, but delivered by two different methods. Premeditated and calculated. Did the killer switch to a bomb to kill Thomas because he knows he failed to kill Cooper with the rifle? Or is it two different killers?"

Behavioral 'tells' of the criminal always showed up in the victim's crime scene and method to deliver the crime. In this case, it seemed odd that one assassin would use two different methods, but like Liv pointed out, maybe the suspect had simply chosen the bomb in order to be sure he didn't miss this time.

"Either way, someone is coming after my team. I've got to shut them down before they can harm anyone else."

5

Olivia took Taz with her when she went to work. The Monday morning meeting was the first thing on the day's agenda, so she went in early and rummaged through the back area containing tactical gear. There in one of the boxes, she found a police dog vest she attached to Taz.

At first, he didn't seem too keen on the idea, standing there giving her an odd look with his head cocked and his ears up as if to say, "What the hell?"

"If you want to hang out with me, you have to make concessions," she told him. "As of this moment, you are a special deputy marshal K9."

He turned his head and sniffed the vest, but then put his ears down and wagged.

That's settled. "Good. Do what I tell you and we won't have any problems. Got it?"

The wagging sped up. He followed her to the door and she went to grab coffee before the meeting. In the kitchen, several of her coworkers commented about the dog, Taz receiving ear scratches and back slaps. "Watching him for a friend," Olivia said several times. "Figured as long as he's trained for police work, he could keep me company today."

No one questioned the lack of a badge on the vest or anything else about Taz's sudden appearance. The dog's quiet, polite demeanor fit with a trained police dog.

Olivia's boss did a double-take when she entered the room, but he was already at the podium calling the meeting to order, so she dodged the bullet of explaining Taz to him.

Everyone took their seats, and Supervisory Deputy Director Abraham Navarro began the Monday morning spiel about recent successes. "Our fugitive taskforce arrested Gerald O'Neil Saturday night for numerous charges including felonious assault and battery against a police officer. We worked with Mexican authorities and arrested federal escapee Ivan Morales who is wanted on a double homicide in Mexico City."

The list went on for another minute, many of her counterparts able to close cases since the previous week. Olivia sipped her coffee and let her mind wander to Victor and the situation he was dealing with. She considered paying Alfie a visit sooner than this evening, but showing up unannounced on his doorstep could lead to trouble. He wasn't under official Justice Department protection yet, and playing a dangerous game with Frankie and Gino in order to solidify the intel the JD needed in order to take down the West Coast Fifty-seven Gang. As far she could tell, Alfie never worked at home because of his daughter, but it was imperative Olivia keep their relationship covert. The dinners were always preplanned and could be cancelled if Alfie was worried about surveillance from his bosses. She couldn't risk blowing his status with his mob group or all the hard work she'd put into setting up the deal with the JD to take Gino DeStefano and his "family" down.

"Does anyone have further updates?" Navarro asked, shuffling his papers.

No one did, and he began listing current assignments. Once again, Olivia tuned out. She had a very special position in the district office, allowing her more freedom than most of her coworkers. She'd done her time serving warrants, arresting fugitives, and transporting prisoners, her total dedication to the job helping her climb the ranks quickly and efficiently. When she'd gone to Navarro and told him about Alfie and the potential use of him as an informant, Navarro had wanted to turn it over to the FBI. Olivia had insisted she was the perfect person to handle the case. After several intense discussions, she'd made the decision to go over Navarro's head and speak directly to the chief director for their territory. Eventually it had gone all the way to Justice. When word had come down from on high that Olivia and her idea had been granted permission, Navarro had let her know how annoyed he was at her. She had no doubt after this case, she'd have to find a new office.

Of course with that permission came the Justice Department's request for her to investigate Victor. No one, not even Navarro, knew about that. Her contact in Washington had made it clear that if she wanted permission to groom Alfonso Barone as a confidential informant, she had to do something for them. That something had been the investigation. No reason had been given, but there was obviously something in Victor's background that had made them suspicious.

Navarro would probably never know about that, and that was fine with her. She didn't want anyone to know. She'd only agreed because she wanted Gino and Frankie B. Buddying up to Victor had been an easy assignment...until she'd figured out what a great guy he was.

If only her contact at the JD would've let her off with her original report two months ago, stating that very fact. Not in those exact words, but a sterile, organizational memo citing that she had found nothing suspicious. The whole thing had set her on edge, wondering if they were hoping to find something criminal where there wasn't anything. It struck her as if they had it in for Victor. But why?

She didn't like it then and still didn't now.

Believing she could exonerate him, she'd continued her investigation. So far, she had done that, but the problem was, now she was having a relationship with him. If they found out, her tail would be grass from the Justice Department on down, everyone suspecting she was simply covering for him.

Olivia had been in plenty of quandaries before, but this one might top them all.

The meeting finally adjourned, and as she rose to her feet, Navarro passed by giving her a wave to follow.

Oh joy. He was going to give her grief about the dog, she just knew it.

As she and Taz took their time leaving the room and heading for Navarro's office, Liv mentally tried out various explanations, feeling out which one Navarro was most likely to buy.

"Shut the door," her supervisor said as she and the dog entered.

She did, leaning against it and hoping this would be quick. Maybe the best defense was a strong offense. As in, steer the topic of conversation right from the start. "Did you hear about the DEA officer who was shot in San Diego yesterday and the bomb explosion this morning that killed an agent?"

He shuffled some papers on his desk, avoiding her eyes, as if she were insignificant. "What's with the dog?"

She sighed mentally. Her distraction had been worth a try. "I'm dog sitting, and he's trained, so I brought him along."

"Trained in what, chasing tennis balls?"

She kept bluffing. "He's a trained police dog."

"And I'm Santa Claus," Navarro said. "What's the latest on your investigation?"

He wasn't going to press her about the dog. She supposed that was a bonus. "I'm looking into the fact that the shooting and bombing I just mentioned happen to be related to the Fifty-seven Gang and Gino DeStefano. I'm meeting Alfonso tonight to pump him for information. He called yesterday and told me Frankie B had put out a hit on a high-level law enforcement officer. I believe it's tied into my investigation. I'd like to head to San Diego this afternoon and speak to some members on the taskforce involved."

Navarro finally looked up, kicking back in his chair. "The SCVC taskforce is under the jurisdiction of Victor Dupé. He won't let you near any of them."

Little did he know... "You know Dupé?"

"Don't you? Weren't you at that hostage situation he was involved in at Christmas with the children's hospital?"

So he remembered. Go figure. "We spoke during and after, which is why I believe he will let me interview his team."

Navarro put on his reading glasses and faced his computer screen. "Looks to me like you better get your admin work completed. I haven't had an official report from you in the past two weeks. Nathaniel is still waiting for you to sign off on that subpoena you served last Wednesday. You need to sit at your desk today and clean it up."

That was the last thing she was going to do, but pushing him wasn't a good tactical maneuver. She knew exactly what was on her desk, and although she hated paperwork, she'd have it done in an hour, maybe less. "I'll clear it before I leave today."

He took her statement as compliance and nodded. "Dismissed."

Happy to bail, she grabbed the door handle and pulled Taz to his feet.

"Fiorelli?"

Damn, she'd almost made it. She glanced at him over her shoulder. "Yes, sir?"

"Do not bring the dog again. This is not puppy daycare."

She didn't like making promises she might not keep, so she

said nothing, hustling herself and the dog out and closing the door behind them.

She stopped at the vending machine and grabbed a bag of crackers and a diet soda before heading to her desk. Taz was ready for a nap and laid down at her feet as she went to work typing up the required forms necessary to get Navarro off her back.

Forty-two minutes and twenty seconds later, she finished the last report, dropped the empty cracker bag in the garbage, and checked to make sure no one was paying any attention to her. Satisfied, she grabbed her half-drank soda and led Taz to the door.

The noonday sun was bright and hot, too hot this early in April, but she had plenty of time to make it to San Diego and back before dinner with Alfonso. It'd be a fast round-trip, but worth it. She was still determined to tell Victor the truth as soon as possible.

Before she and the dog were on the freeway, she sent Victor a text. *On my way. Can we meet?*

For long minutes, there was no reply. The lack of response could be due to any number of reasons, she just hoped nothing else bad had happened to anyone on the taskforce. Flipping on the radio, she turned to the Southern California news station, but soon grew frustrated as the lunchtime talk show focused on the recent robbery of an actor in Beverly Hills, rather than pertinent news.

Taz had his head out the window again. She queued up her favorite playlist and glanced at the navigation system that handled all her calls and messages while she was driving. It would ding to let her know about an incoming text, but she kept glancing at the screen anyway, watching for a reply.

She was five miles into the drive before the text finally came. *"When you hit town, let me know. I'll meet you here."* He sent a link to a small mom and pop coffee shop a few blocks from downtown.

Feeling a sense of relief, but dreading the upcoming conversation, Liv reached over and patted Taz before turning up the music in hopes of drowning out the doubt demons swimming in her brain.

VICTOR SPOTTED Olivia's car across the street as he left the coffee shop with two large Americanos in a tray. He'd told her not to come inside but to wait for him. As he darted through traffic, he saw Taz sitting in the backseat with his ears up and tail wagging.

The combination of Liv and the dog was the best thing Victor had seen all day.

Before he climbed in, he did a casual scan of the area to make sure nothing seemed out of place. No one appeared to be paying him any attention, and he quickly climbed in the passenger seat.

Liv leaned across the console to kiss him as she lifted one of the cups from the carrier. "How did you know I needed a large one of these?"

The kiss had been too quick, too brief. After she'd taken a sip, he caught her by the back of the neck, dragging her face into the center between the seats again, where he laid a proper kiss on her, parting her lips and teasing her tongue with his. She tasted of coffee and comfort, desire and encouragement. When he finally let her come up for air, she looked at him with a deep craving in her eyes and a shy smile. He wanted to freeze that moment and carry it with him the rest of the day.

She's the best thing that's ever happened to me.

The thought struck him as odd. He had a nice life. He enjoyed his job and had good people working under him. He loved his family, and missed them every day. "I brought you a brownie too, if you want one."

"Coffee and chocolate? You really know how to woo a girl."

"Next best thing to beer and cannolis." He fished the folded paper bag of brownies out of his jacket pocket and handed it to her. Taz stuck his head over the seat, licking Victor's ear and making him jump, almost spilling his coffee. "Hey, boy," Victor scratched his chin. "Miss me?"

The dog caught the scent of brownies and nearly came into the front seat. Olivia held them out of reach and used an elbow to keep him in the back. "Down, Taz. No chocolate for you."

The dog obeyed reluctantly, keeping his big face between them. Olivia took another sip and tucked the brownies safely away from the dog's nose. "Where to?"

Paranoia flared again, eating away at his insides. He scanned the buildings nearby, the cars parked up and down the street. "Drive randomly for a few minutes. I want to make sure we don't have a tail."

She put the car in gear and eased into traffic. "I would've been here sooner, but I had to do paperwork to get my boss out of my hair. How are Cooper and Thomas?"

"The doctors are keeping Cooper sedated. He's still in serious condition. I have Thomas at a safe house, and I'm going to insist Ronni join him. Unfortunately, I've spent most of the morning dealing with local law enforcement, the bomb squad, the medical examiner, and a host of others, including dozens of requests from news organizations wanting a statement about my "dead" agent. I'm doing my best to keep Thomas's actual status under wraps as long as possible, but there are too many people involved. Word will leak soon enough." He rubbed his eyes and took a drink of the hot coffee. It was a bit weak. He probably should've gone for straight espresso, but he wasn't choosy at the moment. "It's been a long morning."

She took a left. "San Diego PD have any leads on the bomber?"

"None. The office the taskforce uses for meetings is in a

rundown building that houses a senior center, an ambulance chaser, and an accountant. The neighborhood has no traffic cams, no ATM cameras, or other sources of video. No witnesses have come forward. Thomas immediately contacted the dead agent's superior, obviously, to let him know what happened, and I've gotten an earful from him, but nothing helpful. Agent Marin was undercover in the Suarez cartel, and he left a couple names with Thomas that might give us leads into Cooper's shooting, but we've got nothing else substantial on who planted the bomb."

"You think the shooter might be part of the Suarez cartel?"

"It's the strongest lead we have at the moment and appears more likely than a mob hit. The suspects we had at the park all turned up as dead ends."

Liv's cheek sucked in as if she were chewing on it as she turned the idea over. "Street gang hits are often less precise, so that fits with the different methods and sloppy execution that left both Cooper and Thomas alive."

"Since Marin's death is not public knowledge yet, whoever set the bomb believes Thomas died. One of the reasons I've been running interference hot and heavy with the news media is to keep the idea alive. Eventually, whoever tried to kill Thomas will figure it out, but I'm buying as much time as possible in hopes we find the killer before he can do any further damage."

They flowed with the light afternoon traffic, weaving around the city. Both checked rearview mirrors and kept an eye on cars that followed them for more than a few blocks. None raised flags. After Victor was certain they were not being followed, he directed Liv to Thomas and Ronni's apartment building.

"Celina is still at the hospital, and I put Mitch on bodyguard duty with her so Ronni could be with Thomas. I need to pick up some clothes and things for the two of them. Everyone else is on high alert and laying low. If I had my way, I'd round them all up and put them in the safe house."

"It's natural to want to protect them," she said. "I have to admit, I'm a little surprised you haven't done that already."

"I floated it by all of them and got nothing but pushback. They want to work the case, not hide out, and I understand their motivation. Some, like Cooper, have spouses and kids to worry about."

"They're afraid to leave them vulnerable."

"Exactly. We don't know if this is over, or they'll start targeting family members as well."

"What a nightmare."

His thought exactly. "I've been in touch with a former agent who worked on the taskforce several years ago, and who now runs a security service in DC. I can't get the FBI or Justice Department to release funding for increased security on my agents yet, but if I have to, I'll hire bodyguards for them myself."

She pulled into the parking lot. "Director Allen doesn't believe there will be more attempts on your agents?"

"I spoke to him for the third time today a few minutes ago, and he's unwilling to come out and say someone is specifically targeting the SCVC Taskforce, even though I'm in charge of several here in California and none of those have been targeted. Some days he's more politician than agent."

"He can't possibly believe these are simply random attacks."

A parking spot was open at the end of the first row. "In my time as West Coast director, the only instances when we have butted heads has been when it came to budget restrictions. It's not about what he *believes*, but what will happen if he declares the SCVC Taskforce needs funding in order to protect its agents. In the big picture, he thinks it shows weakness, that my agents can't protect themselves, or are not trained well enough. In that case, they don't belong on this elite group."

"Ah, yes. Appearances in DC are everything."

"I could have two dead agents right now, and he still wouldn't approve funding for increased security for the rest."

She parked and they took Taz and the brownies and went up to the apartment. Thomas had given Victor a key and the access code for the alarm system.

The place was small, but clean and neat. Victor suspected that was Ronni's doing more so then her husband's. While neither of the agents were home all that much, the place had a comfortable feel to it, very inviting. Victor hoped that one day his would too.

Olivia helped herself to a brownie, under Taz's intense supervision, while Victor gathered clothes. He had no idea what to grab for Ronni from her collection of toiletries, and Olivia jumped in to help.

"Ronni has a lot of hair products and makeup," she said, eyeing the full shelves. She picked out several bottles and lifted the bag. "Hope I grabbed the right stuff."

Victor noticed how Taz followed Olivia everywhere. The dog was probably hoping for brownie crumbs, but he also seemed somewhat protective of her.

Maybe I can get her to adopt him.

"Was that a police dog vest I saw on the backseat?" he asked as she took the lead collecting clothes for Ronni, saving him the embarrassment of going through Ronni's dresser drawers for undergarments.

She smiled, swallowing the last of her brownie and brushing her hands on her jeans. "Taz came to work with me today. He's in training, if anyone asks."

Yup, I think I could love her. She found a way to take every situation and make the best of it. He'd tried to do the same throughout his life, taking care of his disabled mother while she raised him and his sisters with no father in the picture and a very limited income.

"You're amazing, you know that?" He smiled at her as he sent off a text to Thomas, telling him they would be at the safe house shortly.

She returned it, then the smile faded. "Victor, there's something I need to tell you."

His stomach went tight at her tone. "What is it, Liv?"

The dog sat at her feet, sensing the unease in her voice. She patted his head, averting her eyes from Victor. "It's just that... Well, you know how I feel about y—"

Victor's phone blared with Celina's ringtone. He snatched it from his pocket. "Sorry. It's Celina."

"Oh, um. Go ahead. You have to take it."

He punched the button. "Celina, how is he?"

Her voice was teary, but with happiness. "He's awake, Victor! The Beast rises. You have to come."

Yes! Everyone on the taskforce referred to Cooper as the beast. "That is great news. Hang tight. I'm on my way."

He disconnected and shoved the phone back in his pocket. "Cooper's awake."

Olivia smiled again, but it was strained. "That's wonderful. I thought they had him sedated."

"I've never known anything that can keep Cooper Harris down, and apparently not even heavy doses of intravenous drugs. I need to talk to him. He might have seen the shooter. It's a long shot, but it's possible he could ID the guy."

She headed for the door. "I'll drive."

6

The marshal was on the move again.

The man watched the red dot pulse on the map, glad he'd stuck the small tracking device on her car when he'd seen her at the hospital. She was proving to be of more value than he'd expected.

Technology was a wonderful thing. A few years ago, he would've had to physically follow her, and she was a busy woman. He would've found himself running all over the place, trying to keep up with her. Today, he had time, so he'd followed her just for fun.

She was an unexpected bonus in this scenario. He hadn't realized she was involved with the director, and his ego smarted a little. The director was a slight impediment on that front, but give the situation time. Olivia would come around.

Now he understood things differently and he was always one to use every opportunity.

Deputy US Marshal Olivia Fiorelli definitely presented a prime one. It was no hardship to seduce her into his web.

She could access important information he needed and assist in his mission with the director, without ever realizing she was doing so. She might also offer a bonus target his superiors would appreciate, but that'd mean putting his quest to win her heart aside.

No way he was doing that. Olivia was his and he would protect her at all costs. She was the woman he wanted next to him when he pushed his bosses out of the way and moved to take over the Southern California quadrant of the Fifty-seven Gang. The DeStefano Syndicate was going down in flames, and the sooner the better.

More power, more money, more security. He could eliminate his enemies in one fell stroke, all thanks to the woman driving the car he watched on the GPS map.

She was headed for the hospital, leading him to believe there were two possibilities. Cooper Harris was dead, or the man was awake and talking.

While he preferred the former, his gut told him it was the latter. Either way, it made no difference. Harris wasn't the real target. Neither were the other taskforce members. In his line of work, a good distraction and sleight-of-hand were the best ways of getting what he wanted. It was unfortunate he'd missed the man's heart by centimeters—another dead agent on his kill list would be a nice addition, especially one as prominent and seemingly invincible as Harris—but in the end, it was the director he wanted gone.

Soon. Very soon.

Everything was going to work out fine. With Olivia providing effective intel, it might be sooner than he'd originally planned. All he had to do was convince her he was the better man.

Which meant finding a way to make Director Dupé look like the bad guy in this scenario.

Hmm...

That would take some doing, but it wasn't impossible. The man turned over options and ideas as he tracked Olivia's progress. Watching the red dot make a turn off the main road, he wondered if she would return to Carlsbad yet tonight. She had a meeting later; would she put Dupé over her job?

His phone rang with a call from one of his superiors. He thought about letting it go to voicemail, yet believed in taking care of things immediately and not letting them pile up. He'd have to talk to the man sooner or later, might as well get it over with.

As he watched the red pulsing dot arrive at the hospital parking lot, he answered with a statement. "Nothing to worry about, boss. I have everything under control."

The man on the other end seemed to disagree, launching into a series of arguments and accusations. The red dot stopped.

Interrupting his superior wasn't the best idea, but he wasn't in the mood for being berated by a man who sent others to do his dirty work while he enjoyed the power and profits his position allowed.

"I told you I have everything under control," the man said. "Let me do my job."

"Where are you?" his superior asked. "We should meet. Now."

Not going to happen. "I'm in San Diego," he said, staring at the red dot. "I should have more information after tonight. I'll be in touch."

He disconnected, knowing it was a bad idea, but the other man didn't realize his days were numbered. Soon, he'd be nothing but another mark at the end of the riflescope.

Because taking out Victor Dupé was only the first step in the overall plan. Soon, DeStefano and Molina would join him six feet under, somewhere in the desert.

His superiors were shortsighted. They were intent on controlling the micro aspects of California, they kept missing the bigger picture.

He sat back and took a swig of whiskey. He could appreciate the director's position as head of the entire West Coast FBI, but he needed a source inside the Bureau to smooth the way for certain transactions. From all accounts, Director Dupé was not that person. He couldn't be bribed or threatened into cooperating.

Which only left one option—someone needed to take his place.

Taking another sip, he sat back, eyeing the GPS as a new thought came to him. If Dupé had feelings for the marshal, that could work to his advantage, at least in the short term.

Liking this recent turn of events in more ways than one, he smiled to himself.

Yes, Olivia Fiorelli definitely offered many opportunities, and he was going to make sure she ended up on his side of the law very, very soon.

COOPER HARRIS WAS INDEED AWAKE, but extremely groggy according to Mitch Holden, who met Victor and Olivia as they stepped off the elevator. Mitch's handshake was firm and quick. He frowned slightly at Taz's presence, but said nothing, giving the dog a pat on the head before he directed all of them down the hall toward the ICU.

Olivia planned to stay in the waiting room with the dog, and at first, Victor didn't seem to notice she wasn't right behind him. She'd just settled into one of the worn waiting room chairs when he popped his head back in.

"What are you doing?" he asked. "Aren't you coming?"

The ICU floor limited how many people could be in a patient's room at one time, and with Celina and Mitch already here, Victor would max that number. Plus, law enforcement was a funny thing. She knew Cooper and Celina casually, but she wasn't part of the team. It could make things awkward. "They won't allow Taz into ICU."

He seemed genuinely surprised. "I'm sure the rules forbid it, but since when has that stopped you?"

She smiled, but stayed put. "I'll hang out here with your dog. I know when to push it, and when not to. Go talk to your agent and tell him I said hi."

After he left, she checked her emails as Taz lay at her feet. A minute later, Dr. Emma Collins came strolling into the waiting room.

"Hello, Olivia." Emma was dressed in a peacock blue skirt and matching jacket. Her blond hair hung loose around her shoulders, and a pair of blue framed glasses sat on her nose. "I didn't expect to see you here today."

"Lending moral support," Olivia said. "How is he doing?"

She leaned down and patted the dog's head. "Cooper? They don't call him The Beast for nothing. He's one tough guy, and I suspect he'll be up and running in no time."

"And Celina? How is she holding up?"

Emma glanced out the window. Olivia had the feeling she wasn't seeing the view from this floor. The doctor had some interesting experiences in her background, all of which would leave a normal person with severe PTSD, so Cooper wasn't the only tough one around here. "There are times when it's harder on the people around the injured person, because of the emotional strain, than on the person themselves."

In other words, Celina was still a hot mess and probably would be for quite a while. Seeing the man you love shot in the heart right in front of you and your child was about as traumatic as it could get. "Victor hoped she might talk to you about what happened, so I'm glad you're here. How is Jett?"

Jett was Emma and Mitch's son, about the same age as Cooper and Celina's daughter. The two kids had been fun to watch back at Christmas, and Olivia was once again grateful that no one had gotten hurt that night at the hospital.

"He's a handful," Emma said, bringing her gaze back and smiling at Liv. "I wouldn't trade him for anything."

There was that look in her eyes that parents got when they talked about their kids. Olivia wondered if her dad had ever looked like that when he'd told someone about her. "I don't suppose he takes after his dad in the 'handful' department?"

The smile grew. "I'm surrounded by a lot of testosterone at the ranch. You should come out sometime. Do you like to ride?"

"Horses? Never been on one, but they look…nice." She preferred dogs over just about anything, and found herself automatically reaching to pet Taz. "Does Jett like them?"

"Loves them. Mitch will have him riding before he's walking, I'm afraid."

Rarely did Olivia feel comfortable chatting with another woman about normal things like family, but Emma had a way of putting even a workaholic outsider like Olivia at ease. "A couple of daredevils, huh?"

She chuckled and took the seat next to Olivia. "I'm glad you and Victor are getting along so well. Thank you for being here for him with this. He's not one to ask for support, if you know what I mean. Are you two…?"

Seeing each other? The invisible words hung in the air. *Are we actually a couple?* Sure felt like it, even though they'd only really shared a couple of intense lovemaking sessions and lots of texts and phone calls. It almost felt like being in high school instead of a mature relationship. "We're taking it slow."

What a lie. She wasn't even sure what "it" was, but they'd jumped into a physical relationship so fast, her head still spun. That was not how she took it 'slow.'

But then again, she hadn't had a real relationship since…

Damn. She couldn't even remember the guy's name it had been so long. Dean? Dan? No wonder she was starved for attention and super-hot sex with a good-looking, powerful man. Her library card was way past due on getting stamped.

Emma smiled again, this one more placid, psychologist-like. "Nothing wrong with slow. I would expect nothing else from Victor. He's not one to rush into a relationship. He's a good man, Olivia. He deserves a strong, honest woman like you."

And whoopsie, another lie. This one of omission, but a mistruth nonetheless. She was strong, yes, but she was *not* honest. She still hadn't told Victor about her investigation into him for the Justice Department.

A man hustled past the door, coming back and peeking his head around the frame a second later. "Dr. Collins?"

Emma stood and brushed down her skirt. "Dr. Walsh? What are you doing here?"

He was tall and lean, the hint of a beard covering his jaws. He seemed to fill up the room as he entered, extending a hand to Emma. "I have a theory to run by the director." He glanced at Olivia and offered his hand to her as well. "Roman Walsh, Director of the Southern California Domestic Terrorism Taskforce. You're Olivia Fiorelli, correct?"

The DTT was under Homeland. Olivia rose to her feet and shook his hand, wondering where he recognized her from. Had he been at the Christmas party? "I don't believe we've met before, have we?"

A commotion sounded in the hallway. Victor appeared at the door. "They're moving him to the cardiac floor. Since he's awake but still in serious condition, that's the best place to keep an eye on him."

"That's good news," Olivia said.

Victor stepped aside as Cooper was wheeled by, Celina following. "Roman, good to see you," he said. "You mentioned in your text earlier you had information I needed? We have time to catch up—the nurses say it will be half an hour or so before we can talk to Cooper again. Once they get him situated, the doctor wants to check him over."

Roman glanced around, noting the waiting area was empty

outside of the four of them. Still, he seemed to think it better if they had privacy. "Any chance they have a conference room available?"

"On the first floor," Emma volunteered. "I'll get someone to open it for us. That'll give Cooper and Celina time to adjust to the new room before Victor questions him."

She led the way, Roman on her heels. Olivia grabbed Victor's hand before he could follow. "I should probably get going."

He looked disappointed. "You sure? I could use your input on whatever Roman has found."

Hearing that he wanted her in on the meeting caused a flush of heat to her chest. "Dr. Walsh might feel differently. I may not have clearance for whatever he's going to talk about."

"If you're with me, he'll grant you clearance. All I have to do is say the word."

The warmth spread lower. "Do you know how sexy that is?"

"What?"

"The way you swing your power around like that."

He chuckled and tugged her after him.

They caught up with the others at the elevator and rode down to the first floor, Taz bracing his feet at the drop and giving Olivia a worried look. Emma texted someone she knew and, by the time they arrived at the conference room, her friend had unlocked it and placed several bottled waters on the credenza for them.

Victor sat at the head of the table and Olivia took the chair to his right. Emma sat next to her and Roman paced the floor. Taz wedged between the table leg and Olivia's chair, laying his head on one of her feet.

"Did Cooper see anyone?" the head of the DTT asked Victor.

"He did," Victor answered. All eyes swung to him. "At least, he thinks he did. Everything happened fast, and his memory is blurry. We only spoke for a minute or two before the nurses kicked me out to move him, but what he told me is, he believes he saw a Suarez gang member as he and Celina walked to the park.

The male suspect is approximately 5'7", Hispanic, and clean shaven. He wore a red baseball hat cocked to the left over a purple bandana wrapped around his head. He sported a flame tattoo on one arm, and was wearing a leather vest with the gang symbol on the back. The guy walked past the park entrance, looked square at Cooper, and jumped into a rusted out, late 80s, Pontiac Grand Prix that pulled up to the curb. No license plate. The car circled the park once, then disappeared."

Roman stopped pacing and pulled several papers out of his briefcase. "You like this kid for the shooter?"

Victor shrugged. "I do. He's the best lead we've got and it jives with some of the intel we've received."

Roman handed out papers to each of them and took a seat. "Preliminary report on the bomb that blew up Agent Mann's car this morning. I put a rush on it."

Like the others, Olivia scanned the chain of command, agency number, and the brief description of the scene. Explosive device specialists had examined what the crime scene technicians had recovered, which wasn't much. It appeared to be an IED and had been sent to the FBI's Terrorist Explosive Device Analytical Center to see if they could match it to anything in their database.

The homemade improvised explosive device was simple in its makeup and yet had caused the death of an agent. In Olivia's mind, it made no difference how it was designed or what materials had been put into it—the result was the same.

"There weren't any large enough remnants of the bomb to provide us with fingerprints," Roman said, "but the bomber left us a different kind. The explosive was placed in a backpack we assume was tossed under the car. It appears it was triggered by the call from a cell phone."

They all looked at him, waiting, anticipating. What kind of fingerprint was he talking about, and how did this help the case?

"Is this bomb similar to others you've investigated?" Victor asked.

"The bomb itself is pretty generic; it's what it was carried in that gave us a clue."

"The backpack," Olivia said.

Roman nodded. "Several fibers and the zipper were recovered from the blast site. They happen to match those from another car bombing two months ago in Oceanside. Polly, my CSI expert, caught the similarities. She also did some cross-matching and discovered this particular brand of backpacks has been used by the Suarez Kings for running drugs across the border, and carrying their own shake and bake meth labs."

'Shake and bakes' consisted of a two-liter bottle, cold pills, and a couple noxious chemicals. Drug users loved the simple method, but it was highly explosive, much like the more complicated meth labs.

"They're recycling the drug backpacks for bombs?" Emma asked.

"The last one was used to take out Giada Russo."

Olivia sucked in a breath. Giada was Frankie Molina's little sister.

Taz lifted his head and came to sit beside her, nuzzling his nose against her arm. She petted him absentmindedly. "The Kings killed Giada? I thought her case was unsolved."

"It was," Roman said, "until now. The problem is we don't have an individual to arrest. Like I said, no actual fingerprints, DNA, or witnesses. But I've forced the local detectives to reopen the Russo case and I'm trying to get some FBI involvement."

Because the woman involved was a known criminal, like her brother, the cops weren't all that eager to solve Giada's murder.

Victor sat forward. "I'll make sure the investigation becomes a top priority."

Roman turned to Emma. "Giada Russo was the sister of high-ranking mob boss Frank Molina. The two of them worked like a team up-and-down the West Coast for several years under the guidance of Gino DeStefano until Giada married Tony Russo. The Russos stayed under the radar, supplying military grade weapons to various motorcycle gangs and survivalists. We're not sure if the Kings were purposely trying to take her out, or simply send a message to her brother."

Emma stacked her papers neatly. "What kind of message? Is Molina interfering with the cartel's business?"

"That's what we're hearing through the grapevine." Roman pointed at Olivia. "As I'm sure Deputy Marshal Fiorelli can explain in more detail, Gino DeStefano and his right-hand man, Frankie, want to stamp out the Suarez Kings and use their infrastructure for the same businesses—drugs, money-laundering, and human trafficking."

"It's easier than starting from scratch," Olivia added, "which is what Gino and his made family have been trying to do for many years and failed. The Mexican gangs, motorcycle gangs, and other enterprising criminal syndicates have made it extremely difficult for the traditional Italian mafia bosses to take over. Giada probably broke completely with Frankie when she married Tony Russo and he continued supplying the motorcycle gangs and survivalists with guns."

"Olivia, our own rock star agent here, has played a huge part in stopping them as well," Victor said.

Olivia had challenged every guy she'd dated, although few, searching for her soulmate. She'd refused to settle, or maybe she'd simply been terrified of having a lasting relationship. Her father's ghost hanging over her shoulder never helped either. Maybe that was why she constantly sabotaged herself and couldn't even remember that last guy's name. Although there'd been few men on her dance card, no one had measured up to her ideal.

Until now.

One of her biggest fears was not being special. Silly, but true.

She was always trying to prove herself in her work, in her life. Hearing Victor's compliment made her feel more than special.

But also a tad embarrassed. Did he mean it? Or was he saying it because...

Because he's sleeping with me.

Taz laid at her feet again, shoving himself against her leg. Oh, she needed to get over herself already. Maybe in the end, it wasn't the men in her life who'd never measured up —

Maybe it's me.

Taz started snoring. All eyes were on her, and heat flushed her cheeks, her throat constricted. She once again reminded herself to stop overanalyzing everything and just go with it. "I do what I can."

Roman's phone rang and he glanced at the caller ID. "That's one of the reasons I'm glad you're here, Olivia. Everything we've uncovered so far points to the Suarez Kings being involved in both hits against Victor's taskforce. If things are heating up between them and DeStefano's Fifty-seven Gang, I want you on board. I already have a call into my boss at Homeland. I want to put together a special taskforce to investigate these crimes, and I want you on it."

He didn't wait for her response, standing and walking away as he answered his phone.

Olivia looked at Victor, then her watch. It was getting late and she had a two-hour drive, more if traffic was bad, to Carlsbad. And when wasn't it between here and there?

He understood her code. "I know you have a meeting, but let's talk afterwards, okay? I'll get the details from Roman about this new taskforce and fill you in."

They all stood, and Olivia mentally smiled at the thought of Navarro getting wind of this. "Of course. I'll call you when I'm done."

The dog jerked upright from his sleeping position and nearly tumbled over himself as Olivia shifted and pushed the chair in.

She said her goodbyes to Emma and headed for the door behind Victor.

In the hallway, he tugged her close. "I'll walk you out."

"That's not necessary." *But please do.*

"I have time to kill before I can see Cooper again. I want to check your car."

Ah. "Afraid there might be an errant backpack under it?"

He took her hand and led her and Taz outside. In the sunlight, he paused and took a deep breath. "I know you're on alert and don't need me hovering, but it's a good excuse for me to spend a few more minutes with you, so don't give me grief, okay?"

She grinned at him. "I might have seen something in the back. Maybe we should both climb in and check it out."

He returned the grin, understanding her invitation. "It's a big backseat. Might take fifteen minutes or so to investigate properly."

God, this man. How was she going to keep him in her life? He made her laugh and feel incredibly good about herself. *All* of herself, from her obsession with work to her generous curves he couldn't seem to get enough of.

I'll tell him the truth as soon as I can, but not today. Handing him Taz's leash, she dug out her car keys. "Fifteen minutes might not be quite long enough for what I have planned for you, but I'll do my best."

He slapped her playfully on the ass as she walked away, making her laugh out loud.

7

Victor stood at the hospital entrance watching Olivia drive off. He hadn't been joking about checking for bombs but he'd never dreamt she'd invite him into the backseat. The last time he'd fooled around in a car was ages ago. High school.

Completely unprofessional. What is wrong with me? he asked himself for the umpteenth time.

The cool thing was, after their initial make-out session, they'd started talking and ended up doing nothing more than spooning in the backseat. Just holding each other.

It was...nice.

Better than nice.

Olivia brought him peace even when he was in the midst of chaos. Her presence calmed him. Rejuvenated him.

Still feeling the aftereffects, he didn't hear Roman approach from behind.

"Sorry about the interruption," Roman said. "Clearance just came down for a temporary taskforce to dig deeper into this situation. We've got forty-eight hours to come up with solid leads."

It wasn't much, but they'd worked with less. "Thank you. We

have the information Thomas got from Agent Marin, and a possible connection between the Suarez Kings and the Fifty-seven Gang, or at least the California branch run by DeStefano and Molina. We also have the description of a member of the Kings that Cooper saw at the park, along with the car he left in. I have clothes and some other stuff to bring to Thomas and Ronni at the safe house. Why don't you follow me and we'll set up an office there to start digging and find where the connections lead?"

A large black limo pulled up to the curb as Victor spoke. A second later, the driver jumped out to open the door for the passenger in the backseat. As Victor saw the long legs emerging from the car, Roman's answer turned into background noise.

Tracee Tyson loved the spotlight and called attention to herself anywhere, anytime, even when exiting a car. Her long dark hair had gentle waves in it, like she'd just come from the beach, but her makeup was perfect, and the short skirt and tank top she wore were clearly designer. Her 5'10" frame didn't need a height boost from the three-inch heels on her feet, but they accentuated her toned calves perfectly.

"Is that...?" Roman's voice drifted off, a common occurrence when Tracee appeared. People—especially men—suddenly became tongue-tied, her beauty and fame merging into a lethal cocktail that left them speechless.

With the tilt of her head, she smiled at Victor and those long, sexy legs of hers carried her right to him. "Vic, sweetheart." Eye to eye with him, she air kissed his cheeks. "It's so good to see you."

"Tracee? What are you doing here?"

His famous ex-fiancée gave him a pouty look. "I heard about your friend and knew you'd be here. That's the kind of person you are, and I wanted to lend my support. It's awful what happened." She ran a hand along his forehead, smoothing his brow. "How are you holding up?"

She was a damn good actress, and that had always been part of the problem when they were dating. He never knew when she was acting and when she wasn't. At first, he'd believed everything she'd said. Later, when their relationship began to struggle under the weight of his job and her career, he became jaded enough he didn't believe anything.

He hadn't seen her in nearly three years, except on the covers of magazines and in movie trailers. Her light brown skin and gorgeous turquoise eyes were as youthful as ever. She was in her early thirties, but could still play the role of a twenty-something with ease.

She turned to Roman, sizing him up. "Hi, I'm Tracee, and you are?"

Roman seemed to snap out of his star-induced haze, shooting Victor an inquisitive look, but catching on quick. "A friend. I'll leave you two to catch up. See you inside."

Victor knew he wasn't intentionally being rude by not engaging in small talk with Tracee, he simply didn't want to waste time on it. The clock was ticking, and they all had work to do.

And Victor knew his ex had not made a special trip from LA to support him. "You could have called."

She gave a halfhearted shrug. "I was in the neighborhood. What kind of friend would I be if I didn't stop by to see how you're doing? You still mean a lot to me, Vic."

In the neighborhood. There was the real answer. Her favorite spa, which doubled as a high-priced rehab center, nestled in the desert not far from the city. Her drug problem had started at a young age, and deep in his soul, Victor had naïvely thought he could save her when they were together. They were quite the power couple, after all, and he was good at saving people.

How many times had he covertly checked her into the spa? How many times had he helped her through withdrawal? Even threatening to put her in jail hadn't done the trick, and eventually, as their relationship continued to fall apart, he'd thrown her dealer in prison. Within days of completing yet another rehab stint, he'd found her passed out on the bathroom floor, cocaine dust under her nose.

Tracee never went anywhere without paparazzi following her, and sure enough, as he scanned the parking lot, he saw a man with a camera duck behind an SUV. A car trolled the lot, bypassing open spaces, probably another tabloid reporter.

Great, that's all he needed. "It's good to see you," he lied, "but I have to get back to work."

He turned to go and she grabbed his arm, stopping him. "Vic, I'm sorry. I really am. Don't go. I want to talk. Like the old days. I'm clean now, and I'd really like us to try again. I mean it. For real this time. You were the best thing I ever had in my life. I know that now."

The same old words. He remembered the hope he'd always felt when she said them. *I'm clean. I'm sorry. Let's try again.* Now, all he felt was an odd detachment.

"I'm seeing someone." *And even if I wasn't, there's no way I'd go down that rabbit hole with you again.* "But I wish you all the best, like always."

It wasn't often he admitted defeat, but when it came to Tracee, he'd already slotted her into the lost cause category.

"Oh, I see." She looked truly surprised. Probably was, considering she knew he was a total workaholic. But also, somewhere deep inside, her ego probably convinced her he could never care for anyone else as much as he did her. "That's great. I'm happy for you."

Her acting skills couldn't carry her this time. She stepped back and gave him a sad smile. "Anyone I know?"

"No." He wasn't about to discuss Olivia with her. "She's devoted to the job like I am. We make a good team."

Tracee nodded, avoiding his eyes as she tried to make a clean escape. "I hope it works out for you. You deserve some happiness."

"Thank you." He felt like a heel, even though he didn't know why. She'd shown up unexpectedly and tried to manipulate him. "Tracee?"

Her driver opened the door for her and she glanced back, placing a hand on it, hope in her eyes. "Yes?"

"Take care of yourself."

Her smile faltered. Without another word, she slipped into the limo.

He didn't wait on the sidewalk for it to drive away. He'd cared deeply for her once, but she'd cared more about getting high. He knew it was an addiction, but he couldn't play second fiddle to cocaine, and he'd tried his best to help her find meaning to her life that didn't involve escaping reality. She had advantages other people who resorted to drugs never had. She had fame and fortune, opportunities, friends and contacts who could help her whenever she needed it. A lot of time and frustration had passed, but he'd realized cocaine was a crutch, a way for her to play the victim. He hoped one day someone could help her, but bottom-line, she had to help herself.

On the cardiac floor, he located Cooper's room. Roman was inside, discussing theories with him and Celina. Celina looked almost as bad as Cooper. Dark shadows hung under her eyes, her normally tawny skin was sallow.

She got up and motioned Victor to her chair. "I'm going to take a bathroom break. Back in a few minutes."

Cooper was half sitting in the hospital bed, his brow furrowed with a mixture of anger and stress. A morphine drip was taped to his arm, but he wasn't using the little button to medicate himself. "Roman told me about the backpack link to the bomb. I need to get my files from the office, see if I can figure out which one of the Kings is directly involved."

Victor appreciated his commitment, and understood his drive to be involved in the case. Revenge was an intense motivator, but rarely an effective one, regardless of what Hollywood liked to advocate. "Roman and I are headed to the safe house to meet up with Thomas and Ronni. Thomas has already been digging into your files, so far to no avail, but I'll crosscheck all of the taskforce cases in the past year with the FBI database intel on the Suarez gang. Your job is to stay here and follow doctor's orders."

Cooper started to argue. No surprise there. Victor held up a hand. "Save your breath, take some morphine. This isn't just about you, Cooper. Nothing is anymore. You have a wife and daughter, and they need you. If nothing else, you need to do what I say in order to help Celina and Via. They need you healthy. *I* need you healthy. We will hunt down whoever shot you. We will find the bomber as well. You are no good to any of us, if you end up dead, especially if it's due to your bullheadedness."

Celina rushed in, holding up her phone so Cooper could see it. "Sophia called. Via wants to see her Daddy!"

The little girl's face was on the screen and Victor heard her giggle and say something. She was still too young to actually make sense, but her baby talk was enough to light up Cooper's expression. "There's my girl!"

As Celina leaned over the bed and the two of them Face-Timed with their daughter, Roman and Victor waved a silent goodbye and left the room.

Outside in the hall, an orderly rushed by, followed by a nurse. Roman and Victor moved aside before loitering a few rooms down.

"If I didn't know better," Roman said, "I would swear you had that planned down to the very second."

"What do you mean?"

"It was like you scripted the whole thing. You were talking about his family and, bam, a second later the kid is on the phone, wanting to see him. I knew you had skills, Director, but that's pretty damn impressive. Not to mention the fact Tracee Tyson shows up here to say hi? Damn."

Sometimes the universe worked in his favor, keeping the others looking up to him. He clapped Roman on the shoulder as they headed for the elevator. "That's how we do it at the FBI. You ever decide to jump ship, I've got a place for you on my teams."

AT SEVEN THAT evening in Oceanside, Olivia walked through the back door of Alfonso's house and drew up short as the scent of homemade Italian gravy hit her. Americans called it spaghetti sauce.

She closed her eyes and breathed deep. It was the same every time, the scent transporting her back to her childhood with her mother and grandmother fussing around the kitchen all day long, the gravy warming in a big stock pot. Rainy days when she would come home from school to be enveloped by her grandmother's loving arms and fresh cookies. Holidays, where fifty people would be crammed into their house, the food and drinks flowing as easily as the laughter.

"Did you bring the wine, doll?" Alfonso called from the kitchen.

She carried in the two bottles she'd picked up at the local liquor store, one Merlot and a Cabernet, setting them on the counter. Alfie wore his usual dark dress pants and button-down shirt with an apron that said "Kiss the cook. I'm Italian."

He was generously handsome. Dark hair, dark eyes, a sculpted Italian nose. He worked out regularly and filled his shirt to the max, his body moving with easy grace around the kitchen.

Alfie was her age, and they'd both grown up with hitmen for fathers. Alfie had gone to law school, gotten married, and had a daughter, but had ended up back in the "family" after his wife died in an unfortunate car accident involving a drunk semi driver delivering fresh produce to a major grocery store chain. He claimed to have returned to the Fifty-seven Gang because Frankie Molina had kept him from wallowing in severe depression after his wife's death. Supposedly, Frankie had made him realize how much his daughter needed him.

Alfie had sued the grocery store company and won several million dollars. His dad was incarcerated at that point and Frankie had offered Alfie his father's job, alluding to the idea that Frankie would keep Lorenzo Barone safe in prison and keep his father's spot in the mob family open so when he got out, he could return to the family. But only if Alfie took his place until Lorenzo was released. Lorenzo had received a sentence of seventeen years, and still had ten left. One thing was for sure, Alfie protected his family.

Grabbing a bottle opener, Olivia went to work on the Merlot's cork. "Where's Mary Margaret?"

Alfie pulled down two wine glasses and set them next to the bottles. "She's at a birthday sleepover. Kid was all excited about it. She keeps to herself most of the time, a real introvert, and doesn't make friends easily. I don't understand it. She's bright, cute, and funny. What's wrong with kids these days?"

So it was just the two of them tonight. She'd left her weapon in the car down the street, not sure if the girl would be inside. They'd only met a couple of times briefly. Alfie always made sure Mary Margaret was safely out of the house whenever Olivia was coming over. "Kids are tough on each other, especially girls. It's good that she's at a friend's, for her and us. We won't have to censor what we talk about."

"True." Alfie grinned, and went back to stirring the gravy. A timer dinged on the stove. He turned off one burner and drained the pasta. "but first, we eat and have a decent glass of wine."

As if she were back home, Olivia took the two glasses to the table and laid out place settings while Alfie brought out the garlic bread and salad. He loaded two plates with pasta, sprinkling shredded parmesan on top of his amazing sauce and hustled them over. Shucking off his apron, he sat, then lifted his glass in salute. "To strong family alliances."

Olivia raised her fork instead of her glass. "We are not family, Alfie."

"You wouldn't be disrespecting me at my own dinner table, now would you? We're not enemies tonight. Quit trying to pick a fight and be nice. I made you food. We're family."

Family was an elusive word. She had one, but she didn't. She wanted one, but she didn't. What was it about this guy that made her put down the fork and raise her glass? Maybe she could blame it on her good manners, rather than him pulling on her heartstrings.

He clinked his glass against hers and drank half in one gulp. Working his lips around, his brow knitted. "Where did you get this? Tastes like cheap ass crap."

"I'm all out of the good stuff."

He eyed her as he shoveled pasta into his mouth and chewed. "I like that stuff from the Sacramento winery."

So did she, but he'd finished off her last bottle during their previous meal. "That's my favorite too, but I don't have any more. You drank it all."

He grunted. "When you heading north again? Next time you hit the winery, buy extra."

"I'm a little busy down here, in case you haven't noticed."

He handed her the basket of garlic bread. "You work too much."

"I have a lot of mob guys to put behind bars."

He rolled his eyes and continued to eat. "We need to find you a safer job."

The pasta was awesome, and the garlic bread homemade. Olivia savored the blend of bread and butter, trying to ignore the emotions Alfie's concern elicited. He sounded like her mother, like her brother, God rest his soul.

It's fake. Don't be gullible. "I wouldn't have to work so much if you would get me the evidence I need against Frankie B and Gino."

His dark eyes scanned her face, as if he were trying to read her mind. "DeStefano didn't kill your brother, you know."

The words attacked her like a sharp knife slicing into her stomach. She could barely find her voice. "You know who killed Dezi?"

He waived off the question. "Course not. If I did, I'd take the guy out for you. What I do know is that Gino DeStefano didn't pull the trigger."

Her stomach felt like she'd eaten ice cubes rather than pasta. In her mind, she saw her brother on the ground in that wet, dark alley, his blood running into the puddles around him. "How do you know? Who did pull the trigger, Alfie?"

"Someone—not Gino, though—wanted to send a message to your old man. Dezi got caught in the crossfire, simple as that."

Everything in her continued to feel cold as ice, frozen. Alfie had never volunteered information about her brother's murder. She hadn't realized he even knew the specifics of what had happened. "What message?"

He gave an exaggerated shrug. "Felix was always pissing everybody off. He had big plans, you know. He liked to push people around, get rid of those who didn't agree with his vision of how things should be. My guess is he pushed the wrong person and they pushed back. Might not have even been anyone in the family. Maybe it was a dirty cop or something."

"My father was a hitman in Chicago with the Carlota syndicate, in direct competition with the Fifty-seven Gang. It was someone in the mob, I'm sure of it."

"Maybe. Whoever did it wanted your dad to back off, but he didn't."

"Yeah, well, the job always came before the family."

Alfie reared back. "You really believe that?"

"He should've protected Dezi. That's what fathers are supposed to do! Not put their kids in the line of fire."

"Your brother knew what he was getting into when he

followed in your father's footsteps. You can't go blaming the whole thing on your dad."

The ice cubes melted and turned to a blazing fire. "Are you defending him? Seriously? You don't even know him. You have no idea what he put me through—us through."

He went back to eating, avoiding her anger. "All I'm saying is there are two sides to every story, doll, sometimes more than two. You're right, I don't know Felix, but I understand him better than you think. He loved you and your brother. Don't you ever doubt that. For sure, there were things he could've done differently and maybe they would've made a difference, but you can't blame him for every single thing that went wrong in your life."

There was no way she could eat now, and she needed to detach from this whole situation. *Do not get emotionally involved.* It was the only thing that kept her focused on her job dealing with a killer minute by minute. "You're lucky I don't rip the gun hidden under the table out of its duct tape and shoot you right here."

His brows rose, and he swallowed his pasta. "You been snoopin' around again?"

Alfie was always prepared. He had weapons hidden all over the house in case anyone ever surprised him. Olivia was also prepared and had noticed a couple when she had been checking things out, but she imagined he had many more. "I'm doing my job, keeping an eye on you. Enough about my family. You got a name for me?"

"Just like that? You're back to being Deputy US Marshal Olivia Fiorelli? You can't sit and enjoy a good meal and pleasant company?"

His tone was teasing now, as if he could shift gears with ease, while she sat seething and only pretending to have her emotions under control. "Who is it that Gino and Frankie are going after? You said it was a high-ranking Fed putting the screws to the cartel."

Making a disgusted sound, he wiped his hands on a napkin

and dropped it on the tabletop. "It's not a Fed. My guy ponied up a little more. The target is a DEA agent."

Cooper. "Did your *guy* say anything else? Like who actually did the shooting?"

"You think that agent in San Diego was the target? I don't know, he doesn't seem right for it."

"Why not?"

Alfie turned his hands up. "I've never even heard of the guy, how big and important can he be? Plus, if the hit had already taken place, I would know. It's gotta be someone else."

"And you're sure Frankie's going after a DEA agent?"

"Look, I don't have a direct line to Frankie's every thought, but he likes to talk, and my informant is close to him. He hears a lot. I'm only passing on what he said."

She reached for her last ounce of patience. "Any other details? Such as, when is the hit going down? Who's executing it? Where's it going to take place?"

He shook his head. "There was nothing else."

Of course not. Was he simply dicking her around? "Doesn't sound like this guy has a clue to me. I think he's yanking your chain, Alfie."

Irritation crossed to his face before he forced it away. "I'll keep working on him. Give me some time."

He started to say something else, but his phone rang and he fished it out of his pocket. Another wave of irritation crossed his face. "Sorry, doll, I need to take this. Back in a second."

It rang two more times as he headed down the hallway. She heard a door slam.

Dinner was a bust, but maybe she could get something worthwhile before she left. Tossing her napkin on the table, she rose and quietly tiptoed down the hallway. Outside the closed door, she turned her ear toward the office and listened.

"No, it's not a good time. I'll call you back as soon as I can." A pause. "Yeah, yeah, did you do what I told you to do? ... Good. You earned your reward, but you got to stay with him, get close again."

Was he talking to one of his cronies? Sounded like a subordinate. What was this "reward"?

"Look, give me an hour and I'll deliver the stuff personally." A longer pause. "You haven't been out a day and already you're desperate? Tough, you'll survive. I'll text you when and where, and no bodyguards, you hear me? Just you and me, but listen up. You got to bring me more next time or the supply is going to be cut off. You have to pay for the product, one way or the other. I don't want your money, I want information, and you're the one person who can get it for me."

Bodyguards? Product? She mentally sighed. Had to be drugs.

"Someone new, huh?" Alfie's voice sounded pensive. "Interesting. Don't you worry about that. No guy in his right mind is immune to your looks or charms. You can do this, just keep your head on straight and do what I tell ya."

He was wrapping up the call. Olivia stole back down the hallway and resumed her seat. She even took a sip of the wine, swirling it in the glass in time with her equally swirling thoughts. He was talking to a woman. Not exactly what she'd expected, and doubtful that this caller was the "guy" close to Frankie B, but maybe Alfie was only making her think his informant was a man. Frankie liked the women, so maybe this one was actually female.

Good to know. When she got back home, she'd start checking into Frankie's current and former girlfriends to see what she could turn over. It might be easier to press this woman than Alfie to get valid information regarding the supposed hit that had been put out on a high-ranking DEA agent. No point in calling Navarro. He would blow her off, telling her it wasn't enough to go on. As soon as she left Alfie's, she'd notify Victor instead and let him alert the Drug Enforcement Agency if he thought the intel was legit.

Her host returned to the dining room, clapping his hands together. "Where were we? Do I need to reheat anything?"

Olivia downed the rest of her wine, and set the glass back on the table. "Thanks for dinner. I've got to go."

Offended, Alfie put his hands on his waist. "Are you kidding me? We haven't even talked about the good stuff yet."

"Good stuff? Like what? You won't even be straight with me about this DEA hit. You really think I'm going to stick around and talk about getting you a deal with the Justice Department for taking down Gino DeStefano? I'm sick of playing games with you, Alfie."

"You promised me a deal."

"And yet, you still haven't given me anything I can take to the JD. My boss is breathing down my neck, and the bigwigs at the Justice Department are getting antsy too. Either give me something of value, or we're done. No more dinners, no more wine, no more bullshit."

He gave her a cold stare that lasted for a long, uncomfortable minute. "I have recordings, accounting records, specific information on certain targets, and some other stuff, but I'm not handing any of it over until I hear what the deal is. I have to protect myself and my daughter. They want me to testify? I'm fine with that, but I need some guarantees Mary Margaret will be safe."

Or the same thing might happen to her that had happened to Olivia's brother—she'd get caught in the crossfire. Gino DeStefano was not one to go down without a fight, and if Alfie testified against him, the first target for his revenge would be the little girl.

They were at an impasse. She couldn't give him any guarantee until he handed over the information, and he wouldn't until he had the guarantee.

She headed for the door. "I'll be in touch."

She left and focused on clearing her head as she walked to her car. She drove down the street and around the block, coming back to park in a dark area under a tree where she could watch

Alfie's house. Her stomach growled as she sat there, and she wished she'd snagged a piece of garlic bread for the road. While she waited, she sent a text to Victor, and a second to her contact in DC. Then she settled down in the seat to watch.

As anticipated, Alfie pulled out of the garage forty minutes later and headed for the freeway. Olivia put the car in drive and followed.

8

T his bitch might be more trouble than she's worth.

The man leaned against the wall of the nightclub, deep bass music filtering through the back door and blacked out windows. The spring night was heavy with the threat of rain, and he itched to get this deal over with before it started to downpour.

Not surprisingly, the woman he was meeting was late. He made sure to clear the alley of a few vagrants as well as a couple who had slipped outside to bang each other. They were so high, they wouldn't remember him come morning, but he kept his baseball cap and sunglasses on anyway.

He heard the click of heels as the woman came running toward him. "I got here as fast as I could. Traffic was a bitch."

Traffic had been thick for him too, and he'd had farther to drive, yet he'd still made it in plenty of time. "What's your plan to get close to our guy?"

She had the hood of a jacket up over her head, her facial features tight under the yellowy alley light, her eyes jumping around. Typical junkie. "What do you mean?"

God, she wasn't that much of an airhead, was she? "Don't play dumb. You blew it today. What. Is. Your. Plan?"

"I, uh..." Another darting glance down to the end of the alleyway where she'd emerged from. "I don't know what you want me to do. He has a new girlfriend."

"You know, I kind of thought that training you went through, and all those movies you acted in, would've taught you something about seducing a man. Men cheat on their girlfriends all the time, in case that's news. You know what he likes. Use it to get to him."

He saw her throat work as she swallowed, her eyes now scanning his midsection, searching for his hands, probably. She'd contacted him before she even left rehab, wanting to line up drug deliveries. He didn't need her money, and her fame brought a few challenges, like dodging the eyes always on her. Normally, he stayed far away from face-to-face deals, using random carriers for the dirty work, but with her, he realized she also offered the opportunity to find another way to his mark. If Fiorelli didn't work out in his quest to bring down Frankie B and Gino, the beautiful actress needing her fix in front of him could help him take out Victor Dupé.

She shifted from one high-heeled foot to the other. "Please, I need those drugs."

He brought the bag of cocaine from his pocket and dangled it between them. "You did what I told you to earlier, so you're going to get this, but I expect you to try again, and this time, I want more effective output. I want you to get that Fed back in your bed, make him vulnerable, understand? Wrap him around your goddamn little finger."

Her lips pursed into a pout. "How? He broke up with me because I can't be the woman he needs."

Jesus, did he have to do everything for her? "He's a hero, right? So play up to that. Tell him someone is watching you, following you around. Use those acting chops and pretend you're scared."

"People follow me around all the time. I'm famous. He knows I have bodyguards."

"Tell him it's not the paparazzi. Make out like it's some crazy, homicidal fan. A sneaky fan. No one believes you, but you know he's out there. He shows up everywhere you go. Pretend it's me, and I'm watching your every move. That should give you some motivation."

"But the girlfriend—" she whined.

"The new girlfriend is not a roadblock. Don't worry about her. You focus on your job and let me handle the rest. Otherwise, no more rewards."

She reached out to snatch the bag, and he raised it out of her reach. "And if you don't do what I tell you to,"—he withdrew the gun from his waistband and showed it to her—"It's not the lack of drugs that will kill you, *capisce*?"

The gun didn't even seem to faze her. Once again, she reached for the baggie. This time he let her have it, but he smacked her arm with the gun for good measure. "You know what I do for living, right?"

She tucked it away, her eyes wary. "You sell drugs, duh."

He grabbed her and pulled her close, jamming the butt of the gun under her chin and making her cry out. "I kill people, doll, and I'm damn good at it. You don't want to piss me off."

He shoved her away and she twisted an ankle, unable to stay balanced on the ridiculous heels. Pushing off the wall, she gained her balance once more and took off limping down the alley, throwing a hateful glance over her shoulder at him.

"I'll be in touch," he yelled after her, smiling to himself. "And you damn well better take my call."

He hung around a few more minutes, waiting to be sure she was gone, and no one would see him following her out. A soft drizzle began to fall. The night was still young, and while it had not gone the way he'd expected, he had a good feeling about things. He was going to take over the West Coast Fifty-seven Gang, one way or the other. And then he'd change the name.

To complete the picture, all he had to do was convince Olivia Fiorelli to join him as his partner.

WITNESSES from the park shooting could not confirm the Suarez gang member had been around, although one mother who'd been recording her twin daughters getting ready for the Easter egg hunt caught the car Cooper had seen in a couple frames. The SCVC Taskforce computer guru, Bobby Dyer, had been able to extract a photo showing the backend of the car but they only had a partial plate. At the safe house, Ronni worked with the DMV to track down the owner.

Also at the safe house with Victor, Roman had put his team on searching for Suarez gang members with bomb-making skills and/or past offenses involving explosives. So far, they had four possible perps. None were strong leads, and they were scattered among different localities up-and-down the coast—San Francisco, Los Angeles, Sacramento, and Bakersfield. Since they had nothing to connect them directly to the San Diego bombing, they'd have to pull strings in order to get the local law enforcement agencies to bring them in for questioning.

Good thing both Roman and Victor had pull. They were already working on the necessary red tape to allow the members of Roman's DTT team to follow through.

Thomas was working on the Suarez members Agent Marin had given him before he was killed. Because both were in the San Diego area, and local PD was friendly with the SCVC Taskforce, having worked with them on many cases before, so they were much more cooperative about bringing the men in. First, however, SDPD had to track them down.

While they waited, Victor and Thomas dug into the cases Cooper thought might be relevant. There were several that had peripheral connections to the Kings, but then at least sixty percent of the drug running in Southern California had some link back to the gang. Victor started putting together a list of names to crosscheck against the Fifty-seven Gang and Gino DeStefano.

The Italian mafia was heavily concentrated out East. The five most notable families operated in the upper East Coast and several had crews in other areas, especially southern Florida. There were a few more scattered throughout different states in the Midwest and South. In the West, there were fewer still. Las Vegas was open territory for all of the crime families, but outside of there, the only one that had not gone defunct worked Los Angeles. A few others had tried to infiltrate areas along the California coast, but none had gotten a toehold that could survive. Now, Gino DeStefano, with his Chicago ties, was attempting to give the Los Angeles mobsters some competition, and it seemed like he might just pull it off, especially if he and Molina could remove the Suarez Kings but keep their infrastructures in place.

Needing to give his eyes a break, Victor rose from the kitchen table and went to the refrigerator for an energy drink. He'd been staring at a computer screen for hours, checking databases, talking to the lead detectives in each of the cases, checking in on Cooper and Celina, and trying to keep his mind off where he really wanted to be—back home with Liv and Taz. Even a few hours with them would be nice to clear his head and get some sleep.

As if he'd conjured her, his phone buzzed with a text. It was nearing midnight, but he wasn't surprised Liv was still up and working.

Trying to track down an old girlfriend of Frankie Molina's. Might have info about the DEA agent hit. I have her name and address. Want to go with me tomorrow to check her out?

He quickly typed back, *yes*.

After her call earlier, he'd alerted the head of the DEA, in case Cooper had not been the target Olivia's mafia insider told her about. Victor's gut told him there was something off about the whole situation, he just couldn't put his finger on it. He needed more details about Olivia's informant—he was worried the guy was leading her on in an attempt to further his own causes. Not that she wouldn't see it, but it happened to the best of agents. Victor wanted to be sure the informant was legit.

Tracking down the ex-girlfriend of Frankie Molina might not be the best use of his time, but any reason to see Liv was a good one, especially since he wanted more details about this informant she was protecting.

Roman stood and stretched, yawning. He rubbed his eyes and checked his watch. "I'm heading home for a shower and a few hours of sleep. I'll pick this up again in the morning and be in touch."

He said goodbye to Thomas and Ronni, both looking as tired as Victor felt. There wasn't much they could do now overnight, so maybe he should leave too.

"Same for me, guys," Victor said. "I have an unusual lead to check out with Olivia in the morning. It's a long shot, but it's worth looking into. I'll contact you after I'm done there. If anything comes up in the meantime, call me."

Thomas walked him and Roman to the door. "No one else has had an attempt on their life?" he asked Victor. "None of the agents on your other taskforces in LA, correct?"

"None, and let's hope it stays that way."

"Then it has to be tied to us." He shook his head wearily. "I don't get it. We may have caused the Suarez Kings a few problems along the way, but nothing that warrants this type of strike, and we've never put the screws to the Fifty-seven Gang."

Victor could see something brewing behind Thomas's eyes. "What are you thinking?"

"That it doesn't have a damn thing to do with any of these cases we keep going over. It's not revenge. It's something else."

Thomas was smart and his sixth sense when it came to criminals was excellent. "I agree. If they're going after a high-level DEA agent out of revenge or to get him out of the way, there are others much more detrimental to their gang than Cooper has been. The Kings haven't been the direct focus of any of our investigations, only outliers when we've taken out certain supply channels or Mexican cartels. They may have suffered a temporary interference on occasion, but we've never been able to shut them down."

"This connection with the mafia seems weak to me," Thomas said.

Roman bobbed his head in agreement. "It seems forced, doesn't it? If the Kings and the mob are clashing over who's going to run this territory, it seems like they'd be taking each other out, not focusing time and energy on you guys."

"Could there be another player?" Victor asked.

A long, tired sigh came from Roman. "Either that, or these DTOs are throwing up a diversion to keep us from the real issue."

DTOs—drug trafficking organizations—were constantly in flux, whether they were a Colombian based cartel or a mafia family. Those in power were constantly getting killed off by those trying to take over, even within their own organizations. While they were well-versed in deceiving law enforcement, they rarely had the resources to pull off elaborate sting operations to keep the justice system looking the other way. "Any idea what this *real* issue is?"

"No, but I have the feeling we're only seeing a small part of this picture. We need to think outside the box."

Victor had the same feeling, and hoped Roman's new, temporary taskforce could help fill in the missing pieces. "All right, let's get a fresh start in the morning."

Down the block in his car, Victor sat for moment debating his options. The drive to Olivia's was a lot shorter than to his house.

Plus, if he stayed at her place, he would be there in the morning for them to get an early start.

He laughed at himself as he started the car. As if he would drive all the way home, even if it made more sense. But it was nice when logic and wisdom agreed with his libido. He texted her before he took off.

Are you up for another houseguest?

Her reply came seconds later. *Thought you'd never ask. How soon can you be here?*

He gave her his ETA before heading for the freeway, smiling at the peace seeing her brought. She was everything he'd ever wanted in a woman and more. Someone he could share work and anything else with.

Hell, she even loves my dog.

If things continued the way they were, he could finally settle down and build the family he'd always wanted. As he drove through the night, his mind spun out what his next move would be. He had the house, he had the dog. All he needed was a fantastic woman to share his life with.

First, he had to solve this case. Second he had to get his house in better shape. But after all that was done, he was going to ask Liv to move in with him.

The thought of that scared and thrilled him at the same time. All these years, all the searching for someone who could accept him the way he was, he'd finally found her.

And one thing was for certain, he wasn't letting her get away.

9

The next morning, Olivia left Victor sleeping and took Taz for a run. She normally did three miles a day when she could, and the dog seemed up for the exercise.

Trailing Alfie the night before had yielded mixed results. He'd left his vehicle and gone into an alley where she couldn't shadow him without revealing herself, so she'd waited to see if anyone followed him in. Eventually, she'd been rewarded with a woman in high heels making her way in and not emerging again for several minutes. Olivia had debated whether to sneak in as close as she could and see if she could eavesdrop, but although the daring move appealed to her, it was too risky. Instead, she waited patiently and followed the woman when she came out.

Unfortunately, the woman had slipped into a nightclub a few blocks down and Olivia lost her by the time she parked and entered it. The woman had worn an expensive designer jacket with a hood. The hood had been up the whole time, and the single picture she'd been able to take showed a partial of her face.

Frustration ate at her as she pounded the sidewalk. The woman was tall and thin, but so was half of LA, hundreds of actresses and models starving themselves to death and using dozens of methods to stay skeletal.

She couldn't rule out either as the woman's profession. The expensive clothes suggested a certain level of wealth. She only hoped she could put the partial face she had through facial recognition and get a hit. Or maybe when she visited Marquita Lomas, she would recognize the designer shoes.

"How about we take a stroll through the park?" she asked Taz.

Three blocks from her normal route, she found the spot where Cooper had been shot. A piece of crime scene tape was still hooked around a tree, the end flapping in the breeze. Olivia took Taz and they swept the perimeter, her eyes scanning the area and checking for anything that seemed interesting. She went to the spot where Cooper had stood, the blood stains in the sidewalk having turned a rusty brown.

No one was there this early, and she had a clear view of the playground equipment and the trees and bushes lining the area. A car drove by across the way and she watched it, imagining the gang members who had taken the same route that fateful day. The shooter had nearly pinpoint accuracy, and even though he'd missed Cooper's heart by millimeters, that was still some impressive shooting from a moving vehicle.

She wasn't buying it.

Her gaze drifted to the buildings across the street. There were multiple businesses stacked side-by-side, none higher than three floors. Trees blocked the majority of those windows, but one had a clear view of where she stood.

Taz sniffed at the grass, marking the spot and panting back to her. She needed to get the reports, see if anyone had checked those buildings. With her phone, she took pictures of the clearing in front, then walked across the park, Taz loping along beside her.

A scan of the rear of the buildings revealed standard fire escapes and a couple metal dumpsters. She took out her phone and shot pictures of the iron stairs at the back of the center building—the one with the view of the park. A visual inspection of the steps showed some rusting metal but nothing to indicate it had recently been used as an escape route. Inspecting the dumpsters, she found the normal bags of office waste—shredded papers, stinky food leftovers, and assorted other trash.

Taz sat and watched the show, ears perked as she went back and forth checking sight lines and looking for any trace evidence. She really needed to get inside to the window with the view, but it was early, and no one was there yet. The name of the business, Kogan & Sons, was nonspecific. It could've been anything from an accountant to a realtor to a construction company for all she knew. When she got back, she'd look them up and see if they had ties to any of the other players in this scenario.

When she emerged from the alleyway, she saw a welcome sight. Across the way in the park, Victor stood staring in her direction. He seemed surprised to see her emerge but waved. He was dressed in running gear and must've had the same idea as her. Taz barked once in a happy greeting, tail wagging furiously as he and Liv ran to catch up with Victor.

"Fancy meeting you here," Liv said.

Victor greeted them, giving her a quick kiss and scratching the dog's ears. "Found your note. A run seemed like a good idea to clear my head, so I thought I'd join you."

"I don't think our boys in the car took a shot at Cooper." She shifted to one side and pulled Victor into the spot where Cooper had stood. Pointing through the trees, she showed him the window of the center building. "My guess is the bullet came from there."

He nodded. "I was standing here thinking the same thing."

She pulled out her phone and showed him the pictures of the front and back. "We need to take a look inside, and do a thorough inventory of the dumpsters to make sure our shooter didn't leave evidence. Do you know anything about this business?"

"No," Victor said. "I'll have Thomas get the details for us." He checked his watch. "Any indication when they open?"

She shook her head. "There are no signs indicating what they do or their hours of operation. We'll have to come back."

Her phone buzzed in her hand. Her eyes automatically glanced at the ID and her stomach flip-flopped. The Illinois State Department of Corrections. There were only two reasons they would be calling her. "Um, I need to take this."

She walked a few steps away, hands shaking as her finger hit the answer button. She cleared her throat. "Fiorelli."

"Ms. Fiorelli, this is Dan Hoskins. I have some news about your father."

God, was he dead? Had another inmate killed him?

Her legs turned to concrete. Everything about the environment in front of her dimmed. She could no longer here the birds singing, the cars driving by, Victor speaking softly to the dog. The green of the trees seemed to turn the same shade as the sidewalk she stood on, the colorful playground equipment faded and washed out.

No words could escape her tight throat, as if a boa constrictor had wrapped around her neck. This did not deter Hoskins from delivering the news. "The parole board has granted a meeting with your father on Wednesday. Thought you'd like to know in case you want to be here."

No way. *Well, at least he's not dead.*

But what were they thinking? She forced herself to swallow down her disbelief. "They can't seriously be considering him for parole."

"He's a model prisoner and hasn't caused any problems in the ten years he's been incarcerated. The State takes securities fraud seriously, of course, but in the overall scope of things, we have an abundance of more serious criminals flooding into the system daily. Rapists, murderers, you name it. Model prisoners are paroled early to make room."

Her stomach cramped. She had the evidence to keep him locked up, but hadn't used it when she'd had the opportunity. She couldn't bring herself to testify against her own father. She'd trusted the agents working the case along with the lawyers prosecuting him to find evidence against him in regard to the last murder he'd committed. Most of what they'd had was circumstantial, and he'd pleaded guilty to a lesser charge of securities fraud while setting up his partner, Joey DeMarco. Two days after being incarcerated, Joey had been killed by a fellow inmate. Olivia knew who had been behind the hit, knew her father was responsible. Joey had been a good friend of the family. "He's like my brother," her father often said.

What kind of man had his own brother murdered?

"You can't let him out. He's a stone-cold killer and you know it."

"I'm sorry, Ms. Fiorelli. There's nothing I can do. If you have evidence the parole board should be made aware of, I encourage you to attend the meeting and bring it forward."

The call disconnected and Liv stood frozen in place. She was damned if she did, damned if she didn't.

"Olivia?"

She turned to see the concern on Victor's face.

"Everything okay?" he asked.

Covering up the emotions her father always evoked was second nature. She'd been doing it a long, long time. "Everything's fine."

She put the phone in her armband and started jogging. "Come on. I'll buy you breakfast."

Running would help. She could pound out her anxiety, keep Victor from seeing the fear she knew had to be on her face, and maybe find a way to sort through the sticky, awful confusion in her brain.

Focus on what you can control.

Control, an elusive concept just like family.

Victor caught up to her with ease, the dog as well. "Are we still on to go see Molina's ex-girlfriend?"

"Absolutely. We can pay her a visit after breakfast. I have shooting practice this afternoon but I should be able to help with your investigation after that."

And somewhere in between, she had to find a way to keep her father in jail.

EVERYTHING WAS *NOT* FINE. Ever since the phone call, Olivia had been acting strange. Victor had not intentionally eavesdropped, but had been concerned from the moment he saw the look on her face when the call came through. Her body language had only gotten more worrisome as she had spoken to whoever was on the other end.

You can't let him out. He's a stone-cold killer and you know it.

Who had she been talking about? Someone she had arrested?

As he ran beside her, he figured it was better not to pry. She obviously didn't want to talk about it, even though she was upset. Injustice sucked. He dealt with it every day, and it never got any easier. Bad guys—really bad guys—got off easy, while some folks couldn't seem to catch a break.

They ran an easy pace, Taz staying in stride, his tongue lolling out the side. The dog was so easygoing, nothing seemed to faze him. The only signs of his former life were the scars around his mouth and ears. He didn't seem to hold the past abuse from his previous owner against the rest of humanity, and that made him very adoptable. Only thing was, Victor didn't think he wanted to put Taz up for adoption. Keeping the dog, however, wasn't the most responsible thing to do, since he was gone so much.

"Race you the rest of the way," Olivia said, laughing as she charged ahead full speed, the dog up for the chase.

Olivia was fast, but Victor had been a track star back in the day, and still enjoyed running half marathons. Sprinting wasn't his favorite, but he liked the dynamic, explosive, and precise version of putting one foot in front of the other. He might have been several years older than Liv, but his legs were longer and he liked the chase as much as Taz. He let Liv stay a few feet ahead so he could watch her curvy backside. At the last second, he poured it on and passed her, reaching her front door three steps before she did.

She bent at the waist, panting. "You...cheated."

He laughed, feeling better than he had in the past couple of days. The earlier phone call aside, he felt hope with the new leads. If indeed someone had shot Cooper from that building, it opened a whole new can of worms, and put them on the right track. All the threads they had crisscrossing with the Suarez Kings and Fifty-seven Gang had not produced the results he wanted. One of the reasons he'd gone to the park that morning was to do the same thing Liv had—stand where Cooper had and get a feel for possible options. She seemed to think along the same lines he did, and now they had an alternate possibility. Some days, that was the thing that blew the lid open on a case.

They bathed together, and Victor enjoyed taking advantage of her wet, naked body as he helped wash her hair, as well as the rest of her. The water festivities ended up taking longer than expected, and they grabbed protein bars on the way out the door to track down Olivia's lead.

A car was parked behind Olivia's blocking it in. A sandy haired guy with a beard and a slim frame leaned against the hood. "Hey partner," he said to Liv. Then he looked over Victor. "I see why you haven't been answering your phone."

Olivia didn't hide her surprise. Taz stopped next to her, his hackles rising. "Danny, what are you doing here? I didn't realize you were back in town."

He ignored her question, pushing off the car and holding out a hand to Victor. "Danny Rossiter. How ya doin'?"

Olivia stepped forward. "Danny, this is Director Victor Dupé. Danny is my partner."

Shaking the man's hand seemed to make both Olivia and the dog relax. Danny kept up a relaxed posture too, although behind his eyes, Victor saw annoyance. "Right," Danny said. "FBI Director Dupé. I've seen you around, we've never had the chance to work together. Nice to meet you."

His tight tone suggested that was a lie. "The marshal and I are on the way to interrogate a possible informant. What can we do for you, Danny?"

The annoyance in the man's eyes became even clearer. He smiled through it. "My *partner* and I need to have a little chat." He swung his gaze over to Olivia. "Adams called in sick. The boss wants us to handle transportation for Henry Valiant this afternoon."

Victor signaled Taz. "Come on, boy." To Olivia, he said, "We'll be in the backyard if you need us."

"It's okay," she said. "Stay. This will only take a minute. Danny, I'll meet you at the courthouse. What time?"

Danny obviously wanted to talk to her alone and hesitated, looking down the block as if deciding how hard to press her. "Four o'clock. You *will* be there, right?"

Now it was Olivia who didn't hide her annoyance. "Of course."

He scratched at his neck, once again seeming to take in the setting. "Heard about your old man. Think he'll get out?"

Olivia's poker face was pretty damn impressive, but Victor saw a tic start under her left eye. "Not if the state of Illinois has an ounce of intelligence. Look, we need to leave if I'm going to be back in time to help you with Valiant."

Danny wasn't easily put off. "You know, all these mobs guys you're trying to put away out here can't hold a candle to your dad. Maybe you should head back to Chicago or New Jersey or wherever you hail from originally and worry about getting your own house in order instead of chasing Gino DeStefano."

A tight smile crossed her face. "We haven't been partners that long, Danny, so I'll let that obvious *none-of-your-fucking-business* opinion pass." She took a step toward him, staring him directly in the eyes. "But I strongly suggest you keep your nose out of that business and don't bring up my family again."

He stared her down before taking out his keys and opening the door to his car. "Answer your phone once in a while, Fiorelli. I don't have time to hunt you down every time we have a job to do."

She stood with feet planted and watched him pull out of her drive.

Victor moved to stand beside her. "Nice guy."

"Oh yeah, he's a real peach. Came from Arizona a few months ago and doesn't like the way I work. Seems to think I need someone to keep me under control and make me follow the rules."

"Rules aren't your thing."

She released a deep sigh. "Oh, I love rules, love the law. It's something to hold onto when there's anarchy all around, but sometimes you have to bend a few protocols and procedures to get the bad guys where it really hurts them."

He wanted to ask about the reference to her dad, but decided she would open up when she was ready. It wasn't hard to figure out—her father must be close to getting paroled. That would explain the earlier call at the park and her reaction to it.

"You still game to go talk to Molina's ex-girlfriend?"

"Damn skippy, I am." She hit the fob for her car and the doors unlocked. "Have you heard from your team?"

"Cooper is stable. The others are working with Roman's team, following up on leads involving the Suarez Kings and who may have set the bomb. Ronni is tracking down the owner of the building across from the park. So far, it's a dead end. The former owner was a tax attorney who went bankrupt and disappeared.

The bank foreclosed on the loan, but nothing's been done with the property. We're trying to get a warrant to search it. If you and I can figure out this shooter angle, we may be able to tie the two together and get a better handle on who's behind both."

They got in the car, Taz riding in the backseat. Olivia backed out of the drive. "Our gal is Marquita Lomas. She officially dated Frankie B for three years, enjoying a nice penthouse suite, maxing out several of his credit cards, and getting dumped for his current girlfriend, who by the way, has a ring on her finger and is making plans to marry him later this year."

Victor thumbed through the file on his phone she had sent him. "And how is it Lomas has information about the shooting?"

"Alfonso Barone, the mob guy I'm pumping for information, is the one who put me onto the hit against an upper level DEA agent. Claims he heard about it through someone close to Frankie. It's possible Alfie is using Lomas to get information he wants, and he's slicing that up and giving me a teaser here and there."

"Why the ex? Why not the current girlfriend?"

"I overheard Alfie talking to a woman on the phone. He was telling her she needed to get close to this guy again, as if they had broken up. He was giving her relationship advice, if you can believe it, but in a manipulative way. Totally using her to get intel. If Frankie still has a soft spot for her, maybe that's how she's able to pump him for information without being obvious, and Alfie is using that for his own purposes. I'm not sure, but my gut tells me this informant he refers to is not part of the syndicate itself, so the ex-girlfriend angle works. Pillow talk, and all that."

"At this point," Victor said, "I'll follow any lead, and I trust your intuition."

She seemed to flinch slightly. "I'm not sure that's a good idea."

"Oh, yeah?" he teased. "Why not?"

She bit her bottom lip and worried it for a moment. Her eyes stayed on the road as she merged with traffic on the freeway. Her knuckles were nearly white from the grip she had on the steering wheel. "Listen, there's something I need to talk to you about."

The phone call? Her dad's situation? "It's okay. You don't have to discuss your family with me, especially the situation with your father. I understand it's private."

Brows furrowed, she glanced at him then back to the road.

He touched her shoulder, not sure about that look. Maybe he'd misread the whole thing. Did she *want* to talk about it? Had they passed an invisible line where she was now comfortable telling him the ugly details? "If you *do* want to talk about him, I'm more than happy to listen."

There. That should cover it both ways. Man, he was rusty with this relationship stuff. All Tracee had ever wanted to do was talk about things. He'd always been a good listener, but eventually he'd started tuning out all the details about her Hollywood peers that she reveled in.

He was used to listening to his agents and hearing the words behind what they actually said. Like a profiler, he could almost read their minds and understand them on a level that was much deeper than the facts they put in their reports.

Olivia eased down in her seat ever so slightly, her grip loosening. "My dad is a subject that is usually off-limits, but I appreciate the offer. Bottom line, the facts are very straightforward. He was a mafia hitman for twenty-some years. I didn't even realize he wasn't like a normal dad until I was eight or nine. For a long time, I couldn't reconcile what he did with the man I knew who came home to us every night, who tucked me in and read bedtime stories to me. But as I got older, I began to understand what a monster he was to the rest of the world. He's been in federal prison for ten years on securities fraud, not for all of the murders he committed. I'm told he's been a model prisoner and the parole board is considering releasing him. It makes me sick to my stomach."

As if to emphasize her words, one hand snaked to her lower belly and rested there.

He knew there was much more to the story, but wanted to give her space. "Totally understandable that you don't want him out."

"What about your dad?" she asked, abruptly.

Her need to deflect and change the conversation to something not about her did not escape him. The subject was a touchy one for him too, his dad not exactly an upstanding role model either. "My father suffered from manic-depression and alcoholism. He tried to take his own life when I was ten, my mother tried to stop him, and she ended up with a bullet in her spine that left her paralyzed from the waist down. After he shot her, he ended up murdered—the case is still unsolved. He left me and my four sisters behind. My mother has spent her life in a wheelchair, and if it hadn't been for some close relatives taking care of us kids, she probably would've lost all of us to the foster system. As soon as she was out of the hospital and able to return home, I insisted on going back too. My aunt and uncle, who I was living with at the time, refused to let me, so I ran away and made it home to her. I refused to leave her and eventually got all four of my sisters under the same roof with us again. It was a rough life, but we all ended up okay."

"*Okay*? I'd say you've done better than that, Director."

"Still haven't solved my father's murder—for years, I wasn't sure I wanted to. I had a lot of hang-ups about the night my mother was shot. But all in all, the important thing was not letting it tear us apart."

"Your sisters must absolutely adore you for keeping the family together."

He smiled, thinking about Brenda, Danille, Ruth, and Nikki. Four amazing women who gave him nothing but hell all the time about working too hard, too long, and still being single. His mother usually led the charge. "We are a close-knit family. I think you'll like all of them. They're strong women, like you."

She took an off-ramp. "I'd like to meet them, you know, when and if you want me to."

He definitely did. "As soon as we're done with this case, I'll plan something, okay? Maybe I can finish painting the house and have a picnic." He'd never planned one in his life, but suddenly, it seemed like the domestic thing to do, right up there with introducing his new girlfriend to his mom and sisters. "How about you? Any siblings?"

She stiffened again and took another right turn, craning her head as if she were looking for the correct street. Maybe she was. "I had a brother. He's dead."

No emotion crossed her face, her eyes scanning house numbers. Another touchy subject probably best left for a different time. "I'm sorry to hear that."

"Sixty-three thirty-seven. Here we are." The car slid up to the curb. "I'll take lead, okay?"

Yep, she definitely didn't want to talk about her family any longer and he didn't blame her. "Lead the way, Deputy Marshal Fiorelli. I'm right behind you."

10

Victor wanted her to meet his family.

Olivia's pulse jumped around, her heart too. She'd felt things were serious, but the ins and outs of relationships were so complicated, and she was so bad at them, she was still in shock he'd suggested such a big step already.

How sad was it that this was a first for her? She'd never gotten serious enough with anyone to receive such an invitation, and even the one or two who might've been candidates had run the opposite direction once they knew who her father was.

Not only had Victor not seemed to care about Felix Fiorelli's current state of incarceration or his mile-long rap sheet, he'd actually invited her over for a family picnic.

Victor had picnics? She almost chuckled out loud at the thought of Mr. Suit & Tie FBI Director hosting a backyard barbecue.

Marquita's home was small and shabby, squeezed in among other postage-stamp sized houses on a dead-end street. A couple rusty cars missing tires and other pieces of equipment populated the tiny side yard. A bedraggled Christmas wreath hung on the cheap wooden front door, faded in the afternoon sunlight.

The porch was nothing more than a square section of concrete barely big enough for Olivia to stand on. The sound of music, heavy on the bass, seeped from inside. Olivia knocked and waited, Victor hanging near the car, his eyes scanning the area. Taz hung his head out a back window, panting and watching both of them.

After a minute, Olivia knocked again, harder this time. "Marquita? Are you home? This is Deputy US Marshal Fiorelli. I'd like to speak to you for a moment."

The music softened, the deadbolt *thunked*. A crack appeared as a short woman with dark hair peered out at her. "What do you want?"

"I'd like some information on Frankie Molina. I know you used to be close."

Her eyes were a honey brown, her features pretty, but haggard. "I ain't got nothin' to do with him anymore."

She started to close the door but Olivia stuck her foot in the crack, keeping it open. "You know about him wanting to take over the Suarez Kings, don't you?"

Marquita pressed on the door, squeezing Olivia's foot. "I don't know anything," she insisted. "Leave me alone."

"How about Alfonso Barone? What can you tell me about him? You're working for him, right?"

The pressure stopped. Marquita once again appraised Liv from head to toe. "Alfie? Why would I? He's nothing but a weasel who thinks his balls are bigger than everyone else's."

No argument here. "I know he's got you pumping Frankie B for information. I want to know why."

Marquita swore under her breath in Spanish. "I don't know what you been smokin', *chica*, but I wouldn't give Alfie the time of day, and if I were back with Frankie, do you really think I'd be livin' in this dive?"

Maybe that's why she was trying to get close to Frankie again. "I have reasonable suspicion you're buying drugs from Alfie.

Maybe I should come inside and confirm that. What do you think, Marquita?"

She wondered if the woman would call her bluff. The best defense was a good offense, so Olivia beat her to it, turning toward Victor. "Bring the dog," she said, waving at Taz. Turning back to Marquita, she hitched a thumb over her shoulder at both of them. "Good thing I brought the drug dog. You know he can sniff out things like crack and weed a hundred yards away. He's been on alert since we came around the block, and I'm guessing he'll find some good stuff inside this house, won't he?"

The door crack widened slightly and Marquita's hand shot out as if blocking Taz's approach. "I don't do no drugs. He's probably smellin' the neighbor's stash. You don't need to bring him in here. I swear to you, I don't do that stuff no more."

How many times had Olivia heard that in her line of work? She held up her phone with a picture of the woman who had met Alfie in the alley. It was grainy due to the low lighting, and the woman was mostly hidden by that damn jacket and hood, but Liv waved it in front of Marquita's face. "I recorded your little meeting with Alfie last night. Stop playing games."

Victor and Taz came up the sidewalk, and the woman's eyes went wide with fear. She gave the photo a quick glance before her gaze went back to the dog, who was now straining against the leash to get to Olivia. Marquita probably assumed he was following the scent of her drugs. "That's not me. I never left the house last night. And look, *chica*, that woman is way taller."

It was true, but Liv pressed on, hoping to ruffle the woman's feathers enough to get something out of her. "She's wearing three-inch heels. The picture's distorted. Are you telling me you don't have shoes like that?"

"That's not me, I swear. I got nothing to do with Alfie, I ain't got no drugs, and I don't know anything about the Suarez gang." She glanced at Victor, then did a double take. "Hey, you're the guy that actress went to see yesterday at the hospital. I saw your picture on the *Red Star Report* this morning. They said you're getting back together."

Red Star Report was a daily online gossip e-zine. Olivia frowned and glanced at Victor. He was definitely Hollywood handsome, but...

The look on his face told her this was not a mistake. Marquita was not confusing him with some headline-making actor. For a moment, Olivia struggled to put two and two together, then remembered that Victor had once dated a very famous young actress.

What was her name...?

The light bulb went off. *Holy shit.*

Tracee Tyson.

Before she could stop them, the words spilled out of her mouth. "She came to see you at the hospital yesterday?"

His tanned skin turned a funny shade of gray. He ignored the question, turning his attention to Marquita. "You have me mixed up with someone else. When was the last time you bought drugs from Alfie?"

Taz sniffed at Marquita's feet and she slid farther behind the door. "Long time ago. He doesn't mess around with people like me anymore. He thinks he's big time, so he moves a lot of product to the rich and famous these days, people who can pay a lot and want larger quantities. What has this got to do with the Kings?"

Olivia was still trying to get her bearings about Victor and the actress. A part of her felt dumbfounded, the little voice in her head telling her he'd been too good to be true, while logic told her there was a simple explanation. "Territory disputes," she said. She flashed the picture in front of the woman's face again. "So this woman met him in an alley. You really think I believe she's some rich and famous gal?"

"I don't know." Marquita shrugged, her nervous eyes glancing at the dog, now sticking his nose through the crack in the door. Olivia kept her foot there to be sure Taz didn't end up with his nose broken off. "He doesn't deliver product himself anymore. If he was meeting her, it must've been a big score for him, but he didn't want to be seen going to her place or meeting her openly. Maybe she's helping him take down Gino."

"Take down Gino?" Alfie was planning to take down Gino all right, but with Olivia's help, wasn't he? Why would he use a junkie, no matter how rich and famous? "What are you saying? Alfie's going after the head of the West Coast Fifty-seven Gang?"

"Look, Alfie is smart and ambitious. He doesn't say a lot, but he's always running a plan to get up the ladder. He gets people under his thumb then forces them to help him."

Tell me something I don't know. "Have you heard anything about a mob hit against a DEA agent?"

"I don't run with that group anymore. How would I hear anything like that?"

Liv pulled out her card and handed it to the woman. "Keep your ears open, and call me if you hear anything about Alfie, Frankie, or Gino. I don't care how insignificant it seems, you get in touch with me, otherwise I'll be back." She patted Taz's head, backing him up and removing her foot from the doorframe. "And I'll bring the dog and a warrant with me, you understand?"

The woman nodded, snatched the card, and slammed the door. The deadbolt cracked loudly as she snapped it into place.

She, Victor, and the dog made their way to the car in silence. As soon as they were inside, Victor said, "Tracee heard about the shooting and happened to be in the area. She stopped by to check on me. That's all it was."

Liv started the car and pulled away from the curb. "That was nice of her."

"I guess the paparazzi thought they could spin the picture and get her fans to speculate we were getting back together."

She drove on autopilot. "You two are still good friends, then?"

"Far from it. I haven't spoken to her in nearly two years."

Olivia was looking forward to her weapons training now even more than usual. She might actually have a face to put on the target. "Kinda strange she'd come to the hospital to find you, isn't it?"

"The reason she was in the area was legit, and I like to think maybe she's realized what a great guy I was, and how she blew it. But the truth is, she was probably looking for a photo op. She always is."

He sent a charming smile her way and she felt the grip on her rib cage loosen. "No chance the paparazzi are correct? That there is some kind of reconciliation going on?"

He shuddered. "Not a chance in hell."

Olivia breathed a silent sigh of relief. "I guess Marquita was kind of a bust. Sorry about that."

"She knows more than she's admitting, and I have no doubt she'll be calling Frankie, or one of the other guys, to fill them in. She seems like the type to bitch her head off about us showing up on her doorstep. You never know, if Frankie slights her, maybe she'll dig up some info and give us a call."

They breezed down the freeway. "Any luck with your other leads?"

He was checking his phone as they drove. "Well, this is interesting."

The way he drew out *interesting* made the hair on the back of her neck tickle. "What?"

"Roman assigned some of his team to follow up on several Suarez gang members who have explosive experience in their background and the use of explosives on their rap sheets. One went to the home of a woman named Kelly Perez to question her, and guess what? She's dead. Two bullets to the heart and one to the head."

"Execution style," Liv said. *Mob style.*

Victor looked out the window pensively before glancing her way again. "What if we've been going at this backwards? What if

Gino and Frankie aren't trying to take over the Kings, but instead, they're working *with* them?"

"But they're fighting over the same territory and resources. Why would they suddenly start working together?"

"I don't know, but I think we better find out."

LATER THAT AFTERNOON, Victor sat at the safe house once more with Thomas, Ronni, and Roman, filling in some blanks for Emma on the other end of the phone. Olivia had shooting practice and then the job at four that afternoon, so he was meeting her at her place that evening.

Meanwhile, Victor had the dog with him. Taz lay under his chair at the kitchen table. It wasn't really big enough for all four of them and their assorted laptops and phones, but they'd squeezed in best they could. Emma was working on a psychological profile for the shooter, and they were feeding her Victor's latest theory about the Kings and Fifty-seven Gang working together.

"Crimes committed across territories by cooperating OCGs—organized crime groups—is nothing new," Thomas explained. "Colombian cartels and Mexican drug-trafficking organizations have been operating within the United States for decades, often working together to advance their mutual goals."

Roman shifted awkwardly, trying to find space for his legs. "Terrorist groups work with drug trafficking organizations in a symbiotic relationship too. For instance, Hezbollah established a strong base in Latin America, working with Mexican DTOs to launder money, finance terrorism, and smuggle people. The Intelligence Community has seen a growing international convergence of OCGs and terrorist organizations taking advantage of the specialized skills and assets of each group."

"The mafia has worked with al-Qaida and outlaw motorcycle

gangs here in the US to carry out criminal operations," Victor added. "All of these groups have diverging interests, goals and philosophies, yet they're working together to capitalize on each other's specific skills or assets."

They heard typing on the other end, Emma making notes. "If you can't beat 'em, join 'em, then, eh? Very enterprising of them, and a little surprising, since I'm sure each group feels they are the power player in any of those scenarios."

Ronni took off her reading glasses and tossed them on her keyboard. "These working relationships are usually short term. It would not surprise me if both the Kings and DeStefano's Fifty-seven Gang are pooling resources, and also secretly planning to wipe each other out once their goal is accomplished."

"It's a possibility we have to consider," Victor said. "Cooper's shooting appears like a mob hit, while the bombing points to the Kings."

Thomas leaned in and took a sip of his soda, staring at photographs from the latest crime scene. "This definitely looks like the work of a mafia hitman."

More typing. "Or someone *wanted* it to," Emma countered.

Ronni sat up and studied the photos too. "That's it. It's possible the two organizations are working together, but it's also possible they're each trying to frame the other for these crimes."

She had a point and Victor rolled both ideas around in his head.

Roman shifted again, still not seeming to find the right spot for his long legs. "We have three other Kings we're searching for in the bombing case that have explosive experience and/or have used a bomb in a crime. So far, none have been home, but my team has all three residences staked out."

"I think it's time to stakeout Gino DeStefano and Frankie Molina too," Victor said. He planned to keep an eye on Alfonso Barone himself, hopefully without stepping on Olivia's toes.

"Thomas, you know all the cartels and their leaders. Is it possible to track down Silvestre Santos?"

Santos was head of the Kings, and much like DeStefano, kept a low profile, moving his home and headquarters around a lot. At any given time, he might be drinking champagne in a millionaire's estate in Bel Air or slumming it with some of his family members along the Mexican border.

Thomas quirked a blond brow. "Track him down, as in bring him in for questioning, or put surveillance on him?"

Victor looked at Roman. "Either way works for me. What do you think? Putting pressure on the leaders of both the mafia and cartel might prove fruitful."

Roman nodded slowly. Victor could see the gears turning in his head, analyzing the options. "I agree. The clock is ticking. Why don't we start with the lieutenants in both organizations and work up from there."

The lieutenants often ran the day to day activities and were easier to track down in most cases. Victor's phone vibrated with an incoming call and he rose from the table, stretching his own long legs and hoping it was Olivia. Taz crawled out from under the chair, stood, and shook himself out. "Good idea," Victor said to the group. "Work out the details. I'll be back in a minute."

As he walked into an extra bedroom, his high spirits sank. He plopped on the bed and the dog jumped up to sit next to him. "Director Allen," he said, answering. "I was about to call you to give you an update."

"I see Dr. Walsh went around the FBI and gained permission to create a special taskforce for this investigation."

Great. Just what he needed, his boss pissed at Homeland. Well, he could be pissed all he wanted. Roman and his boss had made the right call, and Allen would have to suck it up.

"After much discussion, we agreed there was crossover between investigations we've both been working on," he lied. He also preferred to use Roman's law enforcement title. "Agent

Walsh has had positive input on the case so far, and one of his people discovered a possible witness, who upon follow-up, was discovered murdered earlier today by what appears to be a mob hit. It's all tied together."

That told him a whole lot of nothing, but sounded good, which usually resulted in getting the man off Victor's back.

A long pause met his ears and he braced for the yelling he anticipated was coming. "I'm working with the Justice Department on that funding you need for increased security for your agents," Allen said.

Whoa. Wait. Victor had not expected that. On the other hand, Allen never liked to be outshone by any organization and was known in certain circles to enjoy a good pissing match over territories and various cases. Usually those cases involved high-profile victims or clients, but whatever. Victor would take all the help he could get.

"A word of warning," Allen added. "Showing up in the tabloids is probably not in your best interest if you feel like either the Fifty-seven Gang or the Kings are targeting your people. Whoever their high profile target is, it could be you, so maybe you should be laying low as well as your agents."

Victor made a face and Taz whimpered. Shit on a stick. He'd already forgotten about the photo, but now he was going to have to hunt someone down and put the fear of God in them. Or in this case, Victor Dupé.

Maybe this was why the director was suddenly on board with the extra funding—a glamorous actress had entered the equation.

"I didn't realize you were a fan of the gossip magazines, sir."

It was overstepping, but it felt good to get a dig in.

Allen didn't appreciate it. "I suggest you get a handle on your personal life and make sure it's not interfering with this case, am I clear?"

In all his years as director, Victor had never been reprimanded by the top gun about his personal life. He didn't much care for it, especially considering Allen was never on the ground, working with the men and women under him. "I'll take that suggestion under advisement." *In other words, fuck off.* "Will there be anything else, sir?"

"Watch your back. Remember what I said—you could just as easily be in the line of fire."

If he was, whoever was after him was doing a piss poor job. "Roger that, sir."

He'd just disconnected when another call came through. He groaned softly when he saw who it was. He almost didn't answer, but he might need her help shutting down the media problem.

"Tracee,"—he didn't bother with a greeting—"you need to get your publicity person after *Red Star Report* and get the gossip about the two of us shut down."

She sounded like she was in tears. "Victor, you have to come over right now. I have a stalker, I'm sure of it. I need you! I'm so scared."

He shot up off the bed. "Are you at home?"

"Yes. How soon can you be here?"

"Is someone trying to break in? You should call the police, Tracee."

Her voice hiccupped. "No, no. He's not trying to break in, but I know he's around. Everywhere I've gone in the last few days, I've seen him. He's following me. I... I think I picked him up the other day at the hospital. Could it be someone involved with the shooting?"

Victor's stomach dropped to his knees. "Where are your body-guards? Have you reported this to the police?"

"I'm reporting it to you! You know the cops won't believe me, and they'll barge in and ask all kinds of stupid questions. Plus, it will end up in the news, and that's the last thing I need before I take off for my next film. Please, Victor, you have to help me."

He ran a hand through his hair and sighed. What the ever-living hell was going on? "I'm in San Diego. Let me call a friend and I'll send him over to check things out."

"No!" Her voice was sharp. "I don't want anyone else. How soon can you get here?"

He really had no choice. He had to check this out. The last thing he wanted to do was spend time on this, but he owed it to her to make sure she was safe. If someone *had* followed her from the hospital, she could be in danger. "It'll take me three to four hours depending on traffic. Is there anyone there with you?"

"Leon is watching the front door."

Leon was one of her bodyguards and she lived in a fancy penthouse suite with good security. Several other actors lived in the same building. Still, he would have one of the local PD units drive over and keep an eye out until he got there. "Stay inside, keep the doors locked, and stay away from the windows. I'll be there as soon as I can."

11

Olivia scanned the picture on her phone. It was the one from the gossip magazine. Taken from fifty yards away, the photographer had caught Tracee and Victor in front of the hospital entrance. Tracee was leaning into him slightly, looking up with adoration.

The angle was such that Olivia couldn't make out Victor's expression, but he seemed stiff. Or maybe that was wishful thinking.

A call came in from Alfie. She swiped it away, sending it to voicemail. This wasn't the place or time to talk to him. He'd probably caught wind of Valiant's visit with the judge, although everyone was keeping it hush-hush, and there was no way she was discussing the situation in the courthouse in front of her partner.

"How much longer is this going to take?" Danny pushed off the wall opposite her, checking his watch. "I thought the lawyer already had the deal set up. How long does it take for Valiant to spill what he knows?"

Olivia wasn't completely up to speed on Henry Valiant, but what she did know was he'd gotten some information out of his temporary cell partner regarding an ongoing murder investigation. It might help Valiant cut a deal to lighten his sentence.

Information that might also lead to the arrest of Frankie B Molina.

Alfie called again, and she rolled her eyes, hitting the ignore button once more. The mobster had his undies in a bunch, no doubt, wondering if his immediate boss was about to be arrested. If the judge felt Valiant's intel was enough to go after Frankie B, Alfie's confidential informant status was in jeopardy.

Valiant and his lawyer were inside the judge's chambers and had been for the past two hours. The courthouse was already closing for the day, only a couple of security guards manning the exits. Olivia put her phone away, and leaned against the wall. "They can't be much longer," she said, reassuring herself as much as Danny.

Her phone continued to buzz as she stood there and she finally turned off the ringer. It was nearing six before the door opened and Valiant and his lawyer emerged.

"I want protection," Valiant said. He was dressed in prison orange with handcuffs on his wrist and ankles, causing him to shuffle as he walked. "This gets out, I could end up with a shiv in my gut."

His lawyer was short, bald, and heavyset. Sweat beaded on his forehead, and he dabbed at it with a hanky. "The appropriate paperwork will be filed tomorrow morning first thing, and I'll look into getting you into solitary until the detectives have confirmed the information."

Danny met Olivia's gaze and rolled his eyes as he prodded Valiant to move toward the back exit. The man balked, jerking his elbow out of Danny's grasp.

"I'm not kidding," he said to his lawyer. "You promised I'd have protection if I came forward."

Olivia was tired, hungry, and wanted to get this guy back to jail so she could go home. Victor had texted earlier to tell her he was on his way to Los Angeles for a meeting and hoped to be done and to her place in Carlsbad by eight. She barely had time to drop off Valiant, get home and cleaned up before his arrival. Tonight was the night when she planned to come clean.

But that meant getting this bozo to cooperate. "Tell you what." She made a show of pulling out her phone and hitting some buttons. "I'll see about getting you into solitary. Seems to me you're being uncooperative, so I'll tell Gambitt you need to cool your heels in there tonight."

Gambitt, the prison warden, was a hardass and would have no reservations about throwing Valiant into isolation.

A convicted criminal locked eyes with her, seeming to reevaluate who had the power in this group. "You would do that for me?"

She nudged his elbow and they started walking. "Anyone who helps take down Frankie B Molina and his group gets a star in my book."

The lawyer waddled behind them, trying to keep up. "That's really not necessary. I can handle this."

"You're an overworked DA who has better things to do tonight than worry about your client." They were heading for the back door, the transport vehicle waiting for them at the bottom of the steps. Once she had Valiant in the car, the rest would be easy. She held up the phone. "I'm making the call right now, so Henry will be taken directly to solitary upon arrival. I'll handle any necessary paperwork, okay?"

They passed the guard, who nodded, more than ready to lock up and head home. The attorney shrugged but she could see the relief on his face. "I guess that works."

Danny sent the guy a harsh glare. "My partner is doing you and your client a solid. Show some appreciation, huh?"

"It's okay." As the direct line to Gambitt's office went to voicemail, Olivia caught sight of an incoming call from Victor. She accepted it as she maneuvered Valiant between them. "Hey, there, can I call you back? I'm not done with my prisoner transport."

His voice was sharp, demanding. "Where are you?"

Danny pushed open the door and they walked out onto the top of the steps.

"Leaving the courthouse. I won't be home until—"

Danny pulled up short, jerking Valiant to a stop and nearly causing Olivia to stumble into them. The lawyer brushed past her, gaze down as he jogged down the steps.

"Wait!" Danny called to him. At the same time, Victor said, "Stay inside! Thomas just got a tip that something is going down—"

She didn't hear the rest as gunfire rang out.

Valiant's attorney dropped first, tumbling down the last four steps, papers flying from his unzipped briefcase. Across the street, Olivia saw six men dressed in baggy jeans and matching black hoodies. All were armed.

Danny jumped on their prisoner, knocking him to the ground, and yelling, "Get down!"

Bang, bang, bang. As the crack of gunfire continued and bullets smacked into the concrete pillars, sending chunks flying, Olivia ducked behind one. She dropped her phone and reached for her side arm.

On autopilot, she returned fire, wondering in the back of her mind where the uniformed guard inside was. Why wasn't he backing her up? Danny was lying on top of Valiant. They were going to be pincushions, chock-full of bullets if they didn't move.

She nailed one of the men in the firing squad, a direct hit to the chest, knocking him off his feet. The two on either side stopped and reached down to grab him. The others closed rank, protecting their own, but also making it easier for Olivia to take out another.

In the distance, she heard sirens and squealing tires. A black and white must have been close to be there already. No looking a gift horse in the mouth—she would take all the help she could get.

With two men down and the other four helping their injured cohorts, the rain of bullets eased up. They were only a few yards from an alleyway and as Olivia peeked out from behind her cover, she realized they must have a getaway car there.

She wanted to follow them and keep shooting until she had every last one down on the ground, but as her gaze dropped to Danny and Valiant, she saw a dark pool of blood running down the steps.

Shit!

Keeping one eye on the retreating shooters, she stayed low and ran to the spot where Danny lay draped over their prisoner. "Danny!" Olivia shook him, but he was dead weight. She shifted his body and saw his shirt covered in blood.

Under him, Valiant curled into a ball, hands over his head. "Are they gone?"

Olivia checked Danny's pulse, found it to be slow but strong. "Don't you move or I'll shoot you," she said to Valiant. She threw a look over her shoulder at that disappearing firing squad, then placed her hands under Danny's armpits and began to tug him behind the cover of the pillar. He outweighed her by a good thirty pounds or more and she huffed, digging in her heels to slide him across the concrete landing.

She heard Victor's voice and thought it was coming from her phone, but then suddenly he was there, like an apparition bursting out the back door. "Get down!" he yelled, and the next thing Olivia knew, he tackled her, sending her backward as a fresh round of bullets peppered the steps, columns, and exit. Glass from the door shattered, raining down on them, but Victor was on top of her, protecting her.

Her ears rang, her head buzzed from the impact of hitting it on the concrete, and her mind spun. Who was shooting now? She'd seen the firing squad all run off.

Would Danny live?

What about Valiant, still exposed on the top step?

Without warning, Victor jumped up and fired back.

———

OLIVIA LOOKED like hell on wheels. Victor knew that look—like someone with PTSD who was pissed at their own fear as well as the people who'd scared them.

It had been an hour since the shooting, and she was strung out but trying to be tough. Her partner was in intensive care, the prisoner she'd been transporting was dead, and the shooters were long gone. The lone gunmen who'd come back to finish Henry Valiant was already around the corner before Victor could fire.

Olivia swore she'd nailed two of them. All local hospitals had been put on alert for gunshot-wound victims showing up at the ER, but Victor doubted the two Olivia had nailed would be that easy to snatch.

"It was a fucking hit squad," she said. "We were sitting ducks. Maybe if that damn guard hadn't stayed inside hiding like a scared rabbit..."

She pushed out of the kitchen chair, ignoring Victor's protests. He was trying to clean the scrapes on her face caused by flying debris. She'd refused to see a doctor, and by the way she kept holding her head, he was concerned she might have a concussion.

The deputy marshal was on a tear though. She couldn't— wouldn't—sit still.

He sank back into his own chair, tossing the washcloth on the table. They'd already been over this when they'd given their statements at the scene. "Danny will be okay. It's not your fault he was shot."

She rubbed the back of her head again, pacing his kitchen

123

and making Taz nervous, the dog's dark eyes watching her wear a path in the tile floor. "It had to be Frankie, but those guys..."

Her gut was telling her something. She kept circling back to the six gunmen. "What about them? You said they wore bandanas around their necks, gloves on their hands, and sunglasses to cover their eyes. No identifying features were exposed, and they were all dressed alike, except the bandanas were different colors."

"That's just it. They hid every single distinguishing mark. Like they knew I could identify them if I so much as saw an inch of skin." She whirled and looked at him. "Like gang members with tattoos."

He stood and took her hand, guiding her back to the chair and forcing her to sit. "That's a strong possibility."

"But Henry Valiant was tattling on Frankie. Why would a gang try to take him out?"

He resumed washing dried blood from her face and putting witch hazel on the scratches. If he could keep her in the chair and talking, he'd have her doctored in five minutes, tops. "It would make sense for Frankie to send someone to take out Valiant in order to stop his testimony. The judge pulled his cellmate from general population, by the way, in order to protect him, so we still have the opportunity to get the goods on Frankie. But it's possible Frankie used members of the Kings, rather than his own people, to take out Valiant. He certainly made a statement to anyone else who might be thinking of turning state's evidence against him."

Her eyes grew wary and curious at the same time. "Why would six members of the Kings do a hit for Frankie?"

"Roman and I have a theory."

She flinched when he dabbed the cut next to her temple. "Lay it on me."

"We believe the two organizations—the Fifty-seven Gang and Suarez cartel—are working together."

Her spine straightened, drawing her away. "They're sworn

enemies. They hate each other. Gino is trying to run the Kings out of town."

Even banged up and worried, she was beautiful. He wanted to pull her into his arms and reassure her, but the deputy marshal wasn't in the mood for a consoling hug. "They could be working together to capitalize on each other's specific skills and resources."

Disbelief made her shake her head. "No way. They would never do that."

He gave up doctoring her, going to a cupboard and pulling down a bottle of brandy. He fished out a couple of clean glasses and poured them each a shot. Returning to the table, he handed one to her.

His phone rang and Tracee's name popped up on the ID. Damn, with the shooting and the aftermath, he hadn't had a chance to call her. He definitely wasn't driving up to her place at this hour and leaving Olivia alone.

"You should answer that," she said, looking miserable. "It could be Celina or your friend from Homeland."

"It's my ex," he confessed, wanting to keep things as honest as possible. "She's worried about a stalker, but she's fine, trust me. I've got someone watching her place."

When Olivia wouldn't look at him, he took her chin and raised it so she had to. "You're the only one I'm worried about at the moment."

She gave him a hint of a smile. "Your theory doesn't make sense."

He took his seat again. "Criminals do a lot of things that don't make sense, right? But it's not unusual for the mafia to work with other criminal organizations. They've done it with terrorist groups, both international and homegrown, as well as motorcycle gangs, and various other entities."

Tap, tap, tap. She drummed her fingers against the glass before downing the brandy in one gulp. "True, but...if they *are*, what about Cooper's shooting and the bomb meant for Thomas? Are both organizations involved?"

The brandy was warm on the back of his tongue. "Cooper spotted a King at the park before he was shot, and the guy seemed to be sizing him up. Maybe he was IDing Cooper for his counterpart in that building across the street."

She fell quiet for a moment, the wheels turning. "Something my CI said keeps going 'round in my head. I asked him about Cooper's shooting, and he said, 'We never miss.' So maybe it wasn't one of the mafia guys, and it was indeed a King."

His phone quit vibrating, Tracee's call going to voicemail. "Roman's group finally tracked down one of the members who has explosive experience and brought her in for questioning. She did not give up any specifics about the bomb under Thomas's car, but she alluded to the hit squad going after Henry Valiant today. Roman called me just as I hit Los Angeles. The woman had not given specifics about who the hit was on, but I put two and two together, fearing exactly what happened."

She sighed, leaning forward and putting her head in her hands. "And that one came back to make sure Valiant was dead. He tried to put a few bullets in me as well."

He touched her shoulder, pushed some hair behind her ear. "But he didn't."

She raised her head and met his eyes. "Because you stopped him. I owe you my life."

He was desperate to see her smile again. He gave her a cocky grin. "I'm sure you'll find a way to make it up to me."

Her hand grabbed his and squeezed. She threaded her fingers through his. "I'm serious. Thank you."

Coming out of his chair, he leaned forward and kissed her across the table. She tasted like the brandy and he wanted more, but held himself in check. She'd been through too much in the past few hours, so he placed his other hand behind her neck, gently cradling her sore skull. "My pleasure."

She came out of the chair and into his arms. She kissed him, needy and demanding, her hands working over the muscles in his arms, his back.

He broke the kiss. "Liv, I was teasing. You really should take it easy."

She sat on the table and wrapped her legs around his waist, drawing him close as she untucked his shirt. "Screw that," she said. "I'm pissed. I need to work off some anger."

He should argue. Make her rest.

I really should.

Under her assault, though, the voice of reason in his brain went mute. Her tongue tangled with his, her hand cupping him through his pants and squeezing.

Yep, he was gone. Just like that. It was insane—he hadn't had this much sex in ages.

Whatever she wanted, he would give her. He was so screwed.

I love her.

The thought hit him hard in the gut, but he didn't have time to analyze it. She grabbed his hands and put them on her breasts, the soft light overhead making her skin glow. As he massaged the full mounds, his shirt lost a button from her ripping it open. Her lips found his skin, kissing and sucking on his pecs, his neck.

He divested her of her shirt and bra, loving the way her breasts bounced free. He laid her back on the table, trapping one luscious nipple in his mouth.

And then his damn phone started vibrating again.

For a minute, they both ignored it. When it didn't stop, she pushed him gently away. "Your ex is as persistent as my CI. You better answer."

Hating himself, he knew she was probably right. While Tracee was not his responsibility, this new stalker of hers might be. "She's sure someone is following her, and unfortunately, after that picture went viral, I'm afraid it could be tied to this case."

Olivia sat up and handed him his phone. "Then you definitely better take it. She could be in trouble."

Doubtful with his friend watching her place, but maybe if he answered, he could put a stop to her calling.

As he answered, Olivia slid off the table, throwing her shirt on and grabbing her own phone. She left the kitchen, Taz following her.

"Yeah, Tracee, I'm sorry I didn't get there tonight," he said into his phone, "but something happened. I've already made sure you have plenty of police protection. My friend, Detective Gordon, is looking into the situation and keeping me updated. I'll keep you apprised of anything he discovers, but so far, we all believe you're safe."

She sobbed into the phone. "You don't understand, Vic. I need you!"

Drama. There had never been a lack of it with her.

Victor rubbed his tired eyes. "Tracee, if this is a ploy to get me back, I'm not going there with you. You've had stalkers before, and if you can't give me more specifics than you *think* someone is watching you, there is nothing I can do. I'll do my best to come by in the next couple of days, but I'm in the middle of a very serious investigation, and you have plenty of people to help you with this."

The crying lasted several long moments, meant to wear him down. He'd been through this before and knew the way she used emotions to manipulate others. It was one of the things that made her such a good actress.

The sobbing tapered off, and then she whispered, "Goodbye, Victor."

The connection went dead. He blew out a deep breath, slightly uneasy about the finality in her voice. He would have plenty of eyes on her, and if it appeared her stalker was real and had anything to do with the mafia or cartel, he would make sure she was put in protective custody until he wrapped everything up. At the moment, from everything he'd seen and heard, there was no substance to her fear, and nothing he could divert more resources to. Luckily, Gordon was a good friend and willing to keep an eye on Tracee because of it.

Victor went looking for Liv and Taz and found them upstairs in his bedroom. Olivia sat on the edge of the bed, talking to whomever she'd dialed, and the dog lay at her feet. "Thank you, Alfonzo. I will pass that information on... Yes, I told you, I'm fine, but I appreciate your concern." She glanced at Victor and rolled her eyes. "Sure, I'll see you for dinner next week."

She disconnected and tossed it on the nightstand. "Alfie knew about the hit on Valiant today. He called me six times this afternoon, trying to let me know. He had no idea I was one of the deputy marshals escorting Valiant to and from the courthouse, but claims he wanted to prove he's helping me. Oh, and he has it on good authority that it was indeed Frankie who set up the hit."

It was after eleven. He didn't want to wait until the sun came up to go after Molina, but Olivia was beat and he wasn't leaving her. "First thing in the morning, I need to pay Frankie a visit."

She shrugged off her shirt and started undoing her pants. "One more thing, Alfie confirmed Frankie arranged the hit on Cooper."

Victor felt a sudden shift, a little buzz inside him that meant the case had turned the corner and a successful end was in sight. "He has proof?"

"So he claims, but he wouldn't tell me what or how he got it."

"I need that before I go see Molina."

"I'll get it, but you're not going to talk to Molina alone. I'm going with you."

They'd see about that, but for now, if it made her happy, he'd let her think she was his partner.

He helped her out of the rest of her clothes and into his bed. She watched him undress with hungry eyes, raising her hands above her head and showing him her breasts above the sheet.

He crawled in beside her, skimming his hands up her arms and catching his fingers in her hair to bring her face closer to his. "Now, where were we?"

Their bodies came together with the same fiery passion, both shutting out their exhaustion in an effort to forget what happened only hours earlier and to prove to themselves, as well as each other, they were still alive.

12

The next morning, Olivia found Victor sitting on his deck, the dog running around the yard sniffing and digging. Victor was on the phone, and it sounded like he was speaking to Thomas as he went down the list of taskforce members. "How is Ronni?" Pause. "Good. Mitch still okay watching Cooper and Celina?" Pause. "What about Nelson and Sophia? Nothing unusual going on there?"

He was dressed in baggy PJ pants and nothing else, his broad shoulders and chest exposed to the morning sun. Olivia stepped out onto the worn wooden deck in her bare feet, buttoning Victor's shirt that she'd picked up off the floor. It smelled like his soap and she loved being wrapped in it.

She was sore from her tumble on the concrete at the courthouse and had a nice bruise on her left hip and shoulder. The back of her head was tender as well, but at least she didn't have a headache. Victor had done a good job doctoring the scratches on her face, although she looked like she'd been in a catfight. She'd already checked in with the hospital and they'd told her Danny was in stable condition. She planned to drop by and visit later in the day.

As she stood there listening to the soft rumble of his voice, she glanced back at the house. Everything was in disarray, so unlike the director. Her eyes caught on the dining room table, barely visible from this angle. There was a box pushed to one side and papers everywhere. The box was labeled "Ansel Dupé." Had to be the case notes from his father's murder case.

Once this current situation was resolved, she'd help him with it—if he'd let her.

Heading to Victor, she dropped a kiss on his forehead. He grabbed her arm, giving her a squeeze and pulling her face down for a kiss. He was strong and muscular, and she ran her fingers over his chest.

"Sounds good," he said into the phone. "Meanwhile, I'm going to question Frankie Molina at some point today...Yeah, Olivia's CI claims to have some damning information pointing to him being the one who set up the hit on Henry Valiant yesterday. It's possible Molina is also involved in Cooper's shooting."

They discussed Frankie for another minute as Olivia walked into the yard to see Taz. There wasn't much grass, most having died under the hot sun with only sand to grow in. Taz had it all over his nose and paws. "You're going to need a bath," she said to him.

When Victor hung up, she made her way back to the patio. "No coffee?"

He looked tired, a couple days' worth of beard on his chin. "I haven't found the box with the coffee maker in it yet. I usually grab a cup on the way to the office."

She reached for his hand and pulled him out of the chair. "Come on, let's find it."

Inside, he used a towel to get the worst of the sand off the dog's feet, and they began ripping open boxes in their quest for caffeine. As they went, Olivia pulled out other kitchen items, and ended up organizing one shelf with spices. Then she found plates and put those on a different shelf.

Victor found dishtowels and used one to smack her on the ass when she was reaching to place a glass on a high shelf. She grabbed another and started a war with him, laughing at the fact he was a better shot, but was so obviously taking it easy on her, worried about her scratches and bruises.

It was an accident that she found the coffee maker, tripping over a box and knocking it on its side. The contents spilled out, and luckily, the carafe did not break. "Hey, look at that. I found it."

"Now if I can find the coffee," Victor said.

Olivia was slightly dismayed at the state of the coffee maker. It was nothing fancy, that was for sure, and she was even more appalled when Victor handed her a bag of grocery store ground coffee beans. She gave him a horrified look. "You can't be serious. That's not coffee, that's garbage."

He held up a finger. "Wait, Celina gave me some Cuban coffee at Christmas."

Well, that was better, even though it had to be at least four months old.

He looked at the disaster the kitchen had turned into. All the boxes were open now and no Cuban coffee in sight. "Maybe it's in the living room."

They made their way down the hall, finding Taz asleep on the couch. He barely opened his eyes as they started going through those boxes.

"Have you checked on your partner?" Victor asked.

"He's in stable condition. They're only letting family see him right now, but I hope to talk to him later today."

He pulled a blue foil bag from a box. "Aha! Here it is."

Taz sat up at the excitement and the three of them filed back into the kitchen, the dog sniffing at the mess.

"Remind me to buy you a new coffee pot for your birthday," Olivia said. "Something that actually can make a decent drink."

He filled the carafe as she loaded the filter with grounds. "I beg your pardon? What's wrong with this one?"

"Hey, I'm Italian. I want a machine that makes more than watered-down coffee. It should do espresso shots, and have the ability to froth milk for lattes."

"Guess I'm not home that much to have fancy stuff," he said, pouring the water in.

She put her hands on his waist. "We need to change that."

They made out while the coffee brewed. When it was done, Victor broke away and grabbed two mugs, filling each to the top. The smell was full-bodied and strong, just the way Olivia liked it, although the Cuban blend was different than her normal morning sustenance.

"Your confidential informant?" Victor leaned on the counter across from her. "I need to talk to him and find out exactly what he has on Frankie. Getting to Frankie will be challenging. I don't want to give all our intel away until we have an arrest warrant, but I need to be sure I have something damning before I talk to him."

She blew on the hot liquid. "Do you think it's wise to tip our hand to Frankie before we're ready to arrest him?"

"That's a risk I'm willing to take to put pressure on him. I want him to know I'm coming for him, and the sooner the better, since we don't have much time officially for our special taskforce to make progress on this case. Right now, we have extra resources and some leeway with the rules, but that ends by tomorrow morning."

She admired his shoot-from-the-hip style. She'd always approached her targets in the opposite manner, sneaking around and digging up evidence against them before blindsiding them with arrest warrants and handcuffs. "I can set something up with Alfie, but he may only talk to me. He's not exactly friendly with FBI agents, and I don't want him to clam up completely."

Victor nodded. "I don't want to step on your toes, so if you can obtain the evidence on your own, go for it. This guy cares for you, doesn't he?"

All her conflicted feelings about her father and Alfie came rushing to the surface like acid on the back of her tongue. "It's a complicated situation because of my family background. This guy seems to think we have some kind of bond because of the mafia connection, but I'm sure he would throw me under the bus without hesitation. I've only pretended to be friendly because of the information he's been feeding me." *And his sauce is pretty good.* "Half the time, I'm not sure the intel is legit, but enough has proved out that I tend to believe him. He hates Frankie as much as I do, and I'm sure he would love to get him and Gino out of the way so he could take over."

"So Marquita was right? Alfie thinks he can run the syndicate on his own? With all the intelligence he's given you, he doesn't think you'll throw him in prison?"

"He knows I'll never let him become king of the hill. The Justice Department has already agreed to put him and his daughter in the witness protection program if he testifies against Gino when this all goes down. Maybe at one point, he wanted to take over, but he's smart enough to know that's never going to happen."

"What kind of proof do you think he has in relation to yesterday's shooting?"

"He wouldn't tell me over the phone, but I will get it for you, and then we can go pay a visit to Frankie."

"I'd prefer you sit that one out and let me handle him."

"No dice." She took the cup and headed for the stairs to take a shower. "If you want to use my CI to get your evidence," she said over her shoulder, "you get me as a sidekick when you talk to Frankie."

"Package deal, huh?" he called after her, following her up the stairs.

It was kind of like the coffee and the coffee maker. "Yep. You can't have one without the other."

He caught up to her and smacked her playfully on the ass. "You drive a hard bargain, but I guess I have no choice."

No, he didn't. She needed Alfie to come through and she planned to help Victor solve the shooting and bombing. It was the only way she could counter the truth about her secret investigation and hope he would forgive her.

Regardless, she was definitely putting an end to her investigation for the JD, and if they wanted her to take down the Fifty-seven Gang, they better get happy about it.

Package deal, she told herself. One way or the other, she was getting exactly what she wanted—Victor, and the demise of the West Coast mafia once and for all.

ALFONSO BARONE LIVED IN OCEANSIDE, but chose a meeting place several blocks from the harbor. As Victor sat in his car fifty feet away from the shack of a bar, listening to Olivia's conversation with the mobster, he could imagine the smell of stale beer and fried clams. The background noise consisted of multiple conversations, raucous laughter, and the clink and bang of glasses and silverware, even though they were meeting in a private backroom.

Olivia claimed this was one of Barone's favorite hangouts, a place he and his wife visited many times before her death. The two-story building held an apartment upstairs, and Olivia believed Alfie used it for certain business dealings. She suspected he was running his own criminal enterprise here, way outside of DeStefano's territory.

The place had seen better days, and most likely the owners needed Alfie's help with finances to stay open. Restaurants like this were good spots for money laundering, drug sales, and back door deals.

Taz sat in the passenger seat, head out the window, panting. The day was growing warmer and Victor shrugged off his jacket, tossing it in the back. He'd insisted Olivia wear a wire, so he could hear the conversation and record it. She hadn't liked the idea but went along with it when he threatened to come in with her if she didn't.

He got the feeling she was slightly protective of her CI. That wasn't unusual in his world. Most of his agents were as well. She'd told him it had taken months to groom Alfie and she didn't want to blow it. She was closer now than she had ever been to getting an insider to testify against Gino DeStefano, one who had enough evidence against the mafia leader to make sure he went away for good.

"Hey, doll." Alfie must have arrived, Olivia's mic picking up his voice.

Olivia didn't mess around. "What can you give me on Frankie and yesterday's hit?"

Alfie took his time responding, and Victor imagined him sliding into the booth, getting comfortable, and buying time before he spilled whatever he had, if anything. "You look a little rough there, deputy marshal. You sure you're okay?"

"Two men died in front of me yesterday, and my partner is in critical condition. Of course, I'm not okay. I should be at the hospital right now, hanging out with Danny, but I'm here because I need justice and we both need to stop Frankie."

"I'm sorry about what happened to your partner."

"You tried to warn me, and I appreciate that."

They made creaking noises as if one or both of them were fidgeting in their seat.

"Do you have the evidence?" Olivia asked.

"Whoa, there, sweetheart. Can I at least order a drink?"

Some people nearby grew loud, cheering and yelling, drowning out whatever Liv said. Victor was pretty sure it was a curse word.

"I wanna say for the record again that I had no idea you were one of the cops handling Valiant yesterday," Alfie said.

A waitress must have appeared because Victor heard a chipper young female voice. "Hi, Alfie. About time you came around. What can I get you, hon?"

"Ah, Suzie. Looking beautiful as ever. I'll have the porter-house special. Keep it rare. And a beer," Alfie added. "Whatever my friend here wants too, put it on my bill."

"Nothing for me," came Olivia's reply.

Alfie huffed loud enough the microphone picked it up. "Come on, now. At least have something to drink. You're not eating enough, I can see it. Your face is too skinny, you're losing your nice figure."

"No thanks."

"I'll get this order right in," the waitress said.

The wooden booth creaked again and Victor could see Liv leaning across the table with a threatening look on her face as she spoke. "You keep your damn eyes off my figure and stop worrying about my diet. Once I have Gino behind bars, I'll celebrate with a big plate of pasta, okay?"

"Okay, okay. Like I said, if I'd had known you were escorting that dumbass, I would've showed up at the courthouse to protect you myself."

"Right."

"I was trying to warn you so you could catch those idiots and make them confess."

There was a drumming sound, like Liv was thumping her knife on the tabletop. "That would've made things easier for you, wouldn't it, if a couple gang members turned against Frankie? But that's where you're wrong. The Justice Department will still want your testimony, and I want hard evidence about Frankie's involvement in the shooting of DEA agent Cooper Harris. Either you have it or you don't, Alfie, and I'm getting tired of being jerked around."

"You're giving me indigestion and my food hasn't even arrived. Ease up, Liv. I have the information, but you need to be careful with it."

Like most professional criminals, the guy was good at deflecting. Victor didn't know who to feel sorrier for—Olivia, for having to deal with this asshole, or Alfie, for the hell known as Olivia's anger about to rain down on him if he didn't come through.

"I don't want to do this," she said, the thumping growing louder, "but I will bring charges against you for impeding an investigation if you don't cooperate."

"Whoa, whoa. Slow down. You are always pushy, but today, you're really over-the-top, you know that? Is this about your old man? I heard he got cut loose today."

There was a damning pause. Victor held his breath.

Alfie was saved as the waitress returned, apparently with the beer. "There you go, hon. Your food should be out shortly."

"Thanks," he said. A few seconds passed, and he spoke again to Olivia. "Would you put that knife away? You're making me nervous."

The thumping stopped, but Victor knew she was probably thinking about sticking it in Alfie's eye. "This has nothing to do with my father," Olivia said.

"All right, whatever." The mobster must've taken a drink of beer, before clearing his throat. "Nobody likes Frankie, least of all the Suarez Kings, but he can get them access to large quantities of pseudoephedrine."

"The cold medicine? For meth manufacturing?"

"He's in good with one of the owners of a large-scale pharmaceutical company. Once a month, the guy makes a certain truck disappear from the books, so no one realizes it's gone missing down in Mexico. It delivers a large quantity of pseudoephedrine at a Kings' lab. Their American counterparts benefit from the product they make, and in turn, they do certain jobs for Gino."

"Why would this guy work with Gino?"

A disgusting sigh. "He's got a thing for young girls."

"Gino supplies girls to him in exchange for the meth ingredient."

"The guy's disgusting." Did Alfie have a conscience? Interesting. Olivia said he had a daughter, so maybe trafficking young girls hit too close to home. "I have some pictures that might help you take him down too."

"I'll be happy to arrest the scumbag. Now, what about the proof on the six Kings who showed up yesterday and nearly killed me? Two got shot, but we haven't been able to find them yet. Do you know who they are? *Where* they are?"

There was a pause and Victor heard the crinkling of paper. "This is one of their hiding spots. And this..." Background noise filtered in, and Victor wondered if Alfie was holding up something for Olivia to see. "This is gold. You'll find a phone conversation on here of Frankie giving the instructions to take out Valiant, by any means necessary."

"You bugged Frankie's phone?"

No answer—at least not a verbal one—but Victor wasn't surprised.

"What about the DEA agent? Where's the proof Frankie ordered that hit?"

Once again, the waitress interrupted and Victor heard the sound of a plate hitting the tabletop. "One porterhouse steak, rare, and I threw in extra fries." She giggled and lowered her voice. "Don't tell George, okay?"

Unbelievable. The waitress was hitting on the mob guy while he was sitting with Olivia. The thumping of her knife started up again, making Victor smile.

The sound of clinking silverware came through the wire as Alfie dug in. "You find the goons in the hit squad and you'll find the one who shot your DEA agent. Put the right kind of pressure on that person, and they'll testify that Frankie ordered the hit."

"There were six, Alfie. Can you be more specific about which one I should focus on?"

Alfie's reply was slightly muffled as he chewed. "Actually, from what I know, one is a woman. Served in the Army as a sniper, I believe. You might want to start with her."

The thumping stopped. "What's her name?"

"Sure you don't want to share this steak with me? It's excellent. That's why I come here. Good food and nice service. Here, have a fry."

"Why won't you give me the name? You got a thing for her or something?"

"Try a fry. They're homemade."

"You don't want to betray her, why?"

Another heavy sigh, and loud chewing. "I have no loyalty to any of the Suarez Kings."

"And I'm Mother Teresa. If you're not loyal to her, why won't you share her name?"

Silence.

Olivia tried again. "She's part of the family, isn't she?"

"Was."

Meaning what? This woman had been part of the DeStefano family? Victor sent a text to Thomas, asking him to look into potential candidates who had Army sniper experience and any link to the DeStefano syndicate. She could be tied to them because of a relative.

Olivia's voice lowered. "When I find her, I'll keep your name out of it, deal?"

For some reason, that seemed to do the trick. "You might check with Frankie's ex-girlfriend, Marquita Lomas. She can give you details."

"Marquita? She knows the sniper?"

"Calls her 'sister.'"

"Why that little..." Olivia's voice trailed off. "You're not sending me on a wild goose chase here, are you?"

There was a strained silence. "Marquita and her sister have both been in deep with Frankie. One slept with him, and the other—a member of the Kings—works for him."

"Marquita was protecting her sister."

That was said more to herself than Alfie.

"Family takes care of family," Alfie said.

"Save the lecture." It sounded like Olivia stood. "I'll be in touch."

"Don't forget the good wine next time."

When Olivia got into Victor's car, she had to move Taz to sit down. Although she'd only been gone a few minutes, the dog acted like it'd been days, possibly because she smelled like charred meat and fried food. As she tried to get him into the backseat, he was busy licking her face and trying to stay in her lap.

"Looks like we need to pay Marquita another visit," Liv said.

Victor put the car in gear and pulled out of the parking spot. "Her sister's name is Marisol Riva. Same mother, different fathers. She spent four years in the Army and failed sniper training."

"How did you get that already?"

He gave her a rugged grin. "I have my ways."

She smiled back. "Yes, you do, Director Dupé, and they are quite impressive."

13

Neither Marquita Lomas or Marisol Riva could be found. Victor took the taped phone conversation of Frankie putting out the hit on Henry Valiant to a Federal judge and was waiting for the arrest warrant to come through. He didn't want to move on any of the potential Suarez members until he had Frankie in his clutches.

While Olivia understood the strategy and knew it was solid, she itched to hunt down the shooters from the previous evening. That being said, Frankie was the ultimate goal, along with Gino, and taking them by surprise was the only way to make sure they put them out of business for good. If they got wind that the FBI or marshal service was onto them, either could be across the border in no time.

As night fell, Olivia paced the hospital waiting room. Danny was only allowed one visitor at a time, and his wife was keeping vigil. Part of Olivia felt guilty because she hadn't answered Alfonso's calls. She could have prevented the whole thing, but she'd been too wrapped up in her own issues.

Her boss, Navarro, was breathing down her neck, her father had indeed been paroled, and she still hadn't talked to Victor about her JD investigation. She'd had plenty of excuses since things kept getting in the way, but she wasn't letting herself off the hook. It was easy to fall back on those crutches to buy time and avoid the issue, but bottom line, she was just too damn scared to lose him.

Am I in love with him? Her mind kept raising the question, and her heart always sent back the same answer. *Yes.*

Listening to her heart was as scary as admitting the truth to Victor. She wished she could call her mother and get advice, but Mina Fiorelli would be the first person her father would go see. Olivia wasn't taking the chance he'd answer the phone. The very idea made her palms sweat and her heart skip erratically.

"Olivia?" Danny's wife, Carol, stood in the doorway. "He wants to talk to you."

Carol headed for the vending machines as Liv entered Danny's room.

He was hooked up to various monitors, his skin a dull ashen color. "Here I figured you'd have the guys who did this to me rounded up and in jail by now, Tinker Bell," he said from the sterile, white bed.

She let the nickname slide. "Working on it. I have solid intel on where they're hiding out. Just waiting on some red tape and an arrest warrant."

He looked at her through half-lidded eyes. "You know who shot me and you haven't arrested them yet?"

"They're members of the Kings and tied into the Fifty-seven Gang. If we play our cards right, we can nail all of them, including Frankie Molina and Gino DeStefano."

"Fuck that. You're more worried about those gangsters than getting revenge for me? I knew you were a hardass, Tinker Bell, but I didn't realize how bad of a team player you really are. No wonder no one wants to be your partner."

Low blow. *Don't take it personally.* "I know you've been through a lot, but you don't mean that, do you? We're law enforcement agents, we don't take revenge. I promise, I will make sure they pay for what they did yesterday, but we have the opportunity to shut down the Fifty-seven Gang. Regardless of our personal feelings, we have to look at the big picture."

He ran a freckled hand through his hair. "That's all you think about, isn't it? Paying back your old man? Proving how you're so much better than those guys in the mob?" He made a disgusted noise in the back of his throat. "For all I know, they were sent to kill *you*, and I got in the line of fire."

It was growing more challenging to chalk up his attitude to the painkillers. "I'm sorry about what happened, but I have proof they were after Henry Valiant, so you can stop with the victim mentality and quit blaming me for this. I'll make sure you stay updated on the latest, and if you or Carol need anything, you have my number."

Out in the hallway, she stopped for a moment to draw a deep breath. She checked her phone, but there were no messages from Victor about the search warrant. She waited until she was in her car to call him.

"No luck?" she asked when he answered.

"I normally deal with Judge Hardwick, but she's off sick, so I ended up with Ortiz. He thinks there's some legal issues with the recording and now has the district attorney involved. It may be a while."

Damn. The longer they waited, the more likely things were to go south. "Can you put pressure on him from higher up? Maybe ask Director Allen to get involved?"

"Already did. He's working on it."

The tone in Victor's voice suggested that wasn't going to accomplish much. She knew the feeling, having Navarro for a boss.

"What's next? Is there anything we can do?"

"Not tonight. Everything is hinging on this, but we're all on standby to help when the warrant comes through."

And if it didn't? They would lose Homeland's help, and maybe their best opportunity to wrap up this case. She sighed, feeling more than tired and extremely frustrated. "Okay, my place or yours?"

He chuckled, but there was a strain to his voice. "Mine is closer. Meet you there, in say, two hours? I have a couple things to look into, some paperwork to handle."

He had other issues to deal with, being head of the West Coast FBI. Plenty of other cases that needed attention.

So why did it feel like he was blowing her off?

"Um, sure. Do you need me to watch the dog? I am packing it in for the day, so I'm happy to pick him up and head to your house."

"He's already there. I dropped him off earlier."

She didn't have a key, or she'd pick up food and get to Victor's early. "I can head over now and hang out with him until you're done. I'll just swing by for your key, then go feed him, and maybe take him for a walk. He's earned it and I need to clear my head."

"He'll be okay. Look, I got to go. See you in a while."

That was definitely a blow-off and she stared at the phone for a second after he hung up. So, he didn't want her to swing by and pick up his key. Okay, no problem. Message received.

Her stomach growled, and she realized she hadn't eaten since that morning. She tapped the avatar for her browser to look for a nearby restaurant that had a drive-thru.

Except the first thing that popped up on her screen was the picture from the *Red Star Report* of Victor and Tracee Tyson. She hadn't cleared her browsing history.

Her stomach lurched. Why? She was acting like a silly teenager instead of a grown woman. Victor had assured her there was nothing going on between them, but Olivia couldn't help but compare herself to the starlet. What normal woman wouldn't? Tracee was model tall, thin, perfect hair, natural beauty, and had a charisma the camera loved.

Yet, she told herself, *Victor is with me.*

But for how long?

She scanned the picture of the two of them together one more time, trying to see Victor's face. But she couldn't see his features well enough to tell if he still had feelings for the beautiful woman in front of him.

Reprimanding herself once more for acting like a lovesick teenager, she went to clear the browser when her gaze caught on something that made her pause.

Using her fingers, she zoomed in, bringing Tracee's lower legs and feet in view. Her breath caught in her throat, and she quickly left the browser and went to her photos.

"Well, I'll be damned. This is not good. Not good at all."

She closed out the photos and, with her elbow on the door, dropped her head in her hand for a moment. Then she dialed Victor's number.

He needed to know what his ex was up to.

The call went to voicemail and Olivia swore under her breath. She sent him a text, asking him to call her immediately, but before she was done, someone tapped on her window, making her jump.

When she saw who, all the air left her lungs.

She dropped the phone.

The man on the other side smiled and gave her an innocent wave. He wore a ball cap, pulled low over his brow, and sunglasses, but there was no mistaking who he was.

Frozen in place, Olivia didn't know what to do. Her heart felt like it was beating in her throat, her mind suddenly blank.

The man motioned for her to roll down the window. Trepidation swam through her. Should she? Or put the car in gear and get the hell away from him?

Shoving down the shock, she cracked the window a couple of inches.

The man's smile grew wider. He removed the sunglasses, his

eyes slowly scanning her face before coming back to meet her gaze. "Hello, baby girl."

She swallowed hard. The hair visible under the cap had grayed since the last time she'd seen him and the crow's feet at the corners of his eyes had grown deeper.

It took three tries for her to find her voice. "Hello, daddy."

THE RAIN CAME down in sheets, drenching Victor's windshield. The wipers could barely keep up, even though he was idling at the curb outside the high-end wine bar Tracee loved. He'd tried to get her to meet him here, but she claimed she had a migraine and couldn't leave her penthouse.

Roman slid into the passenger seat, swearing and dripping. "You could've picked a better night for this."

The storm had come up quickly, turning the streets to fast flowing streams. Few people were out, and those that insisted on braving the storm wrestled with their umbrellas as the wind tried to invert them. "I appreciate your help with this."

"You think the stalker might be one of the Kings?"

Victor tapped a thumb on the steering wheel. "In all honesty, I'm not sure there is a stalker at all. Something isn't right about this. I spoke to Tracee's publicist, manager, and several others on her team, and none know anything about this supposed stalker. The security agency has no alert, and I spoke to Tracee's regular bodyguard earlier, and he hadn't seen anything unusual, nor had she mentioned being concerned or scared."

Roman wiped his face off with a hand. "I saw the tabloids. Is she trying to get you back?"

"Initially, I thought that might be the case. We were together four years, and we've now been separated for over three. Why she would wait that long is beyond me. I don't believe that's the reason."

"Maybe it took her a while to realize she's really in love with you."

Love. It caused people to do a lot of crazy things, but he suspected there was another reason. He needed to resolve this and get to Olivia. He'd told her he'd meet her in two hours, and he was already running late. As soon as he wrapped this up, he'd call and let her know to grab the extra key from his neighbor, Mrs. Preston, and let herself in.

Should have told her to do that in the first place.

He just hadn't known how this situation with his ex was going to play out, and there was so much riding on the line right now. His taskforce members were still in danger, his boss was not putting any pressure on the judge for an arrest warrant for Frankie, and Tracee had been calling him nonstop all afternoon.

Lightning flashed, and thunder boomed as if mirroring the raging storm in his work and personal lives.

Tracee had sounded sick when he'd spoken to her earlier that evening. Or maybe strung out. "I think my ex is tied up with drug dealers. I'm not sure whether it has anything to do with the Kings or the mafia, but my gut is telling me something is wrong with the whole setup."

Roman sat back, wiping his wet hands on his pant legs. "Off the record, I had Polly check Tracee's emails and recent phone calls. None were to any known criminals."

Victor shot him a look. "You illegally accessed my ex's emails and phone calls?"

"I prefer the term *preemptive* to illegal. As a Homeland employee, I have wide permissions to investigate anyone I believe is in contact with criminals involved in terrorist activities, but it's probably better you pretend I didn't tell you about the invasion of privacy."

In some ways, it was a relief Roman and his group hadn't found any direct contact with the mafia or cartel. "When we were together, she used a burner phone to contact her drug dealer."

"Well, there's still a chance she isn't being completely honest with you, and neither of us wants to walk in blind. I canvassed the neighborhood on the way here, but I'll do another drive-by before you go up. Are you wired?"

Victor handed him the receiver. He wore the same wire that Olivia had with Alfonso. "We should be good to go."

Roman nodded and slipped it inside a jacket pocket. "What's the code word?"

Victor chuckled at the old school tactic. "How about 'help?'"

Under the glow of the streetlight, the HS agent looked disappointed. "Kinda tame, but if that's what you want, okay."

Roman grabbed the door handle. "I'll park as close to the building as I can, but they won't let me in downstairs unless I flash my badge since I don't know anyone who lives there. If you suspect anything, don't be shy about using the signal so I have time to bust in and back you up, partner."

Victor truly hoped he didn't need it.

RAISING a girl in this day and age was harder than planning a coup of a mob syndicate.

Alfie listened to his daughter crying on the other end of the line and silently swore he was going to round up the bullies in her class and teach them all a lesson. "Mary Margaret, you know what I told you about those girls being jealous of you. That's why they say those things. You can't listen to them."

Several girls were harassing her again, and come morning, Alfie would make sure it stopped, one way or another. Either the school was going to take action or he was.

Tracee Tyson sat on her couch, staring at her big-screen TV but not seeming to see it. She'd already gone through what he'd given her the other night and was in the midst of withdrawal.

Junkies were always easiest to manipulate when they needed a hit, and Alfie had decided it was time to use the hand dealt him.

Goddamn me to hell if I raise a daughter as stupid as Tracee.

It took another minute to calm down Mary Margaret and get her off the phone, including several promises to bring home her favorite ice cream. He would do anything for his daughter, and those little brats at school we're going to learn a lesson about messing with her. Their parents weren't going to enjoy it either, because God help him, they were as bad as the kids anymore.

Tucking the phone away, he checked the handgun he'd brought for Tracee. Thanks to a friend, it was registered in her name and backdated to 2016. Everything was in place to take down the FBI director, and it would look like his ex-girlfriend had done the deed before turning the gun on herself.

He wasn't the first in his family to have helped a famous actress die tragically with drugs in her veins, and Alfie hoped this little gig would go off without a hitch. The killing part he didn't mind, but he was a little squeamish about the blood—unbeknownst to anyone in the syndicate—and he had to be sure he took Victor by surprise.

He added a silencer and double-checked his props. Everything was in place and the director was due any minute. As soon as he had Dupé out of the way, Olivia would be all his.

He'd heard through one of his sources that Felix "The Hook" was already in town, looking for his daughter. Alfie had not been expecting this latest complication, but he would deal with it as soon as he was done with Dupé. Olivia would have no one left. She'd be vulnerable and looking to avenge Victor's death, not believing for a moment it was a scorned ex-lover who'd killed him.

And that's where Alfie would come in, sprinkling a few pieces of evidence pointing at Gino and Frankie and sealing the last two nails in the coffin. Somewhere down the road, he would complete his vision of the future by enticing Olivia to run his new syndicate with him. She craved power and justice; he could give her both.

"I...," Tracee rose from the couch, staring at him with cloudy eyes. Her hands shook as she wrung them. "I can't do this."

Here we go again. Leave it to Victor to have an ex with morals. "We've been over this, Tracee, and the deal is the same. You don't have a choice." With some people, he found the best way to recruit them was appeal to their emotions. "This guy doesn't care about you or he would've never left you. You need him and all he's done is blow you off. If he really cared about you, he'd have come to see you several days ago, wouldn't he? Wouldn't he be concerned about your safety? No, he's too busy hanging out with his new girlfriend. It's time you stopped letting him run all over you and push you around. All you have to do is get him inside, lock the door, and let me do the rest."

Her strung out eyes dropped to the gun. "What's that for?"

"Protection." He put it out of sight behind his back. "You don't worry about that. All you have to do is get him in, so I can talk to him, that's all we're going to do," he lied.

Her bottom lip trembled. "And then I'll get unlimited coke?"

Weak women were a real turn off. Weak people in general. But that's what drugs did, making them vulnerable and easy to manipulate. "Lifetime supply guaranteed."

She nodded hesitantly and plopped back down on the sofa once more watching some stupid reality show. It was going to be a relief to pop her a good one and never have to deal with her again.

Never have to deal with Victor Dupé again.

A musical note went off, alerting her that the front desk was calling. Tracee looked at him and he gave her the nod to answer. She spoke to her invisible virtual assistant. "Yes, Ian?" She had named the damn thing after her favorite actor. "What is it?"

A deep male voice responded, sounding like a real person. "You have a visitor at the front desk. Victor Dupé."

"Send him up."

Alfie gave her one more pep talk. "You've got this. Get him inside, lock the door, and offer him a glass of wine or whatever. Keep him occupied until I come out, got it?"

She headed for the door, saying nothing to him, but muttering under her breath. "Everything will be okay. I'm a great actress. I can do this."

Before he slipped around the corner out of sight, he heard her whisper, "I'm sorry, Vic. Please forgive me."

14

It was a sad day when you couldn't invite your own father back to your place because you were scared of him.

Olivia sat with her dad, staring out at the beach from inside her car. Waves crashed against the rocky shoreline, rain pounding against the windows. The streetlights had already come on, throwing muted light across the dashboard.

Even with the hat and sunglasses, she couldn't take the chance anyone would recognize him, so she'd driven through the city and to the coastline, where they could sit and see the ocean. A part of her yearned to get as far away from him as possible, but she had to deal with the situation. The question was, how? She was a law enforcement agent and he was a felon breaking parole by leaving the state. She was also his daughter, and no matter what, she wasn't going to send him back to jail before hearing him out.

Ten years ago, she'd been ready to graduate high school when he'd been arrested. She'd actually had her gown on and was standing in line to walk onstage when the cops pulled up, sirens blaring, and cuffed him there in front of everyone.

He'd missed that and so many other important moments in

her life. Not that he'd been around for many previous to his incarceration, but she had held out hope all those years that somehow she could make him change his ways. That by being the perfect daughter, he'd realize how important it was to her that he become a law-abiding citizen and stop killing people.

See how that worked out?

"I thought your hearing wasn't until Wednesday. How did you get out early?"

"What, you think I escaped?" He started. "Always thinking the worst of me, huh? Now, why would I go to all that trouble if they were planning to parole me?"

"Just answer the question. How is it that you're sitting here when you should still be in a federal prison in Chicago?"

Her dad looked amused. "I have my ways."

He acted as if this was a joke, like they were sitting around on a Sunday afternoon teasing each other.

When she didn't respond other than to glare at him, he relented. "They bumped me up, that's all. I had my meeting yesterday, and I have friends who owe me plenty of favors. They helped me out."

Like helping him get to California? Someone probably flew him in on their private jet. "The day after you're released, you violate parole and cross state lines to come here? I should call your PO."

"Always one for rules and regulations." His accent was more Chicago than East Coast. "I came for you, Livvy."

That was not exactly reassuring. "I don't need you."

He reacted like she had slapped him across the face. "You need protection."

"I need a better explanation, or I *will* call and report you. I'm breaking the law by not turning you in. They could have my badge for this."

He leaned his elbows on his knees and stared at the wild

ocean for a moment before turning serious eyes on her. "Do you want to take down Gino DeStefano or not?"

Of course she did, but was selling her soul to her own father worth it? He definitely had something up his sleeve, and she doubted it had anything to do with protecting her. "What exactly do you think I need protection from?"

"Not what, *who*. You're dealing with dangerous people."

Tell me something I don't know. "You're an expert on them, aren't you, dad?"

He didn't like being mocked, especially by his own daughter. His upper lip screwed up and he reared back in the seat. "I've made mistakes. Never said I was a saint. But I take care of my own, and I know a few things about what you're doing. This man you're using to get information on Gino and Frankie is a dangerous fellow. He'll stop at nothing to become boss, and he's using you to help him."

"Using me?" He had her attention, but she was still reluctant to believe anything he said, and it wasn't as if she didn't know Alfie was untrustworthy. "How?"

"How much do you know about Alfonso Barone?"

"You think I don't know the man I'm working with to take down Gino and Frankie? That I'm gullible and letting him manipulate me?"

"You always did your homework, even when you were a kid. I suppose you know a lot, but like I said, I have friends. Friends in the know about him and what he's up to."

Why did every conversation feel like a sparring match? "What's he up to, Dad?"

"The Suarez Kings weren't after Henry Valiant, Olivia."

A sick feeling clawed its way into her stomach. It warred there with apprehension that he was the one manipulating her, like he'd done so many times before. "Enlighten me, then. Who were they there for?"

"You."

She didn't know whether to laugh or give into the chill creeping over her skin. "And you think Alfie sent them after me?"

Her father nodded.

"That's an interesting theory, especially since Alfie called six times to warn me there was going to be a hit at the courthouse."

"Is that so? Why six?"

"Because I didn't..." *answer.* Alfie refused to leave messages because he claimed they could be used against him. But how did she know for sure he had indeed planned to tell her about the hit? "I have intel that Frankie planned to kill Valiant and sent six of the Suarez Kings to take him out."

"Did that come from Barone?"

Dammit. How did he know? "I'm not stupid, Dad. I don't trust Alfie any more than I do you."

He blanched. "The Kings weren't meant to kill you, but they were supposed to hurt you. He wanted them to scare you a little, and kill Valiant, of course."

The temperature in the car had dropped several degrees, the windows beginning to fog. Olivia started the car and hit defrost, turning up the temperature. Her fingers were cold, and she held them to the vent. "Why in the hell would he want to scare me? I'm his ticket to witness protection when he testifies against his bosses."

Her father gave a shrug. "My guess? Barone wanted to play your shining knight riding in on his white horse afterward, except your FBI friend came to the rescue and superseded him."

"Shining knight?"

"If you see him as a good guy, you're less likely to stand in his way when he takes over."

"Takes over the Fifty-seven Gang? He's going to testify against Gino and Frankie, and then disappear with his daughter. He's not taking over anything, except maybe some beach in a warm climate."

Her dad rubbed a hand over his face and she could tell his patience was waning. "Do you know who killed Barone's wife?"

"She died in a car accident."

"It was made to look like that, but that was the handiwork of Frankie Molina. Lorenzo Barone crossed Frankie back in the day and Frankie took revenge. Not by wiping out Lorenzo or his son, but by taking out Lorenzo's daughter-in-law only a few short months after she gave birth, letting Lorenzo know he could wipe out the entire family. The whole thing was staged, Olivia, and Alfonso knows it. That's the real reason he joined Gino and Frankie—revenge. Got nothing to do with holding Lorenzo's spot until he's out of the tank. It's taken Alfonzo a few years to move up the line, and I think he initially wanted to usurp Frankie, become consigliere to Gino, but Frankie's tough. Tougher than Alfonzo expected. Frankie B got where he is as Gino's right-hand man because he's a cruel, demanding bastard. He doesn't have any weaknesses, not one, and Barone knows it. Alfonzo doesn't want to simply send them to prison and shut down the syndicate. He plans to take both men out, and every single person they care about."

Heavy accusations. "Why hasn't he done it already then?"

"The family is in Alfie's blood now. He's got a taste for the power, the killing. He wants to build his own empire, but to do so, he needs to have everything in place so those loyal to Gino and Frankie won't resist. He needs to have an overwhelming, brutal force to stop any resistance, as well as a stronger network for supply and demand."

Things began to slip into place. "The Suarez cartel."

"He managed to get Frankie and the Kings to the bargaining table, mediated the deal, but Silvestre Santos knows he and his squad are part of Barone's coup to take over. He's promised them a lucrative part of the new business dealings, that's the only reason Santos agreed to help. On top of that, Barone wants a working relationship with law enforcement, so they won't stand in his way. He plans to clean up the cartels he works with, keep their run-ins with the cops minimal, and build an entirely new syndicate. He doesn't just want LA. He wants the entire West Coast seaboard."

A working relationship with law enforcement. Did he mean her? "Alfie knows I would never look the other way for him, no matter what."

What about me? Her dad's glance conveyed the question, the unsaid words hanging in the air between them like a challenge.

She let the silence engulf her, staring out at the rough surf. The waves seemed to match her emotions.

"I'm not proud of all the things I've done in my life," her dad said, "but I've always been proud of you. I know you won't turn a blind eye to Barone's illegal dealings. Problem is, that puts you in more danger. When I got wind of this last month, I deliberately pulled some strings to make sure I could get out as soon as possible. I came here to help you."

"I appreciate the heads up, but I can handle this on my own."

He gave a dismissive grunt. "So stubborn. You need to understand, Olivia, this isn't only between you and Alfonso Barone. He's starting a war, and if you're on the wrong side of it, he'll take you out. He's already working on getting your friend out of the way."

"My friend? What are you talking about?"

Her phone rang before he answered, and she grabbed it, hoping it was Victor. The number was unknown, but it could be the hospital, so she answered. "Deputy Marshal Fiorelli."

"Olivia, it's Roman Walsh. Are you in LA?"

Why was Walsh calling her? A premonition of chills ran over her skin. "Yes." *Sort of.* "What's happened? What can I help you with?"

"I'm at the Wyndham Hotel. Do you know where it is?"

The fancy place that catered to the rich and famous? The

extravagant parties held there were famous in their own right, much less the clientele who rented entire floors.

"I'm familiar with the place."

"Can you meet me there?"

She checked the clock on the dash. The storm had cleared people from the rocky beach, and rush hour was long over. "It'll be ten minutes or so. What's going on?"

"I need you here as quickly as possible. I've got a situation, and need your backup."

"A situation? Can you give me more details?"

Before he could answer, she heard yelling and a gunshot. "Just get here as fast as you—"

The connection went dead.

VICTOR ENCOUNTERED no trouble getting past the front desk, one of the women on duty giving him a bright smile. "Ms. Tyson is expecting you."

She directed him to the slick, glass elevators and put her key in the penthouse slot, turning it and hitting the button. The doors closed, and as the elevator rose, he watched the large entryway disappear. Once on the top floor, the quiet was only disrupted by the sound of the TV coming from Tracee's apartment.

Leon, the bodyguard, came to full attention when the elevator doors opened. Leon had been with Tracee for many years, going back to when Victor had been living with her. They exchanged normal pleasantries before the door swung open and Tracee stood there, eyes red, cheeks swollen. She waved him inside.

The marble tile, and the chrome and glass finishes, were the same. There were several new framed movie posters on the walls, and Tracee's previous obsession with Asian design had been replaced with something more akin to the Greek Isles. Even the fake bamboo in the corner had been changed to a palm tree.

Her hair needed to be brushed and her fingers shook as she swept her bangs out of the way. "You're here," she said. "Finally."

That had been the end of normal. He didn't even make it to the couch when she burst out crying and ran out of the room.

"Tracee?"

A man dressed in black with a ski mask on pulled her back into the room, one arm around her neck and a gun pointed at her temple.

"What are you doing?" Tracee was near panic. "This wasn't part of the deal!"

Victor's hand went to his holster. Deal? Was this the stalker?

"Eh, eh, eh," Ski Mask said. "I don't want to kill her, but I will. Lose your weapon—easy does it—and kick it across the floor to me."

The dead look in his eyes told Victor he had no qualms about killing Tracee, and probably would regardless of Victor's response.

Hostage situations were the worst. "Take it easy." Removing his gun slowly from its holster, Victor held it up by the grip and let it dangle as he lowered it to the floor and kicked it to the masked man. "What do you want?"

Tracee whimpered, Ski Mask forcing her forward so he could kick the gun away. "I finally get to meet the man in person, the one I've heard so much about. Tracee tells me you're a real good guy."

"I'm so sorry, Vic." Tracee's eyes pleaded with him, but was she begging for forgiveness for something else? "I had to do it."

What exactly was *it*?

A dozen different scenarios played out in Victor's mind as he tried to figure out what he'd walked into. "How did you get in here?" he asked the man. "You must work for the hotel or security agency to have access to this penthouse. Did Leon let you in?"

Ski Mask seemed to grin behind the black knit material. "I've got friends everywhere, kind of like you. They owe me favors. I cashed one in, and now I'm about to cash in another."

"You're not stalking Tracee, are you?"

"Ding, ding, ding. Give the director a gold star."

"If you're after me, then let Tracee go. She has nothing to do with my work."

The man rubbed the side of his head against hers, and Tracee began crying softly. "Actually, this is about both of you. Tracee is collateral damage, true, but she brought it on herself, so you can die guilt-free about her impending death."

Tracee made a hiccup-y scream, too soft for Leon to hear. Victor could only hope Roman was already on his way up. "Will you at least tell me who you are before you kill me? I think I deserve to know. Are you the one who shot my San Diego task-force leader? The one who put the bomb under another agent's car?"

Big, fat tears ran down Tracee's cheeks. "He's—"

Shouting came from the hallway, followed by the sound of someone kicking at the door. Ski Mask jerked Tracee backward and pointed the gun at Victor, but the distraction was enough to give him the two seconds he needed to dodge out of the way as the gun went off.

Pfft, the silencer on the end of the gun deadened the sound. A porcelain vase exploded behind Victor's head as he dropped to the floor, using the sofa for cover.

Bam, bam, bam...the kicking continued, accompanied by more shouting. The sound of a gunshot going off on the other side made Tracee scream and then everything seemed to go in slow motion.

Another *pfft* from Ski Mask's gun, the sound of a body crashing into a lamp and sending it to the floor not far from Victor's hiding spot. As the glass shattered, he was horrified to see Tracee's face hit the wooden floor, eyes wide but empty.

"No!"

The door exploded open, Roman running in, gun raised and ready to fire. A woman followed. Victor had seen her before—she was FBI.

"Stop! Homeland Secur—Aw...fuck!" Roman's words were followed by a gunshot, wood splintering, and more swearing. He disappeared down the hallway, the plainclothes agent on his heels.

Staying low, Victor crawled toward Tracee. Her eyes stared at him for a second longer, then fluttered closed.

Glass crunched under his knees, the distant sensation of a jagged piece cutting through the fabric covering his left. He reached her and felt her neck for a pulse. *Do not die on me!*

Blood, thick and dark, pooled underneath her, and he visually searched for the wound, but she was laying on her belly and he couldn't see it.

"Victor?" Roman returned a moment later, dialing his phone. "Are you all right?" He spoke to the operator before Victor could answer. "Get me an ambulance. Now!" He gave the address of the hotel.

Victor felt the slight pump of Tracee's pulse under his fingers and rolled her over. The blood was extensive and soaked her shirt. He ripped it open and saw the wound at her lower left ribs. "She's still alive, but barely. Tell me you got the bastard."

Roman put his phone away. "Sorry, man, I missed the shot."

Victor grabbed a pillow from the couch and put pressure on Tracee's wound. "Is he still here?"

"Jumped off the bedroom balcony onto another one below—I would've fired at him, but there were people on it. He disappeared inside that suite. Nadia has gone after him. I already locked down the first floor. He won't get out of the building."

Victor kept pressure on the pillow and Tracee's ribs, using his chin to point at a turquoise colored throw on the end of the couch. "Grab that. She's lost a lot of blood. We need to keep her warm. She'll go into shock before the ambulance arrives."

Roman scooped it up and snapped it out to lay over her. "I tried to get here sooner, but I ran into some issues—two Suarez Kings took up residence outside the entrance right after you set foot inside. I had to take care of them before I could get up here."

"What the hell were they doing?"

"Backing up our mystery man, I assume. I missed some of your conversation with him due to the flying bullets. Did you get any information?"

"It wasn't so much what he said, but what she did." He looked down at Tracee. From the street, he heard the approach of sirens. "She said, 'this wasn't the deal.' What the hell does that mean?"

Roman sighed heavily. "That she was working with him to get you here?"

"Yeah, I sort of guessed that. This guy was no member of the Kings, though."

"Mafia?"

Victor's head felt like it was going to explode just like Tracee's door, now barely hanging on its hinges. "He was definitely after me, and planned to kill her too. She must've known who he was. He could be our shooter from the park."

"Why does he have a boner for you?"

Olivia suddenly rushed in, her eyes scanning the destruction when she pulled up short. "Oh my God, Victor." She rushed to his side, dropping next to him as she surveyed the blood and Tracee's limp body. "I got here as fast as I could. What the hell happened?"

How had she known he was here? "I came to investigate the stalker and ended up getting Tracee shot."

"Nope," Roman argued. "This whole situation is on me. My backup plan failed."

"The stalker shot her?" Olivia asked.

"Coming through," a man yelled and two EMTs entered with a gurney and med kit. Olivia drew Victor away as Roman filled them in on what happened and they went to work.

The two of them stepped into the large kitchen. Unless Tracee had changed her ways, Victor knew she'd never used it. Outside of making popcorn and pouring herself a glass of wine, she had everything delivered or went out. He rubbed his forehead. "This wasn't a stalker," he told Olivia. "I think this guy is tied in with the Fifty-seven Gang."

Her jaw dropped. "This was a mob hit?"

"Yeah, it was, but unless I can talk to Tracee or we catch this asshole, I have no proof."

She dug out her phone and held up a picture. "Maybe this will help."

He stared at it, not quite understanding. "You're going to have to walk me through this one. What am I looking at?"

"This woman met Alfie in an alley the other night. I think she was buying drugs from him, and he was blackmailing her."

The obvious answer teased at him, but he didn't want to believe it. "You don't know that's her."

Olivia pressed her lips into a thin line and swiped at a couple more photos. "It's not definitive evidence but look at these shoes."

It was the picture the paparazzi had taken of him and Tracee at the hospital. She wore a pair of purple high heels. They resembled the shoes the woman in the first photo wore. "Go back to the other picture."

And yup, there it was. The woman in the hood heading into the alley was wearing the same shoes. "Tracee was mixed up with Alfie?"

Roman's FBI agent walked in, looking equal parts pissed and frustrated. "We can't find him," she said. "It's like he disappeared into thin air."

"Nadia Fernandez meet Victor Dupé and Olivia Fiorelli." Roman motioned between them. "Guys, this is Nadia Fernandez, FBI. She's one of the best."

I've got friends everywhere, kind of like you. The words rang in Victor's mind. *They owe me favors.* "I believe our hitman is

Alfonso Barone, and he had an escape plan that involved someone inside this hotel helping him. We need to interview everyone, employees and guests, and figure out who did it, and if this guy was indeed him."

Nadia snapped to attention. "I'm on it."

"Get Polly and the others here to help," Roman called after her. "I'm going to talk to hotel security."

Olivia dialed her phone. "I'm calling Alfie. We have a system, a code. I don't expect him to call me back, but let's try it anyway."

The EMTs hoisted Tracee onto the gurney and began wheeling her toward the door.

"Is she going to make it?" Victor asked.

One of them gave him a doubtful look. "We need to get her to the hospital, stat."

That was all the answer he was going to get, and it was enough. She was in critical condition.

He turned to Olivia. "I want Alfonso Barone's head on a platter, and I want it now. You know where he lives, right?"

Her throat constricted as she swallowed hard. "Yes, but…"

"You can't possibly still want to protect him after this."

"Of course not." She looked hurt he would suggest such a thing. "I have no problem going after Alfie. It's not that."

He put his hands on his waist, frustration burning in his belly. "Then what the hell is it?"

"It's me," a voice said from the doorway.

Victor glanced over to see an older man rocking back on his heels while scanning the disaster in the room.

"Who is that?" Victor asked.

Olivia released an audible sigh. "That," she said, "is my father."

15

Once again, Olivia found herself at the hospital with Victor. Tracee was in surgery, the shooter still on the lam. Various law enforcement agencies were claiming territory rights to the crime scene while Tracee fought for her life and Victor burned with guilt.

He paced the waiting room, speaking to different people on his phone. His boss in DC, members of the SCVC Taskforce, Roman, and agents who worked with him in the FBI. He'd already spoken to Tracee's manager, agent, publicists, and a whole bunch of other people. Surely, he'd be hoarse soon.

They had all these pieces to the puzzle, but none connected the dots enough to get an arrest warrant for Alfie, who was in the wind anyway, it seemed. He'd not returned her call and it appeared no one was at his house. All they had was inconclusive evidence.

On top of that, she was harboring a fugitive and trying to deal with her feelings about her father who sat next to her in the waiting room reading a Popular Mechanics magazine as if this was a normal occurrence.

"Did you even stop and visit mom?" she murmured under her breath.

He cut his eyes to her for a second before going back to the magazine. "Don't be a smartass. Of course, and she said you haven't called in weeks. What's up with that?"

"All she wants to talk about is my love life, or lack thereof. Can you blame me for not wanting to call her on a daily basis?"

"She's your mother. She worries."

Story of my life. "Why are you both so worried about me? I'm a trained federal agent who is quite capable of taking care of herself."

He made that condescending noise in the back of his throat and turned the page. "You're thirty years old and haven't had a serious relationship since God knows when. You call that taking care of yourself?"

"I just turned twenty-nine!" She wanted to toss her hands in the air, but tamped down her emotions instead. "I don't need a man to take care of me, and my age has nothing to do with it. And, by the way, the reason I haven't had a serious relationship is because of you."

"Sure, blame it on your old man." He flipped another page. "Your dysfunctional relationships are not because of me, and you should stop blaming others and take responsibility like a true adult."

What was this now? "Are you seriously playing psychiatrist with me?"

"Look, kid, I know your career putting us bad guys away has consumed your life. I get it. But maybe you need to knock that chip off your shoulder and find something—*someone*—that makes you happy."

She was getting relationship advice from her father—the irony was almost too much. On the flip side, he and her mother were celebrating their thirty-fifth anniversary soon, and had obviously been through some pretty traumatic experiences together.

She looked at Victor, who now stood at the window, shoulders thrown back and feet planted, as though ready to take on the entire world.

Her dad followed her gaze. "You and the director, huh? He doesn't care you're a hitman's daughter? Did you tell him?"

Oh, Lord. "Of course, I did. He doesn't hold it against me."

"His dad was one of those union guys back in the 80s, wasn't he?"

She cut her gaze to him. "Wait. You knew him?"

Another page flip. "I had to come out and do some business back then for Ralphie. Set up a couple clubs for local contractors. If I remember right, Dupé was part manager of one of the big concrete companies. He and the owners resisted joining."

Everything in Olivia went very still. The "clubs" her father was referring to extorted payoffs from the heads of companies. If the owners refused to pay, the mafia threatened them with physical harm or labor disruption.

If Victor's father had been part of the resistance, then it may have been why he ended up dead. "Please tell me you did not..."

Victor appeared in front of them, sliding his phone into his pocket. His voice was low, controlled, almost automated. "Can I speak to you alone for a moment, Liv?"

She felt a sudden heat rush over her, an old but familiar guilt that her father might be responsible for yet another murder that had ruined someone's life, a whole family's life. She stood slowly, feeling slightly shaky as she did. "Of course."

She followed him to the far corner. The normal light in his eyes was gone. He spiked a hand through his hair and she saw a muscle jumping in his tight jaw. "The judge is going to let me round up the courthouse shooters, but I'm guessing they've already gone to ground, especially if Alfie is behind all of this. Roman is meeting me at the address Barone gave you. It may be bogus, and could actually be a trap, but I wanted to ask if you want in on it."

"Absolutely. Whatever you need. If you want to stay here until Tracee is out of surgery, I can help Roman."

"I don't think I can stand here and do nothing any longer. One of Roman's people looked into Tracee's recent communications and could find no link to Barone, but I'm guessing there's a burner phone in her apartment. I want to go back there and search the place thoroughly."

If Tracee was truly the woman Alfie had spoken to on the phone, then there had to be a burner.

"Why don't I go to the apartment while you and Roman check out the address and find the shooters?" And while she was at it, she was going to hunt down Alfie and threaten his balls to see if she could get the truth from him. Had he been the man who shot Tracee? If not, he still might know who had. It was a stretch, but Olivia still held hope he wasn't orchestrating all of this. "That way, we can cover two places at once."

He dipped his chin. "I do not want you meeting with Barone in person anymore."

Had he read her mind? "I need to find out exactly what his involvement in this is. If he's the man behind yesterday's firing squad, and Tracee's shooting, I'm arresting him as soon as I get my hands on him."

"I have no doubts he's behind everything that has happened this week, which means he's extremely dangerous, Liv. You are not to engage until I have the official arrest warrant, and then he is mine."

She understood his desire to catch the person responsible for everything, but if anyone was arresting Alfie, it was her. "If he's guilty," she said, "then he's been playing me all along. He used me to get to you, just like he used Tracee. Plus, he was totally leading me on about testifying against Gino and Frankie. That means I have no case against them. Months and months of investigating, and all I have is circumstantial evidence that will not put them in prison for life. If Alfie has been betraying me all along, I will be the one slapping the cuffs on him."

Victor started to argue, but before he could, her father cleared his throat loudly, catching their attention. A doctor stood in the doorway.

The look on the man's face told Olivia all she needed to know, and her heart sank.

"Mr. Dupé? I'm sorry," the doctor said. "We did everything we could, and she was a fighter, but in the end, she couldn't overcome the damage done by the bullet. It struck one of her ribs, sending shrapnel into her heart along with pieces of bone, puncturing it in multiple places."

Victor's face was impassive except for the nerve that jumped in his jaw. His voice was barely above a murmur as he said, "Thank you, doctor."

A sympathetic nod. "I've already alerted her agent who is informing her family."

The doctor left, and Victor turned away from all of them, his grief and anger taking him back to the window.

Olivia joined him, wanting to comfort him, but sensing his need to stay contained and controlled. One touch could set him off, make him lose it. "I'm so, so sorry."

Down below, local news vans gathered, along with paparazzi. Many of Tracee's fans who'd heard the news had started filing onto the sidewalks and into the parking lot closest to the front entrance. "This is my fault," he said. "I should have taken it more seriously the first time she called me."

"You looked into it, but there was no evidence she had a stalker. She wasn't being honest, Victor, and put herself in this position. If she's the woman Alfie met, she was buying drugs from him. Earlier that evening, I overheard him talking to her on the phone, and he told her to do whatever it took to get close to some guy. Originally, I thought it was Frankie, like I told you, but it was *you*. I've been sitting here thinking, going over all of these different scenarios, and whatever Alfie's end goal, he's attacking those you feel responsible for. If I were you, I'd get protection on your mother and sisters."

Victor's gaze snapped to hers. "You don't think...?"

But he didn't wait for her response, digging out his phone and dialing.

Olivia resumed her seat next to her dad as Victor ordered police protection for his family. "Tell me you did not kill Victor's father," she said softly under her breath.

"Nah, not me. I never met the guy, but I heard about him. He was murdered on Mother's Day. Can you believe it? That generation that came up during the 80s turned everything on its head. A bunch of reckless kids, trying to be big shots. Showing up their elders, reducing friendship and respect to nothing more than dust under my shoe."

She did not know if it still held true, but it used to be that the mafia did not work on Mother's Day. It was one more irony of syndicated crime. Her father was a killer, but he came from a world that still valued a warped sense of honor within the family, and would rather die than break the code of silence surrounding their criminal activities when questioned by law enforcement.

"Do you know who killed him?"

Her dad tossed the magazine on the side table. "Eh, I can probably find out. Why? Is it that important to you?"

Olivia glanced at Victor, still standing by the window, one hand massaging his temples as he called his family members to explain the situation. She had never seen him look scared, not even during the hostage situation at the hospital when she met him. But now? His body practically vibrated with the need to protect his family. "Yeah, it is."

"I'll put out some feelers, see what I can find out."

If she could give Victor closure on his father's murder when this was all done, it'd be worth whatever price she had to pay, even asking her dad for a favor. "Thank you."

Her dad raised a brow but shrugged as if it was no big deal. "Anything else I can help you with?"

"Yeah," she said. "I think there is."

The slightest tremor of his lips suggested a smile. "Name it, Livvy."

"Come on." She stood and pulled him up by his shirt sleeve. "You're going to help me double cross a certain mafia gangster."

YEP, it was hell raising a kid these days, especially a girl. Even worse, raising her without a mother.

Alfie sat on his deck with a tumbler of scotch, the night shadows deep as he looked over the lights of the city. His daughter had gone to bed crying, upset over some stupid text from one of her friends, after he'd slipped both of them inside the house.

After this was over, he was putting her in a private school, away from the LA trash. She was sensitive, and longed to be a writer someday, so maybe he could find one of those artsy schools where she would feel more at home.

A matter of days. His plan was falling into place, although the specifics had changed slightly. He'd spoon-fed the evidence to Olivia, framing Frankie without giving her more than necessary. Soon, he would hand her the final nail for Frankie and Gino's coffins. In the process, he'd kept Dupé busy and let him see just how close he could get to those the director cared about. Tonight's showdown had not gone as planned, but nothing was lost. Tracee wouldn't be telling on him, and while the director was still alive, he wouldn't be for long.

The scotch eased his frayed nerves, his mind building the next scenario, locking in his place as the most powerful man on the West Coast. LA was going to be the biggest challenge, but the Kings would make sure he had the manpower. In exchange, he'd help expand their drug business up to San Francisco and down to San Diego, ending their biggest competition.

His phone rang. He let it. After three rings, it went dead. A minute passed, and it rang three times again.

Olivia.

She was no doubt calling about Tracee Tyson. Again.

He finished his scotch before returning the call. When she answered, he played it cool. "Did you catch any of those bastards from the other night, marshal?"

Her voice was tense. "Working on it. Where are you?"

"Home, dealing with a hysterical thirteen-year-old girl who didn't get invited to a friend's birthday party, and then was texted by the so-called friend, telling her to quit being a whiny baby and go kill herself. Got to tell you, kids these days. Someone ought to smack her upside the head."

"The world is a brutal place. You want me to talk to her?"

He sat up, placing his glass on the table next to him. She wanted to come over? Not exactly what he'd expected, but he needed to pretend he'd been home all evening. Maybe if he got her here, he could work on his plan of seducing her. She was a tough one. And not only because they were on opposite sides of the law. Her father had sure done a number on her head.

Still, it meant a lot that she'd consider talking to his daughter. "You'd do that?"

"I picked up some of that wine you like and thought maybe we could discuss the Suarez Kings in more detail. Have you seen the news?"

"With all the drama in my house tonight? Why? What happened?"

"Tracee Tyson was murdered in her penthouse. You wouldn't know anything about that, would you?"

He frowned into the dark shadows below the deck. Why did she suspect he would know about it? Had he inadvertently left something behind that would tie him to it? "The actress? She's dead?"

A strained silence followed before Olivia said, "I think it was one of the Kings. A drug deal gone bad. A couple of his pals were watching the front entrance and tried to take out a Homeland agent."

Alfie relaxed, his frown turning into a smile. Another thing the Kings were good for was taking the fall for pretty much everything. "Jesus, they're getting ballsy. What was a Homeland agent doing there? They got terrorists in the hotel?"

"Can we talk about this in person?"

He puffed out his lips and made a soft sighing sound. "Sure, doll, but honestly, it's been a long day and it's not over yet in the teenage drama department. I may not be able to talk much about what happened unless we get Mary Margaret calmed down."

"I'll bring some Ben & Jerry's. That'll take the edge off."

She really would make a great mother for his girl. "A female touch is what she needs, I'll admit it. She may be daddy's girl, but she could use a woman to confide in."

Olivia sounded confident. "I'm on my way."

———

"This is the mic I'll be wearing," Olivia told her father, showing the small device to him and handing him the receiver. "You can listen to everything Alfie and I say, and it will be recorded."

He took it. "I know how it works. I wish you'd let me go in and talk to the SOB. He wouldn't be the first person I got information out of."

"Are you serious right now? Don't even go there, Dad."

She fastened the top button of her shirt, making sure the microphone was sufficiently hidden in her cleavage. "Whatever you do, do *not* get out of the car. No matter what happens, you are not to engage anyone or anything. I don't care if you hear Alfie threaten to kill me, you are not to storm the house or call attention to yourself in any way. I will handle whatever comes up, and I need you to have faith in my abilities."

"Jeez, I do, all right? We may look at the world differently, Olivia, but there's one thing I've always known about you, and that is you are my child. You exceed at everything you put your mind to. But I will not promise to sit by and let Barone kill you. If he so much as threatens the hair on your head, I will be inside that house before he can blink and they'll be the last words he ever utters."

She stared at him. He stared back. Two bullheaded people who loved each other but would never be on the same page. Olivia wasn't even sure they were on the same planet most of the time. "You know, I never doubted your love for me. I know you tried to protect me, and I appreciate that, but I don't need you standing up for me anymore."

"You're my daughter and I'm always going to stand up for you."

"If you interfere in this investigation, it could go badly for both of us."

He looked completely disgusted. "I won't unless I need to, but don't think for a moment that I'll sit here and do nothing if that bastard threatens you. He is *dan-ger-ous*."

In that moment, something in her shifted. She wasn't sure exactly what it was, but it felt...better. Lighter. There were so many holes in her heart when it came to her father, and yet, his standing up for her and insisting on protecting her—regardless of her demands for him to stand down—made her want to smile. He was overbearing and pushy, but sometimes a girl needed that in her life, especially from her father.

"I won't let it get that far, okay?" She needed to make sure he understood her goal with this. "I know Alfie well enough to understand his hot buttons and avoid his triggers. While I want nothing more than to simply slip the cuffs on him and bring him in, this is a fishing expedition only. I'm ninety-nine percent sure he's guilty, but I don't have enough to prove it. He'll point me towards Frankie again and I'm not going to call his bluff yet, but I want to see if I can gain more of his confidence, get him to open up about his plans for Victor."

"You really care about that guy, huh?"

"Victor is very important to me." The shadows down the street seemed deeper, the clouds overhead blacking out any light from the moon and stars. "I kind of got myself in a pickle with the Justice Department and I'm afraid it's going to end badly between the two of us."

Her dad shifted so he faced her. "What kind of pickle?"

She blew out some air between her lips, wondering why she felt compelled to tell her dad about her faux pas, but there it was. "Someone significant in the JD asked me to do an undercover investigation to see if I could find dirt on Victor. I should've said no and dealt with the fallout, but I didn't, and now? I'm in too deep. I've lied to him and there's no way to tell the truth without ruining things between us."

"The Justice Department believes he's dirty?"

"I've found absolutely nothing to confirm that. I know Victor. He's truly a good guy in his career and personal life."

"Wait a minute, does this have something to do with me? Did they blackmail you into doing this investigation on the director?"

She laughed without humor. "No, Dad. I got into this all by myself. I always had my sights set on a bigger role in taking down syndicated crime and I've been overly ambitious. I wanted to get into the Justice Department at some point and bring the hammer down on the mafia throughout the entire United States. The person I talked to offered me a covert operation looking into Victor's work and personal life in exchange for consideration for a job I would love to have. I agreed to do it, not understanding the full scope of what they were looking for or why. Now I've painted myself into a corner and found nothing to indicate Victor's success is anything but well earned."

"Then what would make them want to investigate him?"

"I'm not sure, but I have a weird feeling about it."

Her father tapped a thumb on his leg. "I bet it has to do with his old man and the mafia."

All that had happened three decades ago. "How would that have anything to do with Victor's position as head of the West Coast FBI?"

"I don't know exactly, but they may be digging into his past and wondering if he has his own agenda with the mafia families here."

"I don't think he knows or suspects his father stood up to the family back then. Surely, he'd have mentioned to me if he suspected his father was killed because of it."

"You're sure he's not tied into them, so tell this idiot at the Justice Department the man is clean and move on. What's the problem?"

"The problem is I've been lying to Victor all this time. He thinks our initial meeting was coincidence. It wasn't."

"Why does he need to know differently?"

This was the fundamental distinction between them. Her father was comfortable with deception. She was not. "Good relationships are built on trust. I have to come clean to him, or I can't live with myself."

Her father shook his head in disbelief. "You always did make everything harder than it has to be."

She was about to argue when a car turned the corner at the end of the block, headlights dipping over the sleepy street. It lit up the curb in front of Alfie's house and four men in black trench coats slowly emerged.

"I don't like the looks of this," Olivia said.

One of the men stood at the end of the sidewalk, surveying the house as the other three scanned the houses up and down the block, all of them with one hand inside their coats.

Her father sat forward, but kept his face hidden by the dashboard. "Looks like Alfie's getting a visit from Frankie B."

Her blood ran cold. "An unexpected visit that looks suspiciously like a hit."

The man at the end—underboss Frankie Molina—nodded at one of his bodyguards. They walked to the front door. "Crap. Mary Margaret is in there. I have to do something."

A strong hand landed on her arm. "You cannot go in there," her father said. "Whatever happens, happens. Alfie brought this on himself."

Frankie rang the doorbell.

"Mary Margaret is innocent. I can't let her witness her own father's murder or end up dead herself. Besides, I need Alfie. I need to know if he's behind everything that's happened to Victor, or if Frankie B is really the culprit. If Alfie dies tonight, the truth will die with him, and everything I've been working for will go down the drain."

The front door opened. From this distance, Olivia couldn't see Alfie's face, but she was sure it was surprised. A moment later, Frankie B and three of his goons disappeared inside. The fourth stayed on the front porch, a lookout.

Olivia reached for the door handle and jerked her arm out of her dad's grip. "Call Victor and tell him what's going down. Remember, you're not to leave this car or engage in any manner."

"You can't go barging in there!"

"I'm not going in the front door." She pulled out her gun and took the safety off. "I'm sneaking in through the back and getting the girl out first. I'll be sending her to you, so you better be in this car and ready to protect her, you got it?"

"Olivia—"

She hopped out and closed the door on her father's arguments. Ducking behind the car, she stealthily slipped into the nearby bushes, praying she would be in time to save the girl and maybe Alfie too.

VICTOR'S PHONE rang with an unknown caller. As he and Roman sped through the night on their way to the address Barone had given Olivia, he almost ignored it. It was doubtful any of the Kings where there, especially those involved in the shooting of Olivia's partner and the other two men, but it was a chance they had to take. There was still a possibility Barone had supplied accurate intel and the Kings had no idea they were coming. If they could catch even one of them, he and Roman could break the man—or woman—and get the evidence they needed on the additional shooters and everyone else involved.

The phone rang again, and Victor's gut told him to answer. He hit his Bluetooth. "Dupé."

"Yeah, listen up. This is Olivia's father and she told me to call and let you know something is going down at Alfonso Barone's house. You know the address, right? Frankie Molina just showed up and it looks like Barone could be in a lot of trouble."

Victor exchanged a glance with Roman. "Where is Olivia?"

"My daughter is a gutsy gal, and I want you to promise me that regardless of what she admits to about that stupid Justice Department investigation, you will remember she has sacrificed a lot for relationships in her life."

Confusion clouded his brain. "Mr. Fiorelli, I have no idea what you're talking about, but I agree, Olivia is an amazing woman."

"I'm about to help her out, even though she doesn't want it, and I need you to give her a message if anything happens to me."

Victor gripped the steering wheel tighter, the siren on the roof of his car suddenly too loud in his ears. "Where are you at?

Whatever you're thinking of doing, do not engage Barone or Molina. Do you understand me, Mr. Fiorelli?"

"She says you're a good guy, and she deserves someone who will love her no matter what and support her goals, but if I don't intercede, she's going to end up with a bullet in her forehead. You tell her that, no matter what, I have always loved her, and I always will. I know I wasn't who she wanted me to be, but I hope I can prove to her how much being her father means, and what I'm willing to do to make up for all the crap I put her through. Now do me a favor and get to Barone's house ASAP. Olivia went inside to save the guy's daughter. I'll hold off Frankie B as long as possible."

The line went dead. Instinctively, Victor jammed his foot into the accelerator, taking the speedometer up over 100 mph. "Goddammit. What the hell is she thinking?" He threw a glance at Roman. "Call her."

Roman was already tapping at his screen. "Already did. She's not answering."

"Put out an SOS to everyone in range. Olivia wouldn't have gone in after the girl if she didn't think this was a hit. Frankie must have figured out Barone's about to betray him." He smacked the steering wheel with his hand. They were on the freeway, headed in the right direction, but still a good twenty minutes from Oceanside. "Call the locals and get an Adam unit over there. Tell them not to go inside, but..."

Roman interrupted him. "We do that, and we end up with a hostage situation. Beat cops can't handle this. It's better if we sneak up on them, catch Frankie by surprise, don't you think?"

He was right. Victor couldn't think straight, fear cramping his gut. He hit the callback button on the navigation screen, but it went straight to voicemail, an automated female voice telling him the owner of the phone was unavailable. He switched to calling Olivia, as Roman rounded up as many team members as he could, but Victor only got the same response—no one available.

He kept calling anyway, speaking over the ringing phone in the background. "What did Felix mean about a Justice Department investigation?"

Roman shrugged, dialing the next person on his list. "I have no idea. Did he mean in regard to the mafia?"

"That's the only thing it could be. Because of her background and track record, Liv's been given loose parameters to investigate the Fifty-seven Gang, and from what she shared, her boss at the marshal service isn't all that happy about it, but she's put away enough mid-level mafia guys, that when she wanted to go for the big guns, they agreed."

"Her father said *regardless of what she admits to*. Maybe she's broken some laws in order to take down Gino and the rest."

He wove in and out of traffic. *Come on, Olivia, pick up.* "Probably, but I doubt it's anything significant. Most agents break a few when undercover, and what she's done by cultivating a relationship with Barone isn't much different."

One of Roman's agents picked up and he began reeling off instructions. Victor hit redial again and prayed they wouldn't be too late.

16

An empty glass sat on the table next to an Adirondack chair on Alfie's back porch. The faint scent of cigar smoke hung in the humid air. Olivia peeked through the screen, noting that the hitman had left the glass slider open, as if expecting to come back outside.

He probably had, considering he was expecting her and not Frankie Molina.

The lights inside came from the kitchen and hallway. Men's voices drifted to her from the front of the house where the living and dining areas were located.

It was after ten PM, and she hoped Mary Margaret was in bed. She eased the screen door back, flinching slightly when it squeaked. Freezing in place, she waited to see if there was any reaction from inside the house, her pulse banging away in her ears.

When nothing happened, and the voices continued from the front room, she finished entering and softly closed the screen behind her.

Fingering her weapon, she kept it up and ready to fire as she tiptoed down the hall to the base of the staircase, praying no one came out of the living room, because they were sure to see her if they did. The steps were the next hurdle. She had never been upstairs in Alfie's house, but she had heard him go up and down them enough to know the old wood popped and creaked whenever weight was put on it. Drawing in a silent breath, she sidled up to the wall the stairs attached to, putting her back to it and keeping her gun facing the front room as she carefully picked up one foot and placed it on the next step. As she continued the slow climb, she listened to the conversation filtering out from the living room.

"You come to my house and throw accusations around?" Alfie.

Frankie's voice was more nasally, as if he were impersonating the Godfather. "Come on, now, Alfonso. Gino and I are doing a little housecleaning and it has come to our attention that you are being quite industrious behind our backs."

Yep. This was going to go bad, and it was gonna go bad fast.

Olivia climbed faster.

The two men continued to trade comments and veiled threats, but Frankie must not have any hard evidence about Alfie's misdeeds or he would've simply shot him without waiting for an explanation. That gave her hope. She really wished Alfie wasn't behind everything, but regardless, she didn't want Frankie killing him. With Alfie alive, she could still take down the Gang and make sure Mary Margaret continued to have a father around, even if he ended up in prison. If Frankie killed Alfie tonight, she really had no way to prove he was or wasn't responsible for what had happened to Danny or Victor's taskforce members.

She gently stepped onto the landing just as she heard Alfie say, "Look, my kid's upstairs trying to sleep. I don't want to get into anything tonight. Let's start over. How about a drink?"

That was the thing about Alfonso, he knew how to schmooze with everyone. He was probably thinking the same thing Olivia was—he'd already be dead if Frankie knew about his side dealings.

"I've got the marshal in my pocket like you wanted," Alfie said, and Olivia froze in place once more, cocking her head to listen.

"I'd like you to take her and the FBI director out at the same time." Frankie. "Will that be a problem?"

Take us out? Her hand tightened on the butt of the gun.

"None at all." She heard the clinking of ice in a glass as Alfie poured Frankie a drink. "They're together more than they're apart these days. But if I were you, I'd give her a little more time to come to an understanding with me. She and I have a connection, you know. We can use her to help us handle whoever takes over Dupé's position. It might not even be a bad idea to let him live. Think about it—we control her, and she manipulates him. We get the FBI and all those joint taskforces off our backs."

Her blood started to boil as fast as her pulse beat. If she didn't have to save Mary Margaret...

No. She couldn't take the chance that these two might still end up at each other's throats. If Frankie had simply wanted to discuss business, he would've done it at his office. Not in Alfie's home.

This still had the makings of a hit, and she needed to save the girl.

The upstairs hallway had four doors, two of which were closed. Olivia crept past the bathroom where a nightlight spilled a soft glow onto the carpet runner and eased toward the closed bedroom door. A large poster of Beyoncé adorned most of the wood and homemade door hanger, decorated with pink and purple marker and glitter, declared the owner behind the door was Mary Margaret.

Waking up the girl without scaring her was going to be the next obstacle. With one last check over her shoulder, Olivia tucked her gun away in her holster. She didn't dare knock, and only hoped Mary Margaret didn't scream when she entered.

She expected the girl to be in bed, but as she silently twisted the metal knob and stepped in, she saw a light coming from a desk. She peeked her head around and found Mary Margaret behind the desk staring at her, one knee pulled up to her chest, her foot on the chair. Her cell phone sat on the desktop and she looked like she'd been crying.

Olivia smiled and put a finger to her lips, the universal sign for quiet, as she entered and closed the door behind her.

"Hi," she whispered. "Do you remember me?"

The girl gazed at her solemnly. "You're my dad's friend. He said you were coming over to talk to me."

"That's right. Your dad is downstairs, and he has some unexpected company, so he asked me to take you back to my place for tonight." While Olivia knew Alfie protected Mary Margaret from the truth about who he was and what he did, this was no time to beat around the bush. "We need to move fast and quietly, because the men downstairs with him could be dangerous. Do you understand?"

Her foot came off the chair, her hand closing over the phone. "Is my dad going to be okay?"

The false promise of yes tangled up Olivia's tongue. She bit her bottom lip, glancing around for a pair of jeans or sweatshirt she could grab for the girl. "We're going to slip downstairs as quietly as possible and out the back door, kind of like a game. Three houses down in front of the brown ranch there is a red car with my father in it. He's going to take you to my place and I'll come back here and help your dad, okay? In case those men decide to get cranky."

The girl stood and pointed toward the closet door. "I could just go into the safe room and you could help my dad."

Safe room? Olivia moved to the closet. "What kind of safe room?"

Mary Margaret joined her and opened the closet door. She shoved aside clothes and some boxes, going deeper into the darkness. She tapped on a panel and the thing sprang open, revealing a metal door behind it.

"My dad told me to hide in here if anyone ever came to the house threatening us, and not to come out until he said it was okay."

The small space held shelves of bottled water, various snacks, and there was a small security TV allowing the person inside to see who was on the other side of the door. There was a digital lock and the room had electricity.

It wasn't the best panic room she'd ever seen, but it was efficient and the walls were probably bulletproof. Alfie had set up everything for a temporary hiding place to keep his daughter safe.

For a second, Olivia's mind flashed back to a similar room her father had built in their house. Luckily, her and her mom never had to use it. "Your dad is a smart guy. If there's anything you want for inside, grab it now and get in there."

"My phone doesn't work in there."

Her eyes were bloodshot, and she had dark circles under them. Olivia reached up and pulled a blanket down from the highest shelf and tossed it into the room. "I hear you're having troubles with some of the kids in your class."

The girl sniffed and went to grab a couple books off her nightstand. "Being thirteen is tough. I don't really like it."

Olivia patted the girl's shoulder as she returned to the panic room. "After I help your dad out, maybe we can set a lunch date. Do some shopping, share some girl talk. Would you be up for that?"

Mary Margaret nodded, her countenance lightening slightly. "My dad really likes you. He told me you're an important person with the police department."

Close enough. "I'm going to shut you in now. Lock the door, and like your dad said, don't open it again until you see him, or me, on the other side. If we don't come to get you, there will be a man named Felix or Victor who will. You can trust them. Got it?"

The girl drew a deep breath and spread the blanket on the floor before hugging her knees and opening one of the books. "Got it."

Olivia was sneaking back out of the room when she heard it —a sound that sent her heart triple-timing it and her feet running for the stairs.

Boom.

Gunshot. Outside.

Before the echo died, the men flooded the entryway. The doorbell rang.

Oh shit. Who was joining the party now?

She grabbed her gun and pulled up on the landing, every bone in her body frozen in place. Alfie was at the door, swinging it open. She could only see the bottom half of his legs. Behind him stood Frankie's two bodyguards, the underboss out of her view.

"Hello, boys." Her dad's voice was jovial but had an under-lying menace to it.

No! What is he doing?

Alfie stepped back; through the open doorway, Olivia saw a body lying on the front steps—the other bodyguard.

"Who the fuck are you?" Alfie asked.

Her father pushed inside and smacked Alfie upside the head. "Mind your manners. Who the fuck do you think I am? You're screwing with my daughter and I'm here to put a stop to it."

Jesus, Joseph, and Mary. What the hell? Her dad was going to get himself killed and her along with him. Olivia didn't know whether to rush downstairs and make her presence known in order to stop this crazy train or hang back like a spectator and watch it all play out. It was like seeing a car accident about to happen and not being able to stop it.

Hopefully, her dad had notified Victor, and someone was on

the way to back her up. She had two choices—draw her weapon and try to diffuse the situation with force or play a little game on the gangsters and see if she could get everyone out without violence.

Odds were slim the latter would work, but with her dad in the mix, she couldn't exactly go down with guns blazing and expect a positive outcome.

"Alfie?" She called seductively, walking down the stairs as if she owned the place. "What's all the racket? I thought you were coming to bed...?"

She paused as all eyes turned toward her, equal expressions of surprise on everyone's face. Frankie's two bodyguards already had their weapons out and turned them from Felix to her.

Frankie, hanging back in the living room doorway like the coward he was, sent Alfie a grin. "Didn't realize you had company, Alfonso. No wonder Felix The Hook is at your front door ready to kill you."

Her dad blustered, placing his hands on his hips and sticking out his chest. "You ain't getting in the way of this, are you, Molina?"

Alfie raised a brow at Olivia before turning to face her father. "You're Olivia's dad?"

Her father took a step closer to Alfie, pointing a finger in his face. "You and me got things to set straight. I know my Livvy has feelings for you, and I'm here to make sure you ain't pulling a fast one on her."

Dad was on board with her game. Thank God.

Alfie raised his hands in an act of surrender. "I've got nothing but respect for the lady. She's good people."

Felix got right in Alfie's face. "You sleeping with her?" He shot Olivia a fierce look, acting the part of an enraged father. "You're sleeping with this mutt? I thought you had better judgment."

For a moment, her mind flashbacked to Johnny Valducie and the bawling out the poor kid had taken from her dad, only now she was nearly thirty years old and the man in question was a dangerous mobster.

She came down another few steps. "Daddy! I'm a grown woman. If I want to sleep with Alfie, that's my business and nobody else's."

Alfie's eyes went big as saucers. Frankie seemed to itch to get away from the family drama. He set his glass of liquor on the foyer table. "Alfonzo, it appears I came at a bad time. Let's continue this discussion in my office first thing tomorrow morning." He headed for the door, nodding at his goons to follow. Before he crossed the threshold, he turned back and snickered at Alfie. "That is if you're still alive."

Her dad's stare never left Alfie's face, as if Frankie were merely a pesky fly. "Good to see you again, Frankie."

"Once you get this family dispute worked out," Frankie said as his bodyguards picked up their fallen comrade, "I hope you'll be headed back to Chicago."

"I've got no designs on your territory," her dad replied.

Frankie gave Olivia a slight tip of his head before he went down the front steps and disappeared into the night.

Olivia jogged down the last couple of stairs on shaky legs and closed the door. "Holy shit, that was close. Dad, what the hell were you thinking?"

Alfie shifted away from her dad, giving her another raised eyebrow. "What the hell was *he* thinking? What the hell were *you*? How did you get into the house and upstairs?"

She ignored the question. "Mary Margaret is in her safe room. I thought Frankie was here to kill you. You're lucky dad and I intervened."

Her dad went to the transom window and peaked out, checking to make sure the coast was clear. "We're all lucky we're not dead."

"I need a drink," Alfie said. She watched him walk to the kitchen and disappear. His voice filtered back to them. "You want something, Felix? I've got a good scotch if you're interested."

Her dad looked at Olivia and rolled his eyes. "This is your CI?"

She had a few questions for Alfie and ignored her dad as she marched to the kitchen. "You're going to need more than that, Alfonso Barone. You have me in your back pocket, huh?"

As she swung around the corner, *bam*. The ends of a Taser jabbed her in the stomach. Her body exploded in pain and she fell, jerking and spasming on the way to the floor, her forehead smacking into the corner of the countertop. Her vision blurred, and she felt Alfie grab her around the ankles and drag her to the stainless-steel refrigerator. The bright overhead light made everything go fuzzy. "Sorry, doll," he murmured.

She groaned around her locked teeth and tried to kick him, but saw his expensive loafers walk past her face.

"Got your drink here, Felix," he called to her dad.

Blinking away at the spots dancing in front of her eyes, she reached out to grab his leg, but her body would not respond to her commands. The pain in her head was immense and darkness began to close in, her ears buzzing with a high-pitched vacuum sound.

"No... dad..." she squeaked out, the words muffled as though she were drunk. Fighting her frozen muscles, she turned on her side, clawing at the floor. She had to warn her father, to stop him from coming into the kitchen...

Too late, she heard his voice above her. "Olivia?"

In the next half a second, her vision failed, the world went black, and the last thing she heard was a gunshot.

ALFIE'S HOUSE was dark when Victor and Roman arrived, a light drizzle falling once more. The house was in one of the nicer areas of Oceanside, the lawns well manicured and trees lining the streets.

Thomas, Ronni, and Nelson were already there, along with two of Roman's people, Polly and NSA agent, Winslow de Soto. The five of them were huddled at the end of the block, waiting when Victor pulled up.

He barely put the car in park before climbing out. He itched to be inside the house, to put his eyes on Olivia and make sure she was okay. "Status?" he asked.

Thomas looked down the block to Alfie's. "Place has been dark since we got here. No movement, no noise, no one has come or gone. Are you sure she was here?"

Victor scanned the street, his eyes stopping on the red Nissan at the other end of the block under a tree. He squinted through the rain and shadows, not sure if he was relieved or worried that the car looked like Liv's. "That's her vehicle. Her dad said she was here. Let's do a sneak and peek of the house, just in case they are, indeed, inside."

"You take the back," Roman said, and then motioned at his two agents. "We'll watch the front."

Some of the houses had fences surrounding their backyards and security lights, so Victor led his group through the soggy grass and around them, careful not to raise alarms as they approached the inclined hill behind Barone's lot.

No visible fence here. Victor scanned the area for infrared trip wires or motion detectors but found none. Didn't mean there wasn't a camera watching their every move.

The yard had a swing and playhouse. When no alarms sounded as he crossed into the lot, Victor motioned for Nelson, Thomas, and Ronni to check the first floor windows as he headed for the back door.

The wooden deck was slick in the rain, his shoes slipping slightly as he took the three steps up to the main level. A patio set, a fire pit, and a fancy grill covered the open space, a set of patio doors providing entrance to the house. One was slid back in its tracks, only the screen closed. Victor quietly moved to it and peered in.

The interior was dark and soundless. He could make out the shapes of furniture and pictures here and there as he looked down the hallway that lead toward the front.

Rain began to fall in a steady stream, hitting the deck and roof, but Victor still couldn't hear any sounds coming from inside. He checked the screen latch and found it unlocked.

Feeling more confident that the house was empty, he let himself in, kicking off his wet shoes. They would squeak on the wooden floors and alert anyone who might yet be hiding. Nelson joined him, shaking his head to let Victor know they hadn't seen anything through the windows. Thomas and Ronni were still outside, keeping an eye on the exit.

With controlled stealth, he eased down the hallway, past the kitchen and dining room, checking each room for occupants.

Within minutes, he and Nelson had cleared the whole house. They found no evidence suggesting Olivia had been there, outside of several glasses half filled with liquor. Victor tapped his comm unit. "Place is clear."

"Check the front steps," Roman's voice replied.

The door was unlocked. Victor opened it to find Roman shining a flashlight on a dark substance on the steps. He leaned down and wiped a gloved finger through the stuff before glancing at Victor. "Blood. It's fresh."

Victor's stomach dropped.

Polly's voice came through the comms. "Hey, boss, we found something."

Roman swung around to look down the street and Victor followed his gaze. Polly and Winston were at Olivia's vehicle, waving at them. Polly pointed at the trunk of the car, and Victor's stomach fell to his knees.

He took off running. "Oh, no. No, no, no."

As he got closer to the car, Roman on his heels, he heard banging coming from it. Muffled cries.

"Oh, Jesus. Tell me he didn't stuff her in the trunk!"

Winston held up a keychain with multiple keys on it and hustled to the lock. "I already tried to pop the trunk, but it's locked. Found these hidden under the front seat."

Victor grabbed the keychain and inserted the car key. "Hang on, Olivia."

At least she wasn't dead. The key gave him issues and he swore under his breath, fighting with it. When he finally heard the pop of the lock giving way, he was swamped with relief.

Until he saw who was inside.

"Felix?" The man's feet and hands were bound with duct tape. Another strip was across his mouth. "Where's Olivia?"

Dumb to ask a man with duct tape across his mouth a question. Victor and Roman hauled the older man out and Victor ripped the tape off Felix's mouth.

The man gasped for air, allowing Polly to cut the tape from around his wrists. "Olivia...? Is she okay?"

Another gut drop. "She's not here."

Felix was sweating and wiped at his forehead with his arm. "Damn bastard. He took her."

"Took her where?" Roman asked.

Polly freed Felix's ankles and he almost stumbled. Victor caught him and steadied him until the man regained his balance against the car. Polly reached out and touched Felix's arm. "Take it easy. Are you hurt? Do you need some water?"

"Barone took a shot at me but missed on purpose. He threatened to kill Olivia if I didn't cooperate. That's how I ended up gagged and bound in the trunk. I don't know why he didn't kill me. He tasered her, knocked her out, I think. Goddamn son-of-a-bitch. He's not too bright, let me tell ya, because when I catch him, I will kill him."

"Where would he have taken her?" Victor demanded. "Any ideas?"

"I have no clue where the bastard went." Felix gave them a brief description of what happened earlier with Frankie and Olivia. "Barone's daughter was in the safe room upstairs. Did he take her too?"

Leaving Felix with the other two, Victor and Roman ran back to the house, joining Thomas and Ronni inside to look. Sure enough, they found it in the girl's upstairs bedroom closet, but the hidden room was as empty as the rest of the house.

Alfonso had taken what was important to him and bailed.

Why had he taken Olivia?

While Thomas called it in to have the house and car processed as a crime scene, Victor sagged against the kitchen counter. With the overhead light on, his eyes caught on a streak of blood and a strand of dark hair on the tile floor.

He knew that hair. His heart sank, thinking of Olivia hurt and bleeding. Felix was going to need to stand in line when it came to killing Alfonso Barone.

Where would he take her?

There were too many places. Hell, Alfie might be headed for the border, but if he were going to ground, why kidnap Olivia? Was he planning to use her as collateral to ensure his and his daughter's safety?

He's in love with her. The thought made Victor all the more enraged. Alfonso Barone was clever and cunning, but he was highly loyal and protective of those he loved. Did he envision a world where he, Olivia, and the girl could live as a family?

A damn big stretch, unless Barone was not in touch with reality, yet Victor knew that was far from the truth. The mobster had a plan, and Victor had to figure it out.

Before it was too late.

Felix stumbled into the kitchen and handed Victor a recorder. It looked similar to the same one he and Olivia had used the day she and Alfie met at the restaurant. "Not sure there's anything on here that will help you find her, but there is an interesting conversation between Molina and Barone."

Victor took the recorder, turning it over in his hands. "Olivia was wired?"

"Yeah, but I'm sure she's out of range now."

"That's it. I know where he took her." Victor barreled past Felix, heading for the door and calling to his agents. "The Blue Seagull," he yelled. "Thomas, Ronni, you're with me. Let's go."

Just then, his phone burst out with Olivia's ringtone. He pulled up short at the door and drew out the phone.

Roman came hustling up. "Is it her?"

Victor nearly choked when he saw the text—a photo. "Yes." *And no.*

The picture was of her in front of the wall in his living room with the samples of blue paint framing her face. A gash tracked across her forehead, embellished with a bruise and a lump as big as a golf ball. Her eyes were large in her face, sad and angry at the same time.

Below the photo, a message:

Come alone or you know what will happen.

"You hurt her, and I will feed you your balls," Victor murmured under his breath.

Roman shook his head. "You know where she is?"

Victor put his phone away. "Yeah, I do."

His feet couldn't move fast enough to his car. Roman stayed on his heels. Felix joined him. "You're not going alone," Roman said.

"It's a trap," Felix added.

Of course it was, but what choice did he have?

"That's why he took her." Roman said, crossing the street with him. "He's been after you the whole time."

"Well, he's got me," Victor said, waving off both him and Felix, "and I'm bringing hell with me."

17

Alfonso had gotten her good. Olivia wrestled with total disgust at herself for allowing him to get the jump on her. She'd known not to trust him, and yet, all this talk about family and protecting her had been a smokescreen.

Her head pounded, her guts twisted. If she wasn't tied to a chair in Victor's dining room, she would fall over. Her eyes didn't want to focus, probably due to smacking the countertop earlier.

If I could just stop the pounding and think.

Mary Margaret was upstairs in bed with Taz. The poor girl seemed slightly shell-shocked by her father's behavior. Apparently, he didn't Taser too many people, tie them up, and kidnap them in front of her eyes.

Dad. Was he okay? Had Alfie shot him? She could still hear the sound of the gun right before she lost consciousness.

Being inside Victor's house gave her some hope. He was no doubt on his way already, but he was walking into a trap. He would know it was, but that didn't make it any less safe. Somehow, someway, she had to shake off the side effects and concussion and find a way to get free before Victor arrived.

The man sitting across from her seemed to read her mind—

not that she hadn't made it obvious she was going to kill him as soon as she got loose.

Alfie pointed at the pictures he'd laid out on the table in front of her. The box of reports and evidence about Victor's father sat to one side, pushed there by her captor. "Are you seriously telling me you don't believe me?"

Evidence was a funny thing. Like the photos she had of Tracee meeting Alfie in the alley that night, the truth was there, but surrounded by an absence of details. Very important details.

One photo showed a man that looked like Victor meeting with Gino DeStefano at an undisclosed location, the picture taken from a distance, as if the subjects didn't know the photographer was there.

A second was of Victor with Frankie Molina outside a warehouse by the docks.

The third photo was the one that really blew her away: Victor, Tracee, and an unknown suspect in an alley, with Frankie in the background, appearing to be overseeing the meeting.

"Once you are part of the family, doll, you can never leave. He's been playing you this whole time."

It couldn't be true. Alfie was taking circumstantial evidence and spinning it to create a story. "Those pictures mean nothing out of context."

"I gave you the context." He banged a finger on the center photograph. I took every one of these, because I was there. I was a witness. He's in deep with Gino and Frankie, and you deserve to know the truth. Out of all of these guys, I'm the only one you can trust."

Right! Like that was ever gonna happen. "You lied to me," Olivia said, ignoring the churning in her stomach and heart. "You betrayed me. You tasered me, tied me up, and kidnapped me. You shot my dad! Gee, whatever would make you think I don't trust you, Alfie?" she seethed.

"Calm down. Your dad's fine. Just listen to me. Gino

supported Victor's mom after his father was killed. How do you think ol' Vic put his family back together after his dad died? How did he take care of his disabled mother? He was nothing but a kid, Olivia. You really think he could do all that on his own?"

This was completely crazy. "Even if he took help as a child from Gino, there's no way he's part of the family."

Alfie sat back, totally frustrated. "Victor owed Gino. He's always been under Gino's protection, and in return he's been an insider for him. As he sailed up the ranks of the FBI, he helped Gino rise to power in Southern California, avoiding arrest and prosecution for his crimes. Dupé is the reason the Fifty-seven Gang has been untouchable. Until you came along, anyway."

The pounding in her head went sonic. "Oh, you're good. Totally psychotic, but good. Trying to get that little voice inside my head to doubt Victor instead of you."

But it was working in the tiniest of ways, like a grain of sand between her toes, scratching her skin. The nagging inside her head insisted it made sense. Victor had dodged her questions when it came to how he'd put his family back together as a kid, taking care of his sisters and mother. Doubts crept in like more grains, and she tried to mentally shake them off. *Has to be the conk I took on the head. Victor would never work with the mafia and betray the FBI.*

Yet, wasn't that what the Justice Department suspected? That had to be why they'd wanted her to buddy up to him. Olivia Fiorelli, the rock star of organized crime. If anyone could sniff out a traitor working with the mob, it was her.

Was it possible Alfie wasn't the only one who'd duped her?

No. There was no way Victor was in cahoots with a criminal syndicate of any kind.

"You can't brainwash me," she insisted. "It's sad, you know. For a while, I believed that you honestly wanted to change and get out of the Fifty-seven Gang. I thought you were different, Alfie, but you're not. You're cut from the same cloth as Gino and

Frankie. No different than my dad. You used and manipulated me, claiming to care about me, about my family. In reality, the only thing you care about is yourself."

He narrowed his eyes. "I'm nothing like Gino or Frankie, but maybe I am a little bit like your dad. I do care for you, Olivia, more than you know, and I believe you care for me as well. We have a connection that goes beyond the family. I know we do."

A part of her wanted to sneer in his face, to yell at him for being an idiot. She was an idiot too, believing even for an instant that he could be human, someone she could rely on to help her wipe out the California mob.

But she wasn't about to lose her head. If there was any chance of manipulating him the way he had her, this was it. This wasn't about justice. This was revenge. *Sorry for the lecture, Danny.* "If you really cared about me, why didn't you tell me?"

"You wanted something more than a relationship, and I decided to do my best to make it happen. You wanted to wipe out the syndicate, and together we still can. I'll testify against Gino and Frankie, because I love you and want to make you happy, but I want you to know the truth about Victor Dupé. He does not love you."

Love? She had to keep her jaw from dropping. Was he serious? "You have a funny way of showing that you love me."

"You wouldn't listen to me any other way."

Oh my god. "You shot my father! I may not like the guy, but you're the one preaching forgiveness, and I have to admit, I don't want him dead!"

"It was a warning shot, I didn't hit him. I put him in your trunk. He's fine."

Was that true? How could she believe anything he told her? "You swear you didn't hurt him? He's alive?"

"If I'd shot him, he would be dead, Olivia. Like I told you before, hitmen—at least those of us worth our salt—don't miss. Why would I kill your dad when I'm trying to build a relationship with you?" He leaned forward, his dark eyes searching hers. "Unless you ever do want me to off him. Whatever you want, doll. I mean it. I'm ready to give you the world, Olivia, and help put your demons to rest."

"The only demon I have at the moment is you."

"You want to know who killed your brother, don't you?"

Everything in her went still. "You told me you didn't know who killed Dezi."

"The time wasn't right, but now it is. It's time you know everything."

Her vision swam again, and Mother Mary, it was so hot in here. Sweat beaded on the back of her neck, running down her spine. She felt like throwing up. "Just tell me."

"You're not going to like it."

If she could've come out of the chair and went across the table to grab him by the throat, she would have. "Stop dicking me around."

"When Dez came out here, he was working for your father."

"I already know that."

"He was here scouting for the Chicago mob, and doing a little drug dealing on the side to line his own pockets. You're a smart girl, so I'm guessing you can figure out who one of his main buyers was."

Dez, drugs.

A lump formed in her throat, the connections firing off in her brain despite the pounding. "Tracee," she croaked.

Alfie looked pleased. "And what do you think Victor did when he finally tracked down his fiancée's supplier?"

She felt the burn of tears behind her eyes. "He'd have him arrested."

The flash of car lights splayed across the room. Alfie didn't take his eyes off her. "Hate to break it to you, Liv, but the man who killed your brother is the same one you've been sleeping with."

"That's not true."

Alfie gave her a sad look before he picked up the gun resting on the table and headed for the front door.

"You cannot go in there," Felix said.

Roman joined in, both giving Victor an earful in stereo. "He'll kill you."

"Thanks for the vote of confidence." All he wanted to do was kick the men out of the car and get to Olivia. "I know what I'm doing."

He'd driven past the house, saw the lights on. Now he was parked a block behind his house in order to let them out, so they could cross his neighbor's yard and into his while he went in the front. "I'm wired so you know what's happening, and I'll keep him focused on me while you two sneak in the back." Roman had his key. "Felix, you cover Olivia and get her out as soon as I distract Barone. Roman, you get the girl."

"And who is going to cover you?" Roman asked.

"I can handle Alfie," Victor assured him.

In the rearview, Victor saw Felix shaking his head. "I should go in the front. He's not expecting me and that'll knock him off his game. Then you two rush in the back door with guns blazing. Or, better yet, Victor pretends to be injured and I drag him to the front door and tell Barone I want to exchange him for Olivia."

That actually wasn't a bad idea, but Victor couldn't risk Felix getting hurt. Regardless of her feelings for her father, Olivia would never forgive him if he let Felix join in this charade and ended up with a bullet in him.

Roman's phone rang, and he snatched it up. "Winston, whatcha got?"

Victor white knuckled the steering wheel. He didn't have time for this. The clock was ticking, and Olivia's life was on the line.

"How soon can you be here?" Roman asked Winston. "Good enough."

Victor felt like he was going to implode. "I told you not to bring anyone else. We can't have half of Southern California showing up for this."

"Don't worry about who's coming to the party." Roman put his phone away. "We'll go with your plan, but we'll also have my backup. That's how this works, Director."

Great. He was stuck in a pissing match with a Homeland bigwig and a mobster. Somehow, this was not the team he'd imagined working with.

"I know how the guy thinks," Felix continued to argue. "He may be a few colors short in his crayon box, but I know how to get inside his head."

"I don't want to get inside his head," Victor said. "I want to save Olivia and put Barone behind bars."

"Behind bars?" Felix looked like Victor had suggested making the man president. "He hurt my daughter. He's going six feet under."

Victor sighed, the weight of the world riding his shoulders. "Felix, I want your word you will not kill him."

He sniffed and stuck his chin in the air. "I don't make promises I can't keep."

"Then I will handcuff you to the door and not let you within thirty feet of Olivia."

"You can't...!" the rest of the sentence hung in the air, Felix realizing Victor could indeed do exactly that. He blustered again, mumbling to himself before he met Victor's eyes in the rearview. "Fine. Whatever."

But if the opportunity arises... Victor could see Felix would take advantage of it. All bets were off.

"Everybody out," Victor said.

Roman had the receiver for Victor's wire. Barone would expect it, and Victor didn't want to disappoint. Although he might not be able to get into Alfie's head like Felix thought he could, Victor had more than one trick up his sleeve.

"I could stay hidden in the car," Roman said, "and come running the moment you need help."

"The only help I need is for you to get that kid out of the house, and for Felix to do the same with Olivia."

Roman checked the magazine in his weapon. "I don't like it."

"Your confidence in me is reassuring, but I can handle the situation."

"You just make sure you get my daughter free from that bastard," Felix said.

Oh, for fuck's sake. "She's going to die from old age if you two don't stop henpecking me and let me get her!"

That seemed to do the trick, both men bailing out and slamming their respective doors shut behind them.

Sighing with relief, Victor reset his brain. *Get to Olivia.*

As Roman and Felix disappeared into the shadows, Victor cruised around the end of the block and to his driveway. Alfie's car sat in front of the garage as if he owned the place.

Victor pulled in behind it, making sure the vehicle was blocked in. His headlights shone into the dining room, and through the thin curtains, he could make out a figure sitting at the table. *Liv.*

For half a second before he killed the lights, Victor stared at the shadowy outline. Even though he couldn't see her features, his heart sped up, knowing it was her. Every damn time he saw her, it was the same, regardless of the situation. She made him feel alive, wanted.

No matter what happened, he had to make sure she was safe.

Exiting the car, he raised both hands in the air, drizzling rain falling on him. He knew Barone was watching so he turned in a circle letting the man see he was unarmed. The front door opened, but no one stood on the threshold, Alfie playing it safe.

"I'm alone and unarmed," he called to make sure Barone knew he was playing by the rules. "I'm coming in now."

The door stayed open, Barone saying nothing. Every survival instinct told Victor not to walk through the door, confirming this was a suicide mission. He understood his instincts that so closely matched Roman's. If the situation had been different, and it was one of Victor's taskforce members doing this, he'd have rejected the idea too. It was too risky, too dangerous.

How did I end up here, without any of my agents? Roman was a skilled Homeland agent, but they had never worked in the field together, and then there was Felix—a mafia hitman, who was currently breaking more than a few laws.

But this was Liv inside his house. She didn't deserve this, and somehow, Victor knew it was his fault. She was here under Alfie's control because of him. Just like Tracee's death, this was on his head.

"Don't come in here, Victor!"

Her voice was clearly strained and frantic as it filtered through the door. The hell she must be going through, all of her plans blowing up in her face and subjecting her to Barone's crazy and dangerous ambitions. Victor stepped closer, peering into his house. "Don't worry now, Olivia. Everything's going to be fine."

Where was Taz?

If Barone had shot the dog...

Keep your head in the game.

Hands still raised, he stepped across the threshold, scanning to the right where Barone stood behind the door.

"Welcome home, Director," Alfie said with an affable smile.

Olivia had said he was charming, and he was putting it on full display now. Underneath it, Victor suspected he was shaking in his shoes. The man was a killer because the Fifty-seven Gang had turned him into one, but underneath the skills he'd learned in the mob, he was still a man. A man who had gone to law school, started a family, and lost his wife. A man who had a daughter he wanted to protect and had found a woman to fall in love with again. There was more than just his ambition on the line tonight, and all indications suggested Alfonso Barone didn't want to see his own hard work go up in flames.

The door shut, and Barone came around to stand eye to eye with Victor. He held a .40 caliber Smith & Wesson.

Victor went into profiler mode, his training as a hostage negotiator kicking in. It hadn't worked to save Tracee, but he'd succeed this time. "Neither of us wants Olivia to get hurt. Let her go, and I'll do anything you want."

A rueful smile twisted the corner of Barone's lips. He grabbed Victor's arm and swung him around, patting him down with his free hand. "I want you to tell Olivia the truth."

Victor was now facing the dining room and he caught a glimpse of her head as she leaned across the table trying to see him. For a second, their eyes met, so much unsaid between them.

The gash on her forehead was bright red, the swelling had increased. The bruise had spread down to her eyebrows.

But it was her eyes that told him how much pain she was in, and it wasn't from the bump on her head. She was scared. Not for herself, for him.

As their eyes held, he felt suspended. She was so close, all he had to do was walk ten steps to reach her, yet, the physical distance was deceiving when a madman with a gun was between them.

Alfie's hand slapped Victor's chest and patted again. "Unbutton your shirt."

All part of the plan. Victor did as instructed, revealing the hidden wire.

A knowing smirk parted Barone's lips. "I keep telling Olivia you can't be trusted." He ripped the wire off Victor's skin and held it up in Olivia's line of sight. "You see this? This is what I'm talking about. He lies and deceives. How can you still believe in him?"

What was he trying to do? Make Victor look like the bad guy instead of himself? *Figures.* "You said to come alone, you didn't say anything about not wearing a wire." When Alfie's gaze cut back to Victor, Victor gave him a smile, hoping he could see the 'fuck you' behind it. "If you're going to run a family syndicate, Alfie, you're going to need better communication skills."

Barone cocked the gun and pressed it to Victor's temple. Olivia gasped audibly. "Watch your mouth, smartass." He dropped the wire to the floor and stomped on it. "Who's outside?"

Victor gave him another *fuck you* smile. "No one. The receiver is in my car on the seat. Go ahead and check. I was recording you in hopes of getting you to admit you killed Tracee. That *was* you behind the mask, wasn't it?"

There was a slight tightening around Alfie's eyes. "I have no idea what you're talking about."

Such a liar.

He grabbed Victor and shoved him toward the dining room. "As long as we're talking about your ex, why don't you explain to Olivia how you killed her brother because he was selling drugs to Tracee?"

Victor did a double-take between Olivia, who was tied to a chair, and Barone. "What?"

Alfie held up of a photo in front Victor's nose. "I have it all right here. Dez was selling to Tracee and you got mad, so you had him killed."

The picture was fuzzy, and although Victor could pick out his own face, along with Tracee's, he couldn't place where it'd been taken or when. The clothes weren't his, and neither were the shoes. "Nice work, Alfie. Did you do the Photo Shopping on your own or have one of your minions do it?"

A grunt. "Can you believe this guy?" Barone asked Olivia. "I show him the evidence he was in the alley that night and he tries to spin it. I'm telling you, doll, he's been playing you all along."

Olivia's eyes were unfocused. Conflicted and miserable. They pleaded with Victor, and his pulse jumped at the thought she might actually believe the bastard. Her voice wobbled. "It's not true... Is it?"

Oh my god, was she really buying this? When had he ever given her reason to doubt him? "Of course, it's not. I never knew your brother, never met him, and he wasn't dealing to Tracee that I know of. I put Tracee's dealer in prison. His name is Manuel Leon. You can look it up—oh wait, you can't because Alfie has you tied to a chair. He's purposely messing with you, Olivia, and *you know it*."

Her eyes dropped to the table and the other pictures there. "I know, but...the evidence...?"

No way. She didn't actually believe any of this, did she? Victor took a step toward her, but Barone stopped him. "Unh, unh, unh. The game is up, Director. She knows all about your partnership with Gino DeStefano, how he stepped in and helped your family after your father was killed. I've shown her the evidence and she knows it all makes sense. You purposely manipulated, seduced, and betrayed her."

At the mention of his father, everything inside Victor went very still. "What are you talking about? What do you know about my father?"

Alfie grinned.

The fire inside Victor blazed. "Are you saying Gino had my father killed?"

"I see Tracee wasn't the only actor around here, was she? You've been in Gino's back pocket since you were a kid. He helped you out, got your family back together, and now you help him. That's why you got close to Olivia, you knew she was working to eliminate Gino and Frankie both. They were worried and sent you to cozy up to her and stop her when the time came."

"Answer my question. Do you know who killed my father?"

Barone rolled his eyes. "Of course, I do. Who is Gino's right-hand man and always has been? Even back in the 80s?"

Frankie Molina. Victor felt like he'd been gutted. The man had been under his nose for years and he'd never put two and two together. "How do you know it was Frankie? Maybe it was your dear old sack-of-shit dad."

That got under Barone's skin. His jaw tightened, and he put the gun against Victor's skull again. "I told you to watch your mouth. Your father was a wimp, a milquetoast. He tried to stand up to Gino, tried to keep the union from caving, and look what it got him? A bullet to the head, leaving behind his whole family! He knew it could happen, and he still refused to cooperate. What kind of man puts his pride before his family? What kind of man leaves his wife and kids behind instead of looking the other way over a few measly dollars from the company funds?"

Victor ground his teeth. "He was a man of integrity if he wasn't about to be bought off by a bunch of criminals."

"Yeah, I bet his integrity is keeping him company in his grave. Meanwhile, you and your sisters grew up without a father, and he's the reason your mother was crippled. She had no one but the head of the mafia family to help her."

He had heard all he could take. He stepped toward Barone, disregarding the cold steel against his head. Victor was taller and stared down into the man's hard eyes. "My mother and I never took a handout from Gino DeStefano or any other criminal, and I've heard enough bullshit from your mouth."

He took another step, bearing down on the man, and heard Olivia suck in a breath. "You know Olivia doesn't believe this crap, otherwise you wouldn't have kidnapped her and tied her to a chair. The game is up. You want a go at me? Fine, let's do it, but you take off her restraints and let her pick between us."

Olivia's voice held a fearful warning. "Victor—don't do this."

He'd managed to manipulate Barone so that he stood between the man and Olivia, blocking her from the gun if it did go off. Pushing Barone was dangerous, he knew, but he didn't believe the guy had the balls to blow his brains out in front of Olivia.

And then, he saw the change in Alfie's expression...the hard eyes going dead, vindictive. Hitman eyes.

Had he made a mistake?

Not waiting to find out, Victor shifted, thrusting a hand out to grab the gun.

Boom!

In that instance, everything went to hell.

18

O livia screamed and jumped up, the duct tape around her wrists falling away. She'd managed to work at the binding on one of the chair's rough sides until it broke free while Victor had been antagonizing Alfie.

Damn man. If he'd just played along and let her convince Alfie she believed him...

The first shot had gone right past her into the wall, blowing a hole in it.

Boom! Another rang out, the bullet hitting the plastered ceiling overhead and raining chunks down over the table. She ducked and scrambled around the edge of the big wooden thing. The antique wood smelled like a thrift shop or maybe someone's attic.

Victor and Alfie had fallen to the floor on the other side and she could hear them tussling, see the shadows of flailing limbs. The sound of fists hitting flesh, grunts, and fervent swearing echoed on the heels of the gunshots.

She ducked under the table, searching the floor at the other end. The two men were locked in a fight over the gun. She started to crawl down the length of the table to get to them, but suddenly, there was a set of familiar legs rushing past and then someone grabbed her ankles, hauling her out.

"Olivia!" her dad said, lifting her off the ground. "We gotta get outta here!"

Oh, for heaven's sake. How did he keep turning up in the most unlikely places and times? She fought against his grasp. "I can't leave! I have to help Victor!"

He fought to grab hold of her again. "He's got it under control. Let's go!"

Under control, huh? Chairs crashed to the floor, Taz barked somewhere in the background, the box of Victor's files crashed nearby, sending papers flying everywhere.

Another gunshot exploded, making her flinch and throw her hands over her head even though it was still under the protection of the table. She heard a grunt of pain from one of them. Her dad had a hold of her leg and she kicked at him to make him let go.

"Victor!" she screamed as she flipped over and started crawling. *Please don't let him be hurt.*

Her father came after her, grabbing her ankles and jerking her backward. "I have to get you out of here."

Once more, her foot connected with her father and he let go with a curse. "Goddamnit, Olivia! Why won't you listen to me?"

Ignoring him, she lunged for the opposite end where Victor and Alfie were fighting. Victor had Alfie on the ground, trying to make him let go of the gun. Alfie bucked his hips up, nearly unseating Victor. The mobster jerked his hand away from Victor's grasp. As she was about to launch herself at Alfie, he smacked Victor on the side of the head with the butt of the gun.

Victor, still fighting to regain his balance on top of Alfie, fell to the side. Alfie swung the gun around to point it at Victor, and Olivia dove at him.

Thanks to her unfocused vision, she missed the gun, but managed to snag Alfie's shirtsleeve. He was in the process of rolling to his knees and pulled her with him, her lower back smacking on the edge of the table as Alfie scrambled to his feet.

Victor jumped up, eyes darting from her to Alfie and the gun. "Olivia, stay out of this. Get back!"

She hung on to Alfie for dear life, keeping his gun hand from pointing at Victor. She wrapped her free hand around Alfie's waist, trying to shove him to the floor, but he was stronger and elbowed her in the collarbone. The blow knocked the wind out of her and sent her back on her ass.

Now it wasn't just her head pounding and her eyesight blurry, she felt like she couldn't breathe. Alfie moved, and through the fog and dizziness, she saw him raise the gun to aim at Victor. She screamed, and in her peripheral vision, which wasn't much better, she saw a figure move from under the table to tackle Alfie.

Alfie must have seen her dad coming. He pivoted, and the gun went off.

"No!" Olivia screamed as her father fell to the floor, blood gushing from his chest.

Before she could reach him, the dining room window shattered and the next thing she knew, Victor dropped to the floor. He'd been shot as well, the bullet going all the way through and splattering the wall behind him with blood.

It was a surreal nightmare. She kept hearing screaming as she crawled to her father, and realized it was her own voice. "You bastard," she cried at Alfie. "You fucking bastard!"

Her father's eyes were closed, his breathing ragged. She wanted to help him, get to Victor, and stop Alfie all at the same time. Yet, it seemed like the only thing her body would do was cry as she stripped off her shirt and pressed it against her father's wound.

Suddenly, Alfie squatted beside her. He brushed a strand of hair from her face. "Shh. It's going to be all right. I'll call an ambulance."

Was he completely insane?

Something dangerous took hold of her. Something feral and uncontrolled. Through her tears, she raised her face and looked at him. "How could you do this to me? I didn't have a chance to make amends with him, and now I'll never be able to."

He reached for her and brought her in close to hug her against his chest. "It's not a fatal wound. I made sure to miss his heart. I promise you, doll, we're going to be a strong, loyal family. All of us, including your dad."

As she pretended to hug Alfie back, she saw Victor rise to his knees and relief flooded her. There was so much blood, she didn't know how he was standing. He motioned for her to move as he started to creep up on Alfie, but as she had told him all along, this was her case, her very life purpose.

In one swift movement, she made a fist and jammed it into Alfie's balls. At the same time, her other hand ripped the gun from his grip. He yelped and fell sideways, grabbing his nether region.

Blinking through the tears, Olivia pointed the gun, her hand steady even though the rest of her was shaking.

"Liv..." Alfie reached a hand toward her, a grimace on his face. "I love... you..."

Victor staggered toward her "Don't do it, Olivia. He's not worth—"

Olivia pulled the trigger.

THE BULLET HIT Barone square in his right kneecap.

The man howled in pain, grabbing his bent knee. Roman rushed in, pushing a handcuffed woman in front of him. "Caught the sniper that shot you," he said to Victor. "She's the one you were looking for, once again helping out Barone. You all right?"

Victor nodded, his right hand useless thanks to the bullet that blasted through his shoulder. He hadn't counted on Marisol Riva joining the party as a lookout.

He dropped to his knees next to Olivia, who still held the gun pointed at Alfie. She turned a tear-streaked face to him. "I can't do it. I want to...God, how I want to! He deserves it...but..."

"I know." Gently, Victor eased the gun out of her stiff fingers, the digits so cold, he wondered if she was going into shock. "You did good, Liv."

He handed the gun to Roman then reached for her. She fell into his good arm, sobbing, and he held her as tight as he could. "It's over," he reassured her. "I swear to you, I never had anything to do with DeStefano or the Fifty-seven Gang."

"I think I may have blown my case against Gino and Frankie."

Victor chuckled. Sirens blared in the distance. Thomas and Ronni ran in. "You okay, there, boss?" Thomas asked. "You're looking a little like Papa Smurf, blue around the edges. Or maybe that's from all those blue paint samples on the wall in the living room."

Lightheadedness threatened to topple him over. His blood dripped onto the floor, seeping into his pant leg. "Where's the girl? Is she okay?"

Ronni bent to check on Felix. Roman shoved Marisol into a chair and put a hand on Victor's shoulder as if to steady him. "She's safe with Polly. Ambulance is almost here."

Olivia looked at her father, back to Victor, seemingly torn between the two of them. Victor nodded for her to go to her dad. She peeled away, and he grabbed hold of the table to keep from falling over. Roman's hand tightened on his good shoulder, helping to steady him.

Liv dropped next to her father, feeling for a pulse in his neck. "Don't you die on me, Dad. Swear to god, you deserve some ass-kicking from me, and you better not think for one blessed second dying is going to keep you safe."

Alfie continued to yell and curse at all of them, even as

Roman pulled him into a sitting position and handcuffed him. Victor shrugged off Thomas's help to get into a chair, but nearly keeled over from his stubbornness. The wallop Barone had given him on the head, combined with the loss of blood, was about to take him under. Black spots danced at the edge of his vision.

Flashing lights whipped through the broken dining room window. The previous gunshots had left him half deaf in his right ear, but now the ambulance siren was too loud in his head. As Barone began another tirade against Olivia, Victor found an extra ounce of strength, and, balling his left hand into a fist, reached over and punched the guy in the mouth, knocking the asshole flat. "That's for lying to Olivia about me."

Ronni moved out of the way to allow the EMTs access to Felix, coming to stand next to Victor and help him regain his balance. She pointed at the woman Roman had brought in. "This the one who shot Coop?"

She wasn't wearing standard Suarez Kings clothing or colors, but her dark eyes and general appearance were similar enough to her sister, Victor was sure. "Marisol Riva. Her sister is an ex of Frankie Molina's, and Marisol is one of the Kings."

Ronni turned an evil eye on the woman. "Well, aren't you something special."

Thomas was also staring the woman down, but he put up a hand to stop any designs Ronni had on taking revenge. "While I love a good vigilante smackdown, we're going to let Marisol enjoy the long stay in prison awaiting her."

The EMTs asked Olivia to turn loose of her father's hand, but she gripped it harder and shot daggers at them. "Work around me. I haven't seen this man in ten years, and I'm not letting him out of my sight now."

The female EMT glanced at Victor, her eyes pleading for assistance. Against his better judgment, he pushed out of the chair and made his way to Liv, touching her shoulder with his good hand. "They can't do their job and save your father if you're in their way. You can ride in the ambulance with him, and maybe they can check your wounds on the way."

She resisted, and he saw her bite her bottom lip, conflicted, but then with a heavy sigh, she released her father's hand. Victor slipped his into hers and guided her back a couple steps, leaning on the wall to help keep him upright.

He mentally poured steel into his legs to lock them in place. Olivia turned and grabbed him around the waist. "You're the one who needs medical treatment, not me."

Even with her bruises and the gash on her forehead, she was the most beautiful thing he'd ever seen. Her hair was sticking out all over and there were dark circles under her eyes. The tank top she'd worn under the shirt she'd used on her father was torn and splashed with blood. "You are the most incredible woman...I've ever known." The black dots grew bigger. All he could see was her face as his back began to slide down the wall. "I need to know... that you don't believe Alfie. I would never...work with the mafia..."

She kept her hands on his waist until he was sitting on the floor, her eyes scanning his face. "Victor, it's okay. I know Alfie was lying. Forget about him. Stay with me."

Her face was now only the size of a pinhead. "I...love you...Olivia."

Her hand patted his cheek. "There's something I need to tell you, and you're not going to like it. Stay awake and get pissed at me, you hear? Do not close your eyes!"

He felt someone tugging at his body as though lifting him onto a gurney. The EMTs were shouting things and there was a lot of scuffling, but none of it penetrated the haze of unconsciousness descending on him.

Olivia was holding his good hand like a vise grip. "I am serious, Director, I need to unburden myself before you go falling in love with me."

He tried to grin, failed. "Too late."

"I've been investigating you." Her voice floated in and out of his hearing and all he wanted to do was go to sleep. "There's someone higher up in the Justice Department that suspects you of doing exactly what Alfie accused you of. They sent me to get close to you and see what I could..."

An oxygen mask slipped over his mouth and nose and someone pushed Olivia away. Everything seemed transparent, his body floating into numbness, her words nothing more than an echo in his brain.

19

Two weeks later
Victor's home

"I LIKE SOLAR FLARE," Brenda said.

Victor's other sisters looked on, staring at the living room wall where he'd painted six different shades of orange.

Nikki shook her head. "Hawaiian Sunset is the one. It has enough orange, but not too much yellow."

"Are you kidding me?" Danille stomped over and tapped a finger on a different swatch. "Victor needs more earth tones, like this."

Brenda rolled her eyes and Nikki laughed. "That's Dragon Fire, Danille. Who paints their living room Dragon Fire?"

"It's only a name," Danille argued.

Victor turned to his youngest sister, Ruth. "What do you think, kid?"

She glanced at him with a sullen teenager expression, even though she'd turn thirty soon. Somehow, she'd never quite outgrown looking and acting much younger. "I vote for plain old sky blue. Keep it simple."

Out of all of them, she was the artistic one, the one who wrote poetry and grew herbs in her backyard. He'd expected her to come up with something even wilder than Dragon Fire. But that was his sisters for you—he never could outguess them.

Outside in the backyard, their families were talking, laughing, and the kids were playing. Brenda put a palm to her forehead as if searching for patience. "What do you think, Mama?"

Their mother always had the final say. She'd moved out of her wheelchair and into Victor's new La-Z-Boy that Taz seemed to spend more time in than he did. Her feet were up, and she had a margarita in one hand, smiling at all of her children. "Victor's girlfriend is right. With the lighting in here, something like Dragon Fire is probably perfect. 'Fiery,' isn't that the term she used, honey?"

Yeah, he told her about Olivia and their conversation concerning the paint colors for his living room.

"There you have it," he said to his sisters. "Mama knows best."

Victor bent forward and kissed her forehead, careful to avoid hitting his recovering arm on the chair. He still wore a sling but planned to ditch it soon. He only had to suffer through another week of physical therapy. "Dragon Fire it is," he said to the room at large, and then under his breath to his mother, "and I no longer have a girlfriend."

Danille sidled up to him and wrapped her arms around his waist. "You don't know that. You said things have been hectic for her, dealing with her father's injuries and working a deal with the DA not to send him back to prison. Give her time, she might surprise you."

Outside, an SUV pulled in, followed by a sports car. "Looks like our guests are here for the picnic," Victor said. "I'm really glad everybody could make it today, especially all of you guys."

His sisters huddled around him and their mother, smiling

and laughing, in one of their famous family hugs. Ruth pinched his side. "You just wanted help putting together a party for your friends, and you couldn't do it with your banged-up arm."

"That's what sisters are for," Brenda said, patting Victor's shoulder. "We're glad to help any time. You and your friends have been through a lot in the past couple weeks."

They broke apart and Nikki lead the entourage to the kitchen. "And it's about time we got to see the house, but I draw the line at helping you paint the living room Dragon Fire. Every time I walk in there, I'm going to feel like I'm entering a Tolkien fantasy story. At least if you went with Hawaiian Sunset, we could feel like we're on vacation when we came over."

Victor laughed, enjoying the constant bickering and arguing as the four women filed out. "Let's get you back in your wheelchair, Mama, and I'll take you out to the backyard for the picnic."

"You go meet your guests. I'll be fine here for a few minutes. You can send that Thomas fellow in to get me." She winked at him.

She might be closing in on sixty, but she was as full of spunk and silliness as her daughters. "Yes, ma'am."

It was great to see Cooper up and about, carrying his daughter through the front door as Celina dropped a kiss on Victor's cheek when they entered. Thomas and Ronni came in, bearing baskets and platters of food, and Victor directed them to the kitchen and out to the patio,

For the next twenty minutes, he ran back and forth making sure everybody had drinks and had been introduced. Every few minutes, he checked his phone to see if there was a message or call from Olivia. He'd invited her, but she hadn't responded to any of his texts or voicemails.

Hence, his certainty he didn't have a girlfriend.

She'd visited him once in the hospital, shortly after some minor surgery on his shoulder. He'd been looped out on medication, and even now couldn't quite recall the entire conversation, but had sensed she carried a heavy burden of guilt. Something she had said to him in the dining room the night Alfie took her hostage kept chasing around in his brain as he lay in that sterile bed, but he hadn't quite been able to put his finger on it. He'd thought everything was okay between them, but then she'd disappeared.

The day he'd been discharged, he kept thinking she was going to show up to help take him home. Instead, it was Thomas and Ronni who picked him up and made sure he had his prescriptions filled. His sisters had taken turns visiting every day, bringing food and fussing over him, until he finally insisted he was okay and could handle normal life again. It was hard having them constantly checking on him and hanging around when he knew they were so busy with their own lives, but in many ways, he'd enjoyed spending time with each of them. He only wished Olivia had been around to do the same.

A few days after he left the hospital, he'd received a call from his boss in DC telling Victor he had been under investigation. The previous fall, someone in the Justice Department had received an anonymous tip claiming Victor had ties to the Fifty-seven Gang and Gino DeStefano, conducting criminal activity with them the entire time he'd been with the FBI. The conversation with Olivia that night in the dining room had all come back to him.

She'd been the one covertly investigating him.

No wonder she hadn't returned his texts and phone calls. The whole time they'd had a relationship, she'd been pretending she cared.

He'd spent every minute of the last two weeks going over their relationship in his mind, and maybe he was being an idiot, but he truly believed that she *did* care. Maybe it was his sad ego, needing to feel like he hadn't been tricked, but he remembered what Felix had said to him the night everything went down, as well as some of the things Liv herself had said that sounded cryptic then and now made total sense.

So, against all hope, he'd invited her to the picnic.

As the last of the food was set out and Brenda began calling everybody to grab their plates, Victor went to look out the dining room window. Cars lined the driveway and down the street but there was no Olivia.

His heart sunk, and he dropped his chin to his chest, wondering how he could've been such a fool. His relationship with Tracee had been a disaster, and it had gotten her killed. The one with Olivia had held promise, but apparently, had been based on lies. If his right arm hadn't been in a sling, he probably would've punched the wall. Instead he turned, heading back for the kitchen.

The doorbell rang, stopping him in his tracks. Slowly, he pivoted and stared at the closed door for a moment.

A funny feeling invaded his chest—hope. *You're a fool.* It was probably Roman or one of the other taskforce agents he'd invited.

That reasoning didn't stop him from rushing to the door and throwing it open.

Olivia stood there, in red shorts and a flowery blouse, raising a paintbrush. "Figured you had plenty of food and booze, so I came bearing a promise instead."

He couldn't stop the crazy grin that spread across his face. His heart beat rapid-fire, banging against his ribcage. "A promise?"

"Seems I owe you for getting my dad a deal with the federal government. Because there were extenuating circumstances—he was, quote, *assisting with a deep cover investigation*, per your report to the Justice Department—he's been allowed to return to Chicago and stay on parole. My mom is beside herself with happiness. No charges will be brought against him."

Power was a good thing sometimes. "He *did* assist, and if it weren't for him, who knows what would've happened to you."

Her eyes softened along with her voice. "I can't tell you how much it means to me that you did that. In return, I'd like to offer my painting services."

His heart whacked against his ribcage like it was going to beat out of his chest. He moved back, motioning her across the threshold. "As it so happens, I've decided on a color for the living room with the help of my mother and sisters. It's called Dragon Fire. I think you'll like it."

She entered the foyer and glanced around as people filed in and out of the kitchen near the back door. Celina saw them and waved. "You're late!" she called.

Olivia waved back. "How's Cooper?"

"Come outside and ask him yourself." She disappeared into the kitchen.

"Great idea," Victor said. "You probably need sustenance before you start working, so why don't you join the picnic?"

She stared at the back door, seeming to contemplate it. One of the kids ran in, Taz giving chase. When the dog saw Liv, he let out a happy yelp, his legs spinning as he tried to get traction to run to see her. A second later, he barreled into her open arms and began licking her face as she greeted him. "I missed you, buddy. Don't tell your owner, but you're the real reason I came over."

"He's missed you too."

She finished hugging the dog and rose. "Is he the only one?"

Victor reached out and grabbed her hand, dragging her closer so they were chest to chest, nose to nose. "You better eat a lot, because you're not going to need sustenance just for painting."

She chuckled low and sexy. "I'm really sorry about what happened. I was going to tell you everything, but the timing was always off. I fell totally head over heels for you, Director, our first night together. I didn't trust myself or my feelings and by the time I realized I was in love with you, I'd dug one hell of a hole. Nothing about our relationship was fake on my end. I want you to know that."

He smiled down at her, a sense of completeness enveloping

him. Liv was here in his arms. In the background, he heard the sounds of his family and friends having a good time. Everybody was okay. Everybody was happy.

Now he could relax, at least for a little while. *Maybe it's my turn to be happy.*

Olivia too.

"I have no doubts you're the real deal, Olivia Fiorelli, and I'm hoping you're going to spend a lot of time in this house with me and the dog."

She grinned. "I don't work for free, you know."

"God, I hope not, but you may have to take it easy on me for a while." He lifted his bum arm an inch.

"Excuses, excuses. You're not going to be a wimp about it, are you? I mean, I get that you can't paint right now, but as for the other stuff"—she raised her eyes toward the bedroom—"I need to know you can hold your own."

He tilted his chin down to place his forehead against hers. "What do you say after the party, we do a test run?"

She kissed him, softly, gently, but with promise. As she broke away, she whispered, "I love you, Victor, and I want to spend the rest of my life proving it to you."

As Taz leaned against both their legs, watching them intently, Victor knew this was the future he'd been waiting for. While the two of them still had demons to put to rest about her brother and his father, they had new leads. More members of the Suarez Kings had been picked up and questioned, and with the testimony Olivia had gotten out of Alfie, the Fifty-seven Gang was already being torn apart, Gino and Frankie were both under arrest and facing life in prison. Alfie was in jail too, his daughter now living with his mother in Sacramento.

It was time for a fresh start, a new beginning. Time to let the ghosts of the past rest and build a future with this woman. "I love you too, Liv, and you don't need to prove anything to me. I know you, and what a good heart you have. I've never doubted that for a moment."

"Are you two going to stand there and jabber all day, or can we get this party started?"

Victor looked over to see Cooper standing in the hallway, two beers in hand.

"Good to see you up and about," Olivia said.

Cooper gave a wry smile. "Can't keep The Beast down, Fiorelli. You know that."

"We'll be there in a minute," Victor said. "Go ahead and start without us."

Olivia stepped back as Cooper headed outside once more. "Let's go join the party. I'm dying to meet your mom and sisters. You and I can save our deep *conversations* for later."

"Is that what the kids are calling it these days?" He grabbed her by the hand and guided her toward the stairs. "I need to show you a couple paint samples."

Olivia laughed softly under her breath. "Paint samples, huh?"

They jogged up the stairs, eager to be in each other's arms. Taz chased them, sure of the game. "There are way too many shades of blue. I definitely need help picking the right one for the bedroom."

"And this decision needs to be made at this exact moment?"

He propelled her into the room and to the bed, now officially set up and ready for plenty of *conversations*. "Oh yeah. National emergency. How fast can you get out of those shorts?"

She hugged him, and they fell onto the bed together, Victor ignoring his injured shoulder and stripping off the sling before he began removing her clothes. As he sank into her soft, inviting heat, he felt no pain, no regrets. He was a stronger man because of her and he wanted nothing more than to make her happy for the rest of her life.

There was no time like the present to begin.

226

ROMANTIC SUSPENSE & MYSTERIES BY MISTY EVANS

Spies of Shadow Force (Coming 2019)

Man Hunt

Man Down

Man Killer

Shadow Force International Series

Fatal Truth

Fatal Honor

Fatal Courage

Fatal Love

Fatal Vision

Fatal Thrill

Risk

The SCVC Taskforce Series

Deadly Pursuit

Deadly Deception

Deadly Force

Deadly Intent

Deadly Affair, A SCVC Taskforce novella

Deadly Attraction

Deadly Secrets

Deadly Holiday, A SCVC Taskforce novella

Deadly Target

Deadly Rescue (coming November 2018)

The Super Agent Series

Operation Sheba

Operation Paris

Operation Proof of Life

The Blood Code

The Perfect Hostage, A Super Agent Novella

The Justice Team Series (with Adrienne Giordano)

Stealing Justice

Cheating Justice

Holiday Justice

Exposing Justice

Undercover Justice

Protecting Justice

Missing Justice

Defending Justice

The Secret Ingredient Culinary Mystery Series

The Secret Ingredient, A Culinary Romantic Mystery with Bonus Recipes

The Secret Life of Cranberry Sauce, A Secret Ingredient Holiday Novella

ABOUT THE AUTHOR

USA TODAY Bestselling Author Misty Evans has published fifty novels and writes romantic suspense, urban fantasy, and paranormal romance. She got her start writing in 4th grade when she won second place in a school writing contest with an essay about her dad. Since then, she's written nonfiction magazine articles, started her own coaching business, become a yoga teacher, and raised twin boys on top of enjoying her fiction career.

When not reading or writing, she enjoys music, movies, and hanging out with her husband, twin sons, and two spoiled puppies. A registered yoga teacher and Master Reiki Practitioner, she shares her love of chakra yoga and energy healing, but still hasn't mastered levitating.

Get free reads, all the latest news, and alerts about sales when you sign up for her newsletter at www.readmistyevans.com. To find out more about her holistic healing practice, please visit www.crystalswithmisty.com.

LETTER FROM MISTY

Hello Beautiful Reader!

Thank you for reading Deadly Target! This is my 50th published book and one that is very special to me. I never dreamed I'd be a storyteller when I grew up, but maybe I really never did grow up! Anyway, it is an honor and a privilege to write stories for you.

I hope you enjoyed this book, and I'd like to ask a favor – would you mind leaving a review at your favorite retailer? I'd really appreciate it, and reviews help other readers find books they will love too.

If you'd like to learn about my other books, sales, and special promotions, please sign up for my newsletter at www.readmistyevans.com.

I also have a holistic business, Crystals With Misty, and invite you to check out my website www.crystalswithmisty.com for information on my services.

Thank you and happy reading!

Misty

Printed in Great Britain
by Amazon